MW01657086

12 DUKES OF CHRISTMAS

BOOKS 1-2

ERICA RIDLEY

ALSO BY ERICA RIDLEY

The *Dukes of War*:

The Viscount's Tempting Minx

The Earl's Defiant Wallflower

The Captain's Bluestocking Mistress

The Major's Faux Fiancée

The Brigadier's Runaway Bride

The Pirate's Tempting Stowaway

The Duke's Accidental Wife

The *Wild Wynchesters*:

The Governess Gambit

The Duke Heist

***Rogues to Riches*:**

Lord of Chance

Lord of Pleasure

Lord of Night

Lord of Temptation

Lord of Secrets

Lord of Vice

The *12 Dukes of Christmas*:

Once Upon a Duke

Kiss of a Duke

Wish Upon a Duke

Never Say Duke

Dukes, Actually

The Duke's Bride

The Duke's Embrace

The Duke's Desire

Dawn With a Duke

One Night With a Duke

Ten Days With a Duke

Forever Your Duke

***Gothic Love Stories*:**

Too Wicked to Kiss

Too Sinful to Deny

Too Tempting to Resist

Too Wanton to Wed

Too Brazen to Bite

***Magic & Mayhem*:**

Kissed by Magic

Must Love Magic

Smitten by Magic

The *Wicked Dukes Club*:

One Night for Seduction by Erica Ridley

One Night of Surrender by Darcy Burke

One Night of Passion by Erica Ridley

One Night of Scandal by Darcy Burke

One Night to Remember by Erica Ridley

One Night of Temptation by Darcy Burke

ACKNOWLEDGMENTS

As always, I could not have written this book without the invaluable support of my editor and critique partners. Huge thanks go out to Tessa Shapcott, Erica Monroe and Morgan Edens. You are the best!

Lastly, I want to thank the *Historical Romance Book Club,* and my fabulous street team. Your enthusiasm makes the romance happen.

Thank you so much!

ONCE UPON A DUKE

12 DUKES OF CHRISTMAS #1

ONCE UPON A DUKE

Beware romantic spirits from Christmas past...

Due to the terms of an estranged relative's will, the Duke of Silkridge must revisit the cold, unforgiving mountains where he lost everything he once loved. As soon as he restores his family legacy, he'll return to London where he belongs. He definitely won't rekindle the forbidden spark crackling between him and the irresistible spitfire he'd left behind...

Noelle Pratchett is immune to charming scoundrels like the arrogant duke. He stole her heart, stole a kiss, and then stole away one night never to return. Now he's back—and they both know he won't stay. But how can she maintain her icy shields when every heated glance melts her to her core?

CHAPTER 1

24 December
London, England

Benjamin Ward, the fifth Duke of Silkridge, reached for another bottle of champagne. The guests who filled his home with amusement and laughter weren't the patronesses of Almack's or his peers in the House of Lords. These friends were like him: rudderless in the worst time of the year to be alone.

Christmastide.

Not that this was a *Christmas* house party. Benjamin did not celebrate Christmas or Yule or Twelfth Night or anything else that reminded him of—

"Champagne!" he called out, just before the pop filled the air. A trickle of fizzy foam bubbled out over the edge of the bottle.

A dozen crystal glasses swung his way at once. He grinned at his first-cousins—and heirs presumptive—Nicholas and Christopher, as he refilled their glasses.

"You'd make a splendid footman," Nicholas said with a straight face. "If you tire of the 'duke' thing."

"Alas," Christopher interjected. "Silkridge will never tire of the 'duke' thing. When he is not in the House of Lords, he's discussing politics in gentlemen's clubs. When he is not discussing politics in gentlemen's clubs, he's off in coffee houses interviewing the people *about* politics. When he is not in coffee houses—"

"—he's rebuffing the subtle machinations of matchmaking mamas everywhere," Nicholas finished.

"They're not subtle," Benjamin said with a grimace. "When you're duke, you'll discover what it's like."

"I already know what it's like." Nicholas groaned in commiseration. Although he possessed no title, he was London's most celebrated rake. Doe-eyed debutantes swooned in his wake everywhere he went.

Christopher pressed a hand to his cravat. "You poor lads. How deeply you must suffer, to be so handsome and so powerful that hopeful young ladies pile up about you like snowdrifts. You may *think* you'll never marry, but one day—"

Music filled the parlor, drowning out whatever romantic curse Christopher had hoped to inflict upon them.

Nicholas pointed to his ear in an exaggerated *What? I can't hear you!* gesture, and swung the closest woman before the orchestra to dance. Christopher rolled his eyes in good-natured frustration, and followed suit.

The series of musicians Benjamin had hired to entertain the party over the next several days had, like the rest of the guests, nowhere else to be. The pianist was new to town, the violinist between plays, the flautist a young hopeful dreaming of one day performing at Vauxhall.

If they were a motley crew, well, so were Benjamin's

friends. He and his cousins were the last of their family. The widow in Nicholas's arms had no one at all. Everyone present would have finished out the year all alone, had it not been for the Unyuletide celebration. For twelve days, they'd have each other. No one need fear so much as a whisper of Christmases best forgotten.

As always, the unwelcome reminder of everything he'd put behind him brought to mind a shimmer of the one bright spot in all that darkness. Warm brown eyes, soft pink lips, clever wit... Noelle Pratchett had imprinted on his soul. Benjamin sighed. Despite endless champagne and a house full of music and people, the empty ache inside his chest only grew wider.

He flagged down a passing footman. "John, has the Gazette arrived?"

No need to specify which. Benjamin had been trying to remove his name from the Cressmouth Gazette's subscriber list from the day he'd unexpectedly received its first issue. No matter how many stern letters his man of business sent on Benjamin's behalf, the relentless four-page publication arrived on Benjamin's doorstep every three months without fail.

Until this winter.

"Not yet, Your Grace," the footman answered. "Perhaps they've finally removed your name from the list."

Pity. Benjamin had been looking forward to throwing it in the fire.

Well, after he'd scoured it for mention of Noelle. But there never was.

"I am glad," he informed the footman.

And he should have been. He did not require the unsolicited delivery of a tiny local journal to know what the latest news would be. Cressmouth was colloquially known as Christmas. A pristine speck of a village high atop a lonesome mountain in the northernmost corner of England, punctuated by a folly of a castle amid an endless sea of evergreens.

The gazette's winter edition always said the same things. Although it was always Christmas in Cressmouth, the village additionally hosted a special Yuletide festival every year from the sixth of December to the fifth of January. All were welcome.

Many did. Visitors flocked to the idyllic site from far and wide. The predictable influx of coin supplemented the villagers' income for the rest of the year, until it was time to begin their excessively prolonged Christmastide celebrations all over again.

Benjamin could not think of a worse hell than eternal Christmas. He certainly had no wish to read about it. Unsubscribing from quarterly updates about the cheerful village's Yuletide exploits was a dream come true. He had assumed the feat would fill him with elation, but instead all he felt was… a hole. Yet more yawning emptiness, right there in his chest.

He threw himself into the forced gaiety of his party. What he needed was more music, more champagne, more distractions from old memories that wouldn't stay locked away.

His butler approached with a silver tray and a grave expression. "A message, Your Grace."

"At this hour?" Benjamin lifted the neatly folded parchment with trepidation.

It was too small to be the Cressmouth Gazette, and yet a prickling of the skin warned him that big problems might be tucked inside all the same.

He was right.

Three short lines from Castle Marlowe's resident solicitor: Benjamin's estranged grandfather was dead. Bequests would be read in five days. The will and testament required Benjamin's immediate presence.

He tucked the missive into his waistcoat pocket with a calm he did not feel. "Prepare my coach, please."

"As you please."

Benjamin's cousin Christopher approached the moment the butler left. "Is something amiss?"

"Nothing's amiss," Benjamin lied. He'd never expected to see his maternal grandfather again, so his death did not change their relationship. Rather, the missive gave him hope. Perhaps his grandfather had repented. Perhaps being named in the bequest meant the old man was finally returning the heirloom he'd stolen from his grandchild. The one link Benjamin had cherished above all others. "I have to go."

"Where?"

"Cressmouth."

Christopher frowned. "I thought…"

"So did I," Benjamin said flatly. He'd thought a lot of things that had turned out not to be true.

That he would now have to spend the first few of the twelve days of Christmas traveling to the godforsaken mountaintop where Christmas never ended was the cream on the crumpet.

"Stay here," he told his cousin. After all, Jacob Marlowe wasn't their relative. Nicholas and Christopher were the sons of the previous duke's sister. They needn't be burdened with this quest. Just because Benjamin was suddenly forced to face his past in the back of beyond did not mean he needed to spoil the party for anyone else. "Let everyone know they needn't return to their empty homes on my account. The musicians and caterers have already been contracted, and my staff is more than competent. Everyone is welcome to stay. I'll be back as soon as I can."

With luck, he would arrive mere moments before the bequests were made and leave immediately after. Gone just over a sennight. He could do this.

He'd survived worse.

And yet, as the air grew colder and the countryside bleaker and the passing days grew from two to three to four, Benjamin began to fear that being trapped inside the four walls of his coach for one more hour would drive him mad before he even arrived.

Winter enveloped the frost-tipped forest in its deathly grip as the lone black carriage made its determined way up the side of the frozen mountain.

Benjamin glowered at the sleet obstructing the view from the window. Instead of being ensconced in the dry warmth of his town house in London, he was almost four hundred miles north, heading ever closer to the one place he had vowed never to return.

Cressmouth, England.

The nearer his coach drew to the tiny village nestled on the mountain, the worse the weather became. The cold breeze had turned into a punishing wind, and the endless gray skies above had begun to clot with heavy clouds.

Already, blobs too icy to be rain and too wet to be snow spit down upon him.

Bad weather was a good sign. It meant he was getting closer to his goal. Closer to the end. The sooner he fetched the heirloom that had been stolen from him, the sooner he could return to London. Back to where he belonged.

Benjamin clenched his jaw and tore his gaze from the countryside. He hated to leave his home. This was the first time he'd been called away in years. The first time he'd allowed a deviation from his rigid timetable.

Whether Parliament was in session or not, there was too much work to be done back home. Benjamin was personally responsible for half a dozen committees shaping the country's future. He had no time for distracting quests.

But here he was.

His horses clomped past a large, festive sign held sturdy in the frozen ground by thick wooden posts. Despite the darkening sky and the falling sleet, its boldly lettered words were still legible.

Welcome to Christmas!

"It's *Cressmouth,* not Christmas," he muttered beneath his breath.

But it was no use. The quaint northern village was even worse than he remembered. Brightly colored cottages dotted amongst the white of the snow and the frosted tips of a thousand evergreens.

Everywhere he looked there were sparkling candelabra in windowpanes, curling smoke rising merrily from red brick chimneys, children in colorful woolen mittens pelting each other with soft balls of snow.

"Humbug," he muttered. *He* would not take part.

But it was too late. The Silkridge ducal crest gracing the sides of his stately coach had caught the attention of those he passed. Children smiled. Ladies waved.

"Ho, there," called out a ruddy-cheeked gentleman shoveling snow from his walk. "Happy Christmas!"

"No such thing," Benjamin muttered to his valet.

"Didn't you see the sign?" Doyle answered with a grin. "'Tis eternally a happy Christmas here."

"Humbug," Benjamin repeated, and motioned the driver onward.

He'd never understood the attraction of living out in Nowhereland. Although the area did grow warmer in the summer months, the inhabitants lived as though there were twelve months of Christmas, rather than twelve days. The only explanation for such fervor was a sad and desperate attempt to try to create some sort of advantage to living in the coldest corner of all of England.

Benjamin glared at the snow-dusted pines dipping and curving down the mountain. Cressmouth was in the middle of nowhere. The closest town was Cornhill-on-Tweed. Any further north, and this village would be in Scotland.

A bright red ball sailed from between a pair of cottages and out into the street.

The horses reared in alarm. The driver struggled to keep control of the reins.

From the corner of Benjamin's eye, he caught a flash of movement. A lad scarcely six years of age intended to dart out before the horses in order to retrieve his ball.

"*Stay*," Benjamin barked, not to his horses and driver, but to the child at the edge of the street.

He leapt from the coach and hurled the ball far over the child's head so that he would be forced to run away from the lane to fetch it.

"So kind of you," called a woman from an open doorway. "You saved Nigel's life."

Benjamin might not love the festive season, but he liked children. They did not deserve ill fates. He gave a stiff nod to the woman and jumped back into the carriage.

His shoulders tightened. He was tired of the cold, tired of traveling, tired of waiting this long to regain something he had lost.

Not Christmas. He had given that up on purpose. Benjamin was after something far more precious. In the long ride up, he'd convinced himself that a wrong was about to be put right.

At tomorrow morning's reading of the will, his mother's locket would return where it belonged. To Benjamin's hands. He and the last trace of his mother would be reunited at last.

The dizzying white castle seemed to mock him from the peak of the mountain. That had been his estranged grandfather's home. The same grandfather responsible for reviving what had once been a ghostly settlement into a vibrant Christmas village.

A madman. There was no other explanation.

Benjamin directed his driver toward the winding path up to the castle's imposing portcullis. They would sleep here tonight. There were no other inns. Besides, this had once been Benjamin's winter home.

It was past time to take his birthright back. Not the castle—he wasn't after the old man's riches. He was here for his mother's locket. The one meant for him. The one bearing a miniature family portrait inside, painted mere weeks after Benjamin was born.

It was the only portrait he shared with his mother. His throat tightened. She had died shortly after his birth. That had been Benjamin's first Christmastide. That time of the year had not improved since.

After all these years, it finally seemed possible to retrieve the stolen necklace. Benjamin had begged for its safe return a thousand times. But his grandfather was as immovable as his castle.

The old man always said he'd give the golden locket back to Benjamin over his dead body, and the blackguard clearly meant it. He was dead now. Time for the heirloom to come home.

Benjamin shook off the ghost of his grandfather's memory as he alighted outside the castle's doors. A stream of dapper footmen flowed out to greet him.

Murmurs immediately erupted from a growing crowd of onlookers.

"Why, it's the Duke of Silkridge!"

"Happy Christmas, Your Grace!"

He entrusted his carriage and horses to his driver and the footmen, and made his way inside to see if there was room for him in the castle's crumbling interior.

As he crossed the threshold, Benjamin stared about in disbelief.

The interior was the opposite of crumbling. By all appearances, the abandoned medieval castle had been restored to its former glory and beyond.

In the reception hall, crackling fires roared behind their grates, their orange light dancing over a spotless lake of white marble. From the sound of gay voices, the Yuletide festival was well underway.

Strips of bright blue carpet guided visitors from the door to any number of destinations. An adjoining salon filled with voices and laughter. A great winding stone staircase led from one sprawling floor to the next.

At a large buffet, footmen cheerfully handed out plates of

biscuits and generous ladles of steaming mulled wine. The butler pointed him in that direction after accepting his great-coat and top hat.

Benjamin didn't want warm, sugary biscuits. He wanted a room for the night, he wanted his mother's locket, and he wanted to be gone.

Before he could have any of these things however, he caught sight of golden blond hair and laughing brown eyes. His breath caught. Just like that, his world tilted on its axis.

Noelle was here. *Right* here.

His heart beat uncomfortably fast.

She looked both the same and yet somehow even better than before. Soft curves and gold-rimmed spectacles. Happy and smiling and beautiful. Surrounded by a group of equally cheerful friends.

He'd thought she would be gone. He'd *hoped* she would be gone.

So many years had passed since he'd last seen her. For the longest time, he had expected her to have a Season in the capitol, to take London by storm. Perhaps she had done so, and he had missed it. After all, he spent his days in the House of Lords and his nights in his study.

Perhaps she was now "Lady" or "Mrs." and no longer the Miss Noelle Pratchett he remembered.

He didn't want details, he reminded himself. Learning she'd found someone else would serve no purpose, and discovering she was still unwed would not signify. And yet he couldn't help but gaze at her hungrily as she broke from her friends and made her way to the refreshment table, right in his direction.

The moment she caught sight of him, she pulled up short. All traces of laughter disappeared from her eyes. "Silkridge."

"Miss Pratchett," he replied, bracing himself for the inevitable correction.

It did not come.

"Five years," she said instead. A pearl clip pinned a sprig of holly to her hair.

"You look lovely," he blurted out, and could have kicked himself. She did look lovely. He had not meant to notice, much less give any compliments.

She ignored it. Her lips pursed. "I thought I would never see you again."

"So did I," he admitted. He had missed her so much, those first few months.

After that, he had done his best to push her from his mind. One should not dwell upon things one could not have. Such as a rekindled romance.

Or forgiveness.

She crossed her arms beneath her bosom. "No doubt you're here for the will."

Ten o'clock on the morrow. He wouldn't be a single moment late.

"I shall be gone before you know it," he promised.

"No doubt." Her smile didn't reach her eyes. "You were last time, too."

CHAPTER 2

He was back.

Noelle Pratchett gazed at the imposing, impossibly handsome gentleman before her in disbelief. For years, she had vowed that if she ever crossed paths with the Duke of Silkridge again, he deserved nothing less than the cut direct.

And yet she was rooted in place. Her knees were locked tight to keep from trembling and her traitorous eyes could not be distracted from his form.

Tall, intense, tightly controlled. It wasn't just that his clothing had been perfectly tailored to his lean, muscular body. Every thread, every stitch had been selected with the same care and precision that ruled the rest of his life.

He was never well-dressed; he was *perfectly* dressed. Every fold of his cravat, a work of art. Every crease, starched and crisp. Every hair just so, with nary a tendril out of place. His jaw, smooth and clear of stubble.

He wasn't a fashion plate come to life. The duke was no dandy. Rather, he was the very embodiment of rules and expectations. His hair, the perfect length. His waistcoat, the ideal pattern. His choices in color and style, muted but elegant. Timeless. As if an artist might paint his portrait at any moment.

And this magic, despite having just stepped inside from a long drive on a blustery day. Not even wrinkles would dare to mar the plans of the Duke of Silkridge.

He was not here for her, of course. For a while—a very short while—her naïve heart had once believed such a thing possible.

Back in those days, he was not yet a duke but rather *Benjamin*. Irresistible, despite the same haunted eyes and carefully controlled exterior. If it had not been for that one reckless kiss, she would not have believed passion capable of sneaking past his defenses.

At the time, she had been delighted. It was a fairy story. She, the penniless orphan. He, the handsome prince. What had begun as friendship had turned into so much more. He would not have kissed her otherwise. Surely this meant they had a future.

He had been horrified. They had no future at all. Indeed, the next morning he was in the first coach leaving Cressmouth. That was the last time she saw him.

Until now.

"This is a surprise," came the duke's low, comforting voice. "I didn't expect to see you."

Noelle was not comforted. She was annoyed. She hadn't *wished* to see him.

The time for girlish innocence had long since passed. She had learned her lesson well. If you open your heart, you will be left behind. She would not make such a foolish mistake again.

The duke accepted two mugs of mulled wine from a passing footman and offered one to her.

Noelle had come to the refreshment table in search of biscuits, not wine, but she supposed now was an excellent time to change her mind.

She accepted the warm mug and allowed its fragrant steam to bathe her face. "Is Christmas as you remember it?"

"Cressmouth," he corrected immediately with no attempt to mask a light shudder. "I don't know how anyone could live here."

Her spine straightened. She loved the village. Loved the people, loved the scenery, loved being wanted. That he felt himself above all of that, including her, made her vow to be Christmassier than ever just to vex him.

"I wish it would snow year-round to go with our celebrations," Noelle replied cheerfully. She gestured about the great hall. "Nothing could be merrier than a cold crisp day outside and a crackling fire inside, especially when surrounded by so many friends."

He did not look convinced. "I don't recognize anyone here but you."

Unsurprising. Silkridge hadn't spent any significant amount of time here since he was a child. During his most recent visit—five years ago—he had spent a fortnight almost exclusively in Noelle's company. At first, they had thought their friendship was deepening. During a long moonlit stroll, they'd discovered the connection between them was so much more. That perfect, magical night had culminated with their mouths meeting in a kiss. Of course, he would remember such a moment.

It was unforgettable.

"I suppose this party is in Grandfather's honor?" Silkridge gestured at the long buffet piled with refreshments.

"Not at all," she said, infusing her voice with even higher spirits than normal. "You're looking at the spirit of Christmas. The castle offers libations to weary travelers year-round."

He stared at her. "Biscuits are not the spirit of Christmas."

"How would you know, when you don't have any?" she asked.

His blue eyes narrowed. "Biscuits or Christmas spirit?"

"You appear to be sadly in want of both." She took a sip of the spiced wine. Its warmth was just what she needed. It tasted like home. "The castle's kitchen boasts the finest cooks in the region. These biscuits have no equal, and the rest of the meals are every bit as sumptuous. You will not easily find more accommodating footmen or a more thoughtful and efficient maid staff. *This* is the spirit of Christmas."

His skepticism was obvious. "Cressmouth barely holds a thousand souls. Where would Grandfather even find such a quantity to employ?"

"You said it yourself. Right here in the village. Most of us worked either for your grandfather or for the castle in some capacity."

He looked at her sharply. "You *work*?"

Noelle raised her cup to her mouth. She had not meant to give him any personal details about herself at all.

Especially not information that highlighted the unbridgeable distance between them. To those of his class, "work" was a filthy word fit only for commoners. But here in Cressmouth, work was something everyone did together, making each day even better than the last.

"Noelle," came a breathless voice from just behind her. "Have you seen the duke?"

Silkridge stiffened in affront, no doubt because he was standing within arm's reach of both Noelle and the speaker.

"Not you," she murmured under her breath, then turned to her bosom friend Virginia. "Have you checked the amphitheater? They are setting up for *The Winter's Tale*, and you know how he loves those props."

"You are brilliant," Virginia gushed. "Of course that is where he must be."

She dashed off before Noelle could introduce her to Silkridge. Not that Noelle had any particular wish to ingratiate the duke with her friends. Besides, he would be gone on the morrow. He wasn't here to make friends.

Nonetheless, she performed the niceties. "That was Miss Virginia Underwood. It is a wonder robins and song thrushes don't follow her about, singing on her shoulders. She is one of the kindest and sweetest people in all of Christmas."

He frowned. "She mentioned a duke?"

"You are not the only one," Noelle said. Her attention was caught by another familiar face.

"Noelle, you've outdone yourself." Angelica Parker lifted a china tea plate towering with biscuits. "I could subsist on the cinnamon ones for the rest of my life."

Silkridge choked in disbelief. "Noelle Pratchett is the castle cook?"

Angelica laughed. "Even better. She is the grand architect that made these biscuits possible. Without her, one might as well be greeted with gruel."

"Grand architect?" The duke blinked in confusion. "What is that supposed to mean?"

But Angelica was already gone, and Noelle didn't feel like explaining. The less he knew about her life, the better. The lives of her friends were a much safer topic.

"Miss Parker has the steadiest hand and keenest eye in all of Christmas. I once saw her create an intricate, jewel-encrusted tiara fit for royalty. You should see it."

He lifted his brows. "I find that jewel-encrusted tiaras tend to unseat one's top hat."

No. She would not find him amusing. That path only led to heartbreak.

"There you are," came another familiar voice. This one belonged to Olive Harper. "Azureford won't stop pestering me about my stallions."

"Azureford the *duke*?" Silkridge said in obvious befuddlement. "The Duke of Azureford?"

"I told you," Noelle reminded him. "You're not the only duke in Christmas."

She turned to her friend. "You need an auction, of course. Don't allow him to be the only bidder."

Olive pulled a face. "I haven't time to plan an auction. The stable roof needs to be patched and one of my broodmares is looking breach—"

"I'll organize it," Noelle said immediately. "You look after your horses and I will look after the auction."

"Noelle, would you? I shall owe you any favor you wish." Olive squeezed her hand and then dashed toward the door.

A frown marred Silkridge's ducal brow. Either Christmas familial informality or talk of a breach broodmare had met with his disapproval.

He cocked an eyebrow in Noelle's direction. "Do you allow everyone to address you by your Christian name?"

"Not everyone," she said sweetly. "You may call me Miss Pratchett."

A muscle worked in his temple.

"That was a dear friend of mine," she continued as if his

question had never been spoken. "Miss Harper has a quick mind, an enormous heart, and one of the most sought-after stud farms in all of England. She is a fascinating woman and a wonderful person."

Silkridge seemed amused by this explanation. "You make it sound like everyone in Cressmouth is a fine soul and perfect neighbor."

"Possibly because everyone in Cressmouth *is* a fine soul and perfect neighbor," Noelle agreed. She arched her eyebrows right back at him. "That is, almost everyone."

She knew she was being prickly. But sometimes the only way to protect oneself was to keep a safe distance from those who could inflict hurt.

Unfortunately, she was no longer certain such a distance existed between her and Silkridge. His presence on the same mountaintop was more than enough to send her heart racing.

"Oooh!" Ten-year-old Annie Skeffington pointed her finger at Noelle and Silkridge. "You're standing under mistletoe! Have you kissed yet?"

"What?" Noelle and Benjamin both leapt backward with almost comical swiftness.

"Doesn't count," Annie said firmly. "If you're caught under mistletoe, you have to kiss. Those are the rules."

"I don't think..." Noelle began.

"We aren't a..." the duke stammered.

Annie crossed her arms and arched a brow, clearly intending to stay put until the Christmas spirit was given its due.

Correctly interpreting the ten-year-old's militant stance, Silkridge sighed and took a half step forward. "I'll make it fast."

Noelle forced herself to step forward. "See that you do."

He did. Probably. The problem was that whenever his mouth as anywhere near hers, time seemed to slow to a crawl. The briefest brush of his lips to hers felt like the clock had been wound back. As if this was not a new kiss, but a continuation of the last one, back when they were young and giddy, and still believed moments like these could last forever.

Back when they'd both *wanted* it to.

When he pulled away, his expression seemed as dumbstruck as she felt. Her heart hammered beneath her bodice and her knees were no longer trustworthy.

"Oh, look," Annie said. "Someone else is caught under mistletoe!"

Noelle did not look as the girl ran off. She couldn't break her gaze from Silkridge. Neither one of them had resumed a safe distance.

She forced herself to step aside, out from beneath the mistletoe's shadow. Self-preservation meant more than just avoiding another kiss. It meant nipping any friendliness between them in the bud, before her foolish heart could reawaken its dreams of romance.

"Sorry about the mistletoe," she said as coolly as she could. "It meant nothing."

At first, he did not respond. Only the heat in his gaze betrayed what he might be thinking.

"Will you be attending the reading of Grandfather's last will and testament?"

"Most of the village will be attending," she replied with a noncommittal shrug. "Your grandfather meant everything to Christmas."

"He's gone." The duke's expression shuttered. "You can stop calling it 'Christmas.'"

"Mr. Marlowe was the village's savior, not its dictator," she snapped, defensive. "He didn't just rename us. He gave us Christmas every day."

Noelle could swear Silkridge muttered *humbug* under his breath.

"Then I suppose I will see you tomorrow?" he asked aloud.

Not if she could help it seemed a churlish reply.

"I expect the castle to be packed with people," she said instead. "There will be refreshments after, of course."

He shook his head. "Not for me. By then I'll be on my way back to London."

Of course he would. Their hours were already numbered.

Her lips tightened. She should not even be speaking to him. Having him at arm's reach, knowing his presence was only temporary, dredged up all the old feelings, the hackles, the shields. This was not a reunion. It was a brief, chance encounter between former acquaintances who had just shared an equally brief kiss.

If he would not stay for her before, the promise of a refreshment table clearly would not be enough to tempt him.

She doubted anything could.

"Enjoy being home," she said, reminding herself to embody the Yuletide spirit. "Christmas hasn't been the same without you."

It had been better. Safer.

She straightened her spine. From now until his departure, she would endeavor to avoid him completely. Seeing him ripped open a scar she had believed long healed.

"Cressmouth is not my home," the duke growled. "And don't call it—"

"Happy Christmas!" she chirped as sunnily as possible, then turned her back and walked away with her head held high.

CHAPTER 3

The warm fire crackling in the hearth of Noelle's bedchamber kept the chill of winter safely on the other side of her frosted window panes.

But not even a merry fire could keep her constant thoughts of Silkridge at bay.

Until he had stepped foot inside the castle last night, Noelle had been perfectly content. The ideal number of arrogant London gentlemen in her life appeared to be zero. The sooner he and his kisses were gone, the better.

This morning, she dressed with extra care. Not because she had any wish to cast a favorable impression upon Silkridge, but because she wished to achieve the opposite effect. They were not compatible in any way. She couldn't trace her parentage back one generation, let alone ten. He believed her a country bumpkin living in some forgotten village? She would prove she didn't need him or pretentious London finery to be happy.

She left her gowns and her riding habits and her dashing walking dresses in the back of her armoire and cloaked herself in an old day dress four years out of fashion. The last time he had been here, she had worn all her best garments. They had gone riding, taken long walks… she had even hoped for a dance at the upcoming assembly.

It hadn't come. He had left. She wanted no reminders of the foolish girl she had once been.

She adjusted her dowdy gown before the looking-glass. Her neighbors would not judge her for it. Cressmouth's villagers cared more about a person's interior than her exterior.

Noelle's shoulders curved. When it came to her, it was quite possible Silkridge wouldn't notice either aspect. She had spent more time trying *not* to appear as though she'd been obsessing about him, than he had thought of her in five long years.

Disgusted with herself for allowing his presence to affect her thoughts and actions even for a moment, she spun away from her looking-glass and crossed her bedchamber toward the corridor.

She paused with her fingers above the handle. The duke's guest chamber might be near hers. He could be right outside in the corridor.

The topmost floor on the north wing of the castle was reserved for the family. Noelle had earned such a prestigious spot in exchange for her work in the counting house. Silkridge was guaranteed a place due to being born in the right lineage.

If he was standing on the other side of the door, she might be forced to continue on in his company. After all, they were heading to the same place.

Well, wasn't that what her costume was for? She was nothing like his London ladies and had no wish to be. So much the better if he found her forgettable. She was doing her damnedest to scrape him from her mind as well. No—she was succeeding. Beginning here and now.

The only gentlemen who interested her were locals who loved Cressmouth just as much as she did. The Duke of Silkridge simply did not signify.

She wrenched open the door and strode out into the hall.

The only movement was far ahead where a familiar face in a pale indigo gown headed toward the marble stair.

Noelle hurried to catch up.

"Good morning," she said with genuine warmth as she reached Virginia's side. "Did you find your duke?"

"Indeed I did, the incorrigible scamp," Virginia replied with a smile. "Do you ever wish you had been born a bird so that you could soar over Cressmouth and gaze down upon its beauty from high above the rooftops?"

"I must confess the idea had not occurred to me." Noelle fell into step beside her dear friend. Virginia often spoke as if she were in the midst of a half-remembered dream. She was as likely to look for answers in the palm of one's hands than in the pages of a book.

"Can you believe he's gone?" Virginia asked.

Noelle shook her head. Mr. Marlowe had been the heart and soul of Cressmouth. "The village won't be the same without our leader."

Virginia's voice grew distant. "We are all leaders. Each sparrow takes its turn against the winds in order to guide and protect the others."

That... was an extremely Virginia thing to say. Her frequent aphorisms were one of the many reasons Mr. Marlowe had employed her as his personal advisor. Virginia's methods might be odd, but she was indisputably clever.

Noelle plucked a black cat hair from her friends puffed sleeve. "Did you see the *other* duke?"

Virginia's quick eyes locked on hers. "Your duke?"

"Not my duke," Noelle said quickly. How many people had seen that kiss? Had it looked like her heart was breaking anew? "He belongs to London."

"He belongs to England, and England is part of us all," Virginia amended, her tone pensive.

Usually, Virginia's unusual perspective brought nothing but good cheer. Today, however, her words made Noelle's heart hurt. She was uncertain what was more upsetting, the idea that Silkridge still belonged to her a little, or that he belonged to everyone else just as much.

"Do you know where they put him?" she asked quietly. "Is he here in this wing?"

Virginia shook her head. "He was placed on the wrong floor. The maid who prepared a guest chamber for him did not realize he already had a dedicated room somewhere on this wing."

The last door on the left, to be precise.

Noelle wished she did not remember how she had thrown herself into his path time and time again all those years ago. Her cheeks heated in mortification. She would never again allow herself to behave so rashly.

"Was he upset?" she asked.

"Is a badger upset when it rains?" Virginia answered, trailing her fingers lightly on the balustrade as they descended the stairs.

Noelle blinked. "I have no idea."

"Neither do I," Virginia mused. "I should pay more attention."

"Watch your step," Noelle cautioned her. "Pay attention to

the stairs."

"It doesn't matter if the maid's mistake upset Silkridge," Virginia decided.

That was an unusual sentiment. Noelle raised her brows. "Because he turned his back on the village and never returned?"

"Because it's already morning, and too late to undo. We may be deeply embarrassed for the castle staff to have treated Mr. Marlowe's grandson like an ordinary guest, but he will be gone in a few hours and no doubt has already put the incident out of his mind."

The only thing Noelle was deeply embarrassed about was the probability that Virginia was right.

Silkridge had put Noelle and the entire village out of his mind easily enough once before. It would take him no time at all to do so again. Her stomach twisted. She tried to shake off her disillusionment.

There was no reason for her heart to feel clutched in ice at the idea of being forgotten again within the week. She knew his inevitable dismissal was coming. That was why she needed to avoid him at all costs. It would not feel as though he were abandoning her a second time if she was the one who kept him at bay.

He wanted to be gone. She wanted him gone. For once, they were in agreement.

"Silkridge looked quite dashing yesterday," Virginia said. "Didn't you think he cut a fine figure?"

"I didn't notice," Noelle said quickly. She could recall every stitch, every smirk, every dismissive comment about Christmas from memory. And she had done so all night long.

"It was the top hat," Virginia decided. "The way it was so

perfect, sooty black with a dusting of ice crystals upon the rim, set at just the right rakish angle. Or perhaps it was his cravat. Have you ever seen a knot so intricate? Both elements drew the eye to his face, which I must say is no hardship to gaze upon. Eyes as blue as a great crown crane, cheekbones as—"

"Enough!" Noelle blurted. "I saw him. Fancy ascot. Attractive birdlike eyes. Warm lips. Please don't keep describing him to me."

Virginia narrowed her eyes in consideration. "The two of you would make a striking pair, don't you think?"

"We wouldn't even make it through an afternoon," Noelle said flatly. "He is the last man I'd choose. When I marry, it will be someone who respects me, my village, and everything I love."

"Interesting," Virginia said as if Noelle had helped her to solve a great mystery.

"Interesting that I want a husband who loves and respects me?" she asked dryly.

Virginia's brows arched. "Interesting that when I mention Silkridge, your first thought is marriage."

"He is the embodiment of everything I do not want," Noelle enunciated firmly.

She was in no danger of falling in love with him. Silkridge had not only left her, he had abandoned his own grandfather. That behavior spoke volumes. Noelle rather hoped the duke had been written out of the will completely.

"He hates Christmas," she said. "He's impossible."

"Does he hate *Christmas* or Cressmouth?" Virginia asked.

"Same thing," Noelle answered.

Rejecting Christmas meant rejecting Cressmouth. Rejecting Noelle. She was as much a part of this village and everything it stood for as the mountain breeze that blew through it.

Virginia lifted a shoulder. "Perhaps he has changed."

"He has not," Noelle said. Last night had proven as much. His position on Cressmouth had been clear. "Nor has he given any sign of wishing to bend on the matter."

"Sometimes rigid is good." Virginia's lips curved wickedly.

Noelle slanted her a warning look. "Do not even suggest—"

Virginia blinked innocently. "That nature always finds a way? The woodpecker relies on a beak as hard as stone in order to seek sustenance. Dukes are not so different."

Whatever Virginia meant, Noelle disagreed. Silkridge wasn't seeking anything here, sustenance or otherwise. That was the problem.

She pushed him out of her mind as they reached the bottom of the stair. A queue had formed downstairs in the main corridor. They were early. The doors had not yet been opened to allow in those called for the reading of the will.

"Miss Pratchett and Miss Underwood!" A portly gentleman with white hair and an omnipresent worsted cap atop his head enveloped them in a jovial embrace.

Fred Fawkes was Noelle's mentor, or at least he had been before age had begun to affect his memory and his hearing. Now he went nowhere without a trusty ear trumpet clutched in one hand.

"Good to see you, Mr. Fawkes," she shouted into the ear trumpet. "You are looking handsome as ever today."

She was never sure if he completely understood the things she shouted into his ear, but she did her best to include him all the same. He had been Mr. Marlowe's clerk for decades. One could be forgiven for thinking Mr. Fawkes as responsible for turning Cressmouth into Christmas as his old master had been.

Noelle did her best to be just as indispensable. Mr. Marlowe was gone, and Mr. Fawkes was no longer a clerk, which meant Noelle was now the lynchpin of the counting house.

Or at least, she had been until now. She did not think Mr. Marlowe's will and testament would strip her from her post, but she could not be certain whether the will had been revised recently enough to include her.

The doors opened, and the queue streamed from the corridor into a large chamber with hundreds of chairs.

"Now, Miss Pratchett." Mr. Fawkes pinched her cheek. "I must ask you to mind the counting house for me while I attend the reading of Marlowe's will."

"I have been attending to the counting house since you retired four years ago," she reminded him as gently as one could whilst screaming into an ear trumpet. "All of Cressmouth is under the castle roof attending the same reading."

Mr. Fawkes looked startled. "Is that so? When do the proceedings start?"

Noelle hooked her arm through his and led him into the crowded chamber. "At this very moment."

CHAPTER 4

When Benjamin arrived downstairs for the reading of the will, he was already in a restless mood.

It had begun last night when he was shown to a recently renovated bedchamber in an unfamiliar part of the castle. Though the room and its fire were welcoming, he could not help but feel a stranger in a place where he had spent a good part of his childhood.

The feeling had not abated. He had tossed and turned, torn between his anger toward his grandfather and the wholly unacceptable rush of longing he felt every time he thought of Noelle. Cressmouth was torture.

He was glad this particular trial was almost over. Scant moments remained. Sit through a short reading, collect the locket, be on his way.

At least, that was what he had expected prior to finding himself in an enormous chamber stuffed with countless spectators. Despite what appeared to be the presence of hundreds of chairs, that opportunity had vanished long before

Benjamin had entered the room. He was forced to stand with his back against the wainscoting like a wallflower at her first dance.

"Why is the solicitor primping on a dais in a ballroom as if this were a stage?" he growled to the person next to him.

Belatedly, he recognized the woman as the jeweler who made tiaras fit for royalty, not that there could be much call for extravagance in the middle of nowhere.

Benjamin wished he hadn't recognized her at all. No good could come of making personal connections with the villagers. He would be leaving them behind within the hour.

Leaving Noelle behind was hard enough.

"This village loves the stage," the jeweler replied cryptically.

He snorted. "All the world's a stage, and the inhabitants merely players?"

"Shakespeare." The jeweler inclined her head. "Very nice. Mr. Fawkes would be proud."

Benjamin perked up despite himself. The castle clerk had been dearer to him than his own grandfather.

He scanned the room in vain. "All these people cannot possibly be named in the will."

"We are," the jeweler answered with pride. "Mr. Marlowe would never forget one of his flock."

Benjamin shot her a wry glance. "Because my grandfather was such a good shepherd?"

"Because he loved a menagerie," she corrected with a grin. "He would have turned this castle into a circus if Mr. Fawkes would have let him."

Benjamin was unsurprised to hear that his eccentric grandfather had not become any less odd with age. Nor was he surprised that this characteristic should be met with an indulgent smile and nostalgic tone of voice. Grandfather had been devoted to Cressmouth, and Cressmouth alone.

He was saved from this line of thought by a glimpse of golden blonde hair. Noelle was here.

Of course she would be. The entire village was here. But they were not the ones who made his heart beat faster and his mind empty of reason.

She looked just as beautiful in the morning sun as she had by candlelight the evening before. Even more beautiful, if such a thing were possible. He should look away. And he would, any moment now.

He loved the way she wrinkled her nose any time her gold-rimmed spectacles started to slide. He loved the way she laughed, the way her whole face lit up, the way joy seemed to emanate from her entire body. Not that he could see much of it. She was surrounded by friends and well-wishers.

Benjamin was a moth drawn to her flame, but this community was her butterflies. Colorful and energetic where he was distant and staid. Cressmouth was where and how she thrived. Noelle did not need him disrupting her happy life.

He wished he had not run into her. It would have been easier for them both if he had glimpsed her from afar and slipped away with her none the wiser. Now that he had seen her, had spoken to her, he should let that be enough.

But his feet were moving in her direction as though logic held no sway.

Imbecile. He wasn't edging sideways through a packed crowd just to be closer to a woman who distrusted him, he told himself. He had simply noticed that Noelle stood directly beside Mr. Fawkes, who Benjamin was thrilled to see still grumpy and kicking.

When he got within shouting distance, Mr. Fawkes and

another older gentleman were too engrossed in a lively conversation about the causes and treatments of gout to notice Benjamin's arrival.

Noelle, however, noticed right away.

He could tell by the way her stance stiffened.

"Can the Duke of Silkridge be heading straight for Miss Pratchett?" came a loud whisper.

"Fret not," Noelle assured her friend. "My gaze cannot be turned by London gentlemen."

But her eyes had not left Benjamin.

"What's so wonderful about Cressmouth lads?" he asked as he reached her side.

She narrowed her eyes as if mentally preparing for battle. "They can be counted upon to be here every day, not to give a girl bad dreams at night."

"You dreamt about me," he said with pleasure. At least he was not alone.

"*Bad* dreams," she reminded him. "Ghastly."

His smile faded. He deserved that. She knew as well as he did that if he could be trusted to do one thing, anything, that thing would be to leave.

At least there was honesty between them.

He wished there were also about a hundred fewer spectators. He wished a lot of things.

But he was a man of reason and practicality, not poetry and love. Benjamin's priorities had been predetermined. A duke served his country, not himself. Noelle was not part of the equation. He absolutely shouldn't be fascinated by the wrinkle of her nose or the way her lips pursed to one side when she was thinking.

If the two of them were too different before, the chasm was now impossible. She *was* Cressmouth. She was not for him at all.

He forced himself to tear his gaze from Noelle and concentrate instead on Grandfather's clerk, Mr. Fawkes. Mr. Fawkes still wore that oversized worsted cap, every bit as white and fuzzy as the shock of hair it attempted to corral beneath.

His beard was longer than Benjamin recalled, his cheeks ruddier, his eyes just as sparkly. Seeing him was as if no time had passed at all.

Mr. Fawkes caught a glimpse of Benjamin and broke off the discussion of gout at once.

Benjamin grinned despite himself. It was good to see the old man. "Mr. Fawkes! You haven't aged a day."

"Who's this lad?" Mr. Fawkes demanded to Noelle. "He looks familiar."

Benjamin froze in shock and hurt. Perhaps the years hadn't been so kind after all.

"The Duke of Silkridge," Noelle replied loudly.

Mr. Fawkes furrowed his brow. "Scrooge, you say?"

Benjamin gaped at him. "What the devil is a 'scrooge?'"

"*Silkridge*," she shouted into his ear. "Where's your ear trumpet?"

"You must be mistaken." Mr. Fawkes lifted an ivory-and-silver horn to the side of his head. "The Duke of Silkridge passed away years ago."

"His son," Noelle said into the ear trumpet. "Benjamin. The heir."

Mr. Fawkes's face lit up. "Oh, of course. Why didn't you say?"

Noelle gave a quick curtsey in apology.

Benjamin stepped forward, relieved to have been recognized at last.

"I—" he began.

But Mr. Fawkes did not hear him.

"Suppose you are wanting to know what could bring down a crotchety buzzard like your grandfather," Mr. Fawkes said with a hacking laugh.

Benjamin had no wish for a detailed accounting. "I—"

"Came down with quincy," Mr. Fawkes continued unabated. "Spent weeks with poultices wrapped about his head. Looked like an Egyptian mummy, he did. Except for the size of his neck and chin and tongue. Swelled right up after that abscess on his gum. I'm thinking of having every one of my teeth pulled to be safe."

"Have you enough to bother?" cackled the gentleman who had been debating gout remedies moments earlier.

"Good point," Mr. Fawkes said, slapping his knee. He turned back to Benjamin. "A man must do *something* to prepare for his eventuality, wouldn't you say?"

Benjamin swallowed. "I…"

"This lad takes more precautions than most," Mr. Fawkes boomed to his companion. "Can't blame him. His sire also died during Christmastide. He suffered the ague. Virulent strain even quinine couldn't cure."

This time, Benjamin didn't try to speak. He couldn't. The breath had been robbed from his lungs at the reminder of his loss.

All Christmastide had ever done was steal family members from him. Father's loss had nearly broken him. Becoming duke was easy. Duke was merely a job, a task to perform. But Benjamin had not been ready to lose another parent.

Mr. Fawkes's companion lifted a quizzing glass and squinted at Benjamin. "Didn't the old duke have black hair?"

"That he did," Mr. Fawkes agreed. "My lad here takes after his mother in that regard."

Each word sliced open old wounds.

Everyone Grandfather's age remembered Benjamin's mother. They could tell at a glance which parts of him reminded them of her.

He could not. His grandfather had absconded with the only heirloom he had ever cared about. The one with the portrait of Benjamin's mother inside.

Mr. Fawkes used his ear trumpet to gesture toward Benjamin. "My lad here is the last of his line on his mother's side."

That was why he needed the locket. It would be like having a family again. He tried not to clench his fists at the unwelcome reminder. This quest wasn't just a matter of retrieving something that was lost, but a chance to get his family back. If only as painted miniatures hanging about his neck.

He tried to swallow, but his throat was too tight. How he had hated being estranged from his grandfather. He missed having a family. Would have visited as often as he could if it were possible to be cordial.

It had not been possible. Benjamin's birth had caused his mother's death, and Grandfather had never forgiven him for the loss. He had turned all his love to Cressmouth instead. For Benjamin, there had only been coldness.

Grandfather had once snarled that he would rather have lost his grandchild than his daughter. What use was a baby? She could always have another. Or at least, she might have, had she recovered from Benjamin's difficult birth.

After realizing the depth of his grandfather's hatred, Benjamin had taken his words to heart. He would be as useful as ten dukes. He would make the House of Lords his family, his home, his reason for being. He would not limit his responsibilities to one small village but rather the whole of England. Perhaps in doing so, Benjamin could make his mother's sacrifice worth it.

"Well," Mr. Fawkes's gouty companion said with a smile. "At least Your Grace is still kicking. That makes it a happy Christmas, I say."

"There's nothing happy about Christmas," Benjamin said flatly.

He hadn't expected Mr. Fawkes to overhear him, but the man's eyes had been following Benjamin's lips close. "Now, lad, it isn't all bad. What about the title? You inherited a dukedom."

"And lost my family," Benjamin pointed out. It would be better *not* to love than to have someone unexpectedly ripped from one's life.

"True." Mr. Fawkes leaned forward to pat Benjamin on the forearm in sympathy.

Before Benjamin could answer, the growing crowd of onlookers could not hold their tongues any longer. They interrupted Mr. Fawkes like a basket of kittens, tumbling over each other to present themselves to Benjamin. Before he could object, he was swept away from Noelle and into their midst.

"Your grandfather was the loveliest man I ever met," said a stout woman in a flour-dusted apron. "Christmas wouldn't exist without him."

"Cressmouth," Benjamin corrected firmly. "Let us not overstate the matter."

"He gave me a post when others would not," said a young girl with a scarred face.

"That's because they're foolish where you're from," said the woman in the apron. "Mr. Marlowe wasn't foolish."

"Not one bit," agreed a gentleman leaning on a cane. "Why, without him there wouldn't be an annual biscuit festival."

"Annual biscuit festival," Benjamin echoed, deadpan. "He *did* invent Christmas."

"What was it like?" asked a stableboy breathlessly. "To have a grandfather as wonderful as Mr. Marlowe?"

"What do you suppose it was like?" A man with dirt-stained fingers cuffed the lad on the back of the head. "A miracle, no doubt."

"A marvelous influence, I reckon," a different woman piped in. "His Grace is known as the most powerful lord in parliament. When the crown needs something done, they put the Duke of Silkridge in charge. Who does that sound like, if not our Mr. Marlowe?"

Benjamin ground his teeth. It did not sound like his grandfather at all.

It sounded like a duke who gave up sleep, gave up hobbies, gave up every spare moment he ever had for the betterment of his country. It sounded like skipped meals and ink-stained fingers. It sounded like audiences before the Regent and impassioned speeches to the House of Lords. It sounded like someone who didn't have time for playing at Christmas because he was too busy doing his part to keep England safe and secure for the people in this room and every other corner of the country.

Grandfather hadn't been there for any of it.

"Why is Mr. Marlowe's grandson on his feet?" someone yelled.

"A chair, if you please!" someone else called out. "Mr. Marlowe's grandson needs a seat!"

Benjamin could not believe the reasoning. Here in Cressmouth, he was famous not for being a duke, but for being related to his irascible grandfather.

A young lady popped up from her chair. "You can have mine."

"I'll stand," he bit out. "I will not steal a lady's seat."

"I knew you wouldn't," she said with a self-satisfied smile. "When it is his turn to do so, the sparrow always leads into the wind."

Benjamin stared at her more closely. "Weren't you the young lady hunting for a duke?"

She nodded. "I found him prancing between the verdant tree and fake bear, as a duke is wont to do."

He blinked. "I vow that I have never in my life—"

"You are not the only duke in Christmas," she said vaguely.

"So I've gathered." He couldn't be gone quickly enough. "I suppose there are two of us, then? Perhaps three?"

"There are twelve dukes in Christmas." She cast a proud glance toward her neighbor as if to verify such an absurd claim.

"Twelve dukes of Christmas?" he repeated in disbelief.

Bloody hell, she had actually gotten him to say Christmas instead of Cressmouth.

"It's too bad Tiny Tim isn't a duke," murmured her neighbor. "Then we could have thirteen."

"You're absolutely right," said another. "I suppose we have Mr. Marlowe to blame for that."

It was all Benjamin could do to keep his head from exploding. He was not going to ask who Tiny Tim was, and he definitely wasn't going to ask what on earth his maternal grandfather had to do with anyone becoming a duke.

Benjamin's title had been the last gift from his father. Grandfather had given him nothing but heartache.

A gong sounded on the side of the dais and then the solicitor took center stage.

"Shh!" Several ladies shushed the crowd. "The reading is about to start."

Thank God. Benjamin forced his tense shoulders to relax. In a matter of hours, his carriage would be leaving Cressmouth and he could return to real life.

"We are gathered here today," the solicitor began, "for a reading of the last will and testament of our beloved Mr. Jacob Marlowe, who rescued our failing village and established Christmas in its place. Would anyone like to begin with a few words?"

No. No words. Benjamin tried not to groan audibly. There were a few hundred people stuffed into this ballroom. If everyone said a "few" words, the reading wouldn't be over until nightfall.

Yet he had no choice but to stand there and listen.

To his surprise, the heartfelt speeches indicated that the village did not revere his grandfather as an exemplar of excellence. They simply revered him, oddities and all.

Apparently, in addition to the absurd idea of establishing a village dedicated to celebrating Yuletide year-round, Grandfather had had thousands of other eccentric notions. Plans that the villagers had found creative ways to indefinitely postpone.

Preparing a place from which to launch a hot air balloon for when dirigibles became *de rigueur*.

Requiring the kitchen to dye all food the colors of the flag to show support of Britain's efforts against Napoleon.

Installing water tunnels to turn the castle into a circus, complete with tightrope walkers above a pit of crocodiles.

Good lord. Turning Cressmouth into Christmas was perhaps the sanest of all his grandfather's mad schemes.

"Was he in his right mind?" Benjamin asked the older woman to his left in wonder.

"He was a jolly, mischievous fool," she replied with damp eyes. "I shouldn't be surprised if his will is full of more of the same."

A mischievous fool. Iron encased Benjamin's heart. If he had been summoned all the way to the northernmost peak of England a few days before Parliament was set to start anew, only because his grandfather found it *amusing* to manipulate emotions even after his death—

"And now for the reading of the will," announced the solicitor.

Benjamin listened in growing trepidation as it seemed like every person in the room was named before him. His stomach tightened. If he had come all this way, only to learn that his grandfather had buried himself with the locket as a final selfish insult—

"—and to my grandson, Benjamin Ward, Duke of Silkridge, Earl of…"

Benjamin's head snapped up.

The solicitor cleared his throat. "'Be changed or be cursed. This is your last chance.'"

"Oh, for the love of…" Benjamin ground his teeth.

Of course, Grandfather would choose melodrama in favor of plain English. Mischievous fool indeed.

It was all he could do not to yell, *skip to the part where my mother returns to me.*

The villagers wouldn't understand. He doubted they knew the locket existed or would care even if they did. It was of value to no living person besides Benjamin, who was tired of waiting. He had suffered more than enough Christmas *and* Cressmouth for the rest of his life. As soon as the heirloom was in his hand, he would leave this place and never look back.

The solicitor continued, "'You must complete the renovations on my unfinished aviary.'"

"Complete the what on his what?" Benjamin spluttered in disbelief. "He isn't granting me a bequest. He's asking for a favor. Is that even legal?"

He should not have expected better, and yet he was still bitterly disappointed.

"—I do not grant Silkridge the privilege of populating the aviary with an appropriate collection of birds—"

"Thank God," Benjamin muttered.

"—but in order for restorations to be considered complete, Silkridge must cut open a ceremonial bottle of champagne upon its threshold before witnesses—"

"'*Sabrage?*' I'm to slice the bottle open with a saber, just as Napoleon does when conquering new territories?" Benjamin gaped through the crowd at the solicitor in disbelief. "Shall I design a colonial flag for the aviary as well? What kind of daft restorations are these?"

"—and stock the interior with its first symbolic bird, which must be a—"

"Dodo?" Benjamin guessed. "Raptor? African swallow?"

"—partridge."

Benjamin blinked. He was to break a bottle of wine upon the helm of a landlocked aviary in order to present all and sundry with their first ceremonial... partridge? His teeth clenched.

Of course he was.

"The aviary must open on Twelfth Night," the solicitor

concluded. "Silkridge must remain on premises until that date, or else forfeit forever the gold locket currently held in trust."

"Are you *bamming* me?" Benjamin's blood heated. "I don't have that much time to waste before the new session of Parliament."

The elderly woman patted his arm. "Where there is a will, there's a way."

"That is *not* what that phrase means," he muttered. Where Grandfather was concerned, there was rarely a way.

Muscles tight with anger, Benjamin made his way toward the dais. Grandfather had betrayed him not once but twice, by withholding the locket from its rightful owner first in life and now also in death.

He had obviously taken pleasure in crafting his ridiculous challenge. Benjamin clenched his fists. He hated that his grandfather was making him dance to strings for something that should already be his.

A grandfather was meant to love his grandchild. Not taunt him with the memory of his dead mother.

"Where is it?" he demanded as he stalked to the dais.

The solicitor lowered the papers. "Where is what?"

"The locket," Benjamin growled. "Before I lift a finger, I must verify it still exists and that my grandfather isn't toying with me."

"Mr. Marlowe would never toy with his grandson," chided a kindly voice behind him.

If only that were true.

CHAPTER 5

After stalking out of the reading of the will, Benjamin did not stay to share refreshments with the rest of the villagers. His appetite had been spoiled, and he certainly didn't feel like sharing stories about his grandfather.

Nor could he return to his cold, impersonal chamber. There was nothing intrinsically wrong with the guest quarters. They had clearly been recently renovated and were spotlessly clean. But a bedchamber was all it was.

If he was going to be trapped here for the next few days, he was going to need an office... Or at the very least, a writing desk and stationery. He must send word to London that he had suffered a brief delay but would still arrive well before Parliament opened to continue policy discussions with his committees.

And then he would do whatever it took to make the aviary halfway presentable and shove a partridge inside so that he could retrieve the locket and be on his way. By tomorrow, if possible.

It all depended on the current state of the aviary's reconstruction.

He caught sight of the lead housekeeper. Perfect. No one would know the castle better.

"May I be of service, Your Grace?" she asked.

"I hope so." He tried his best to mask his impatience with his grandfather's machinations. "Is there an empty study I could use or a desk I might borrow?"

"The counting house," she replied without hesitation. "It was your grandfather's primary study. I am confident you will find all you need there."

Of course. Mr. Fawkes had clerked in the counting house since before Benjamin was born. After seeing the state of his health yesterday, Benjamin had assumed Mr. Fawkes had retired at the same time as Grandfather.

No matter. Even if the room had been untouched for some time, the housekeeper was right. It should contain everything Benjamin might need. At least for such a brief stay.

The counting house might be a small chamber atop the south tower, but in some ways, it was the heart of the castle. That was where all the accounting practices took place. The resident clerks ensured every detail was carefully logged in meticulous journals of accounts. Mr. Fawkes and his books boasted an encyclopedic knowledge of every transaction the castle had ever incurred. The room would be empty, but still be well-stocked with supplies.

Benjamin strode to the south tower and wound his way up to the top of the turret. To his surprise, every wall sconce he passed contained a lit candle.

The pale yellow light did nothing to warm the icy tower. Instead, they cast spidery shadows across the gray stone walls, the dark patterns scurrying and leaping in syncopation with each foot fall on the stairs.

Benjamin had always hated the counting house. Too distant, too dark. Too cold. The claustrophobic stairwell and the cramped little rooms made tales of princesses locked in towers seem more like a Gothic mystery than a fairy story. He could not wait to leave it all behind.

When he reached the top, he shoved open the slender oak door.

His pulse skipped. He was not alone. The queen was in the counting house counting out her money.

Or plotting how to rid the castle of an unwanted duke.

Noelle glanced up from whatever correspondence she'd been writing and froze, plume in hand. "What are *you* doing here?"

"What are *you* doing here?" he countered brilliantly. She had always managed to wipe all intelligent words from his mind.

At first, he did not notice her lack of response because he was too busy drinking in every aspect of her person.

The gold-rimmed spectacles were perched on the tip of her pert nose. Her coif, a loose twist. Half a dozen soft tendrils fell against her slender neck or kissed the side of her cheeks. Even scowling at him, she was a vision. His heart thumped.

How he wanted to brush those soft tendrils from her face with the pad of his thumb and lower his mouth to—

"I work here," she said, her voice remarkably even for a woman who likely wished to stab him with the quill in her hand.

He had never apologized for leaving. To do so, he would have to explain emotions he preferred to bury. Like why he could not bear another attachment… and another loss. The fissures she created in the shields around his heart were a liability.

He had not wished to hurt her by leaving. But it had been kinder to leave when all they'd shared was a single kiss. Prolonging the inevitable would have been much crueler. For both of them.

This time, Benjamin would keep his distance.

"If you worked for my grandfather, why are you still here?" He glanced about the otherwise empty room. Being one of Grandfather's secretaries sounded like torture.

"Why wouldn't I be?" She glanced up from her correspondence. "Mr. Marlowe didn't sack me. He died."

"Shouldn't whoever is in charge of the counting house be going through the journals and completing documents?"

He realized his mistake as soon as the words were out of his mouth.

"You work here," he said before she could reply. "You took Mr. Fawkes's place."

"That's right." She bit her lip. "He helped me during the transition. His mind is sharper than his hearing."

Benjamin nodded. "I don't doubt it."

A new silence fell, different than before. Worse, he realized. Noelle was no longer expecting him to apologize for the past. She assumed he wasn't going to.

He wished he could. That there was anything at all that could excuse his absence. From the first, he had enjoyed her company far more than he should.

By the time he'd learned she was an orphan far below his class, it no longer mattered. They were already inseparable. *Too* inseparable. Their friendship would have challenged

Society more than enough. That first stolen kiss had sent him reeling. Retreat was the only safe path for them both.

Gingerly, he stepped into the counting house and seated himself behind the great mahogany desk that had once belonged to his grandfather.

The only items in the room were his large desk, her small desk, a bookshelf, and a pitiful fire spitting orange behind the grate. They were alone.

Very, very alone.

He cleared his throat. "Should you summon a maid?"

She raised her brows. "To watch over me sitting in my chair at my desk as I perform the duties of my post, as I've done alone every day for the last four years?"

Fair enough. Yet they could not continue like this.

He tried again. "Should *I* summon a maid?"

"You're not going to kiss me again, much less compromise me," she said flatly. "Should you working at your desk whilst I work at mine raise any eyebrows, I preemptively decline any resulting marriage proposal. I would prefer to remain a spinster."

That was clear enough.

Benjamin broke her gaze in order to rummage through drawers and pigeonholes for supplies. He found ink and wax. But peace of mind was nowhere to be found.

Being forced to face the woman he had hurt was hell. Especially because he could not make things better or change the past. He wouldn't if he could. Leaving had been the right choice. And going back in time to erase their stolen kisses… Even he could not bring himself to do that.

Before he dipped his quill in ink, he slid her another glance from the corner of his eye. Something was different. Something important. It wasn't her looks; she would be beautiful no matter what she wore. His gut clenched. It was what was missing.

Her smile.

He had never seen her without it for this long. It was one of the first things that had attracted him to her. One of the many reasons he had not wished to disappoint her with a goodbye. Even this morning, she had been in good humor, laughing with her friends.

Granted, he could not count himself amongst that number, but the chilliness emanating from her corner of the room was even frostier than the weather outside.

"Did something happen?" he asked.

"Something happened," she agreed. "You didn't stay for the remainder of the reading?"

"I couldn't." He would not explain the spiral of anger and frustration his grandfather's final game had caused. Even now, he could not be certain that dancing to the old man's tune would result in anything at all. Yet he had to try. "What other tricks did Grandfather leave behind?"

Her expression was grim. "His will instructed me to remain as clerk and personal advisor to you during the reconstruction of the aviary."

"You're my personal advisor," he repeated. What the devil was Grandfather about this time?

She appeared as thrilled as Benjamin was about this new development, which was not at all. "Only until Twelfth Night, when you open the aviary or leave."

"In exchange for what?" he asked suspiciously

"In exchange for nothing." She shrugged. "Those are simply his wishes."

He stared at her. "But you don't have to follow them. Not if there's no bequest hanging in the balance."

"There is a bequest. He has provided me with a generous dowry. It simply is not contingent on any particular constraints. I *choose* to follow his wishes."

Even if it means time spent with you went unspoken.

Benjamin did not ask why her bequest had come freely and his had not. Grandfather was capricious in many ways, but with Benjamin he had always been consistent.

"This won't take long," he promised her. "My presence is required in the House of Lords. I'll employ as many workers as it takes to complete the aviary as quickly as possible. First I will need to make inquiries into what's been done, what's still needed, and where one might find materials and labor nearby."

She laid the letter she had been writing atop similar such documents, tapped them into a neat rectangle, and extended the stack toward Benjamin.

"What's this?" he asked.

She did not respond.

He reached across the desk to accept the stack. His eyes widened in surprise as he riffled quickly through the pages. "This is a detailed summary of the original plans, all completed construction, all pending restorations, workers' names, directions, and wages… and the location of the outbuilding containing all necessary material."

"Yes." She set down her quill. "Everything you need should be in those documents."

She'd gathered all that information in the space of hours? For him? He gaped at her. "How did you… Why did you…"

"It's not a favor," she reminded him. "I'm your clerk and personal advisor until you open the aviary or leave, whichever comes first."

He managed not to wince at the implied rebuke. "Are you going to be here in the counting house every day?"

She arched a brow. "Performing my assigned duties and respecting a dying man's final wishes?"

"A simple 'yes' would do," he muttered. Of course she would be here.

He was stuck, but so was she. Even if Benjamin managed to find some other study to work in, Noelle would feel honor-bound to present herself each day as his clerk and personal advisor. There was no way out. They would be staring across these desks at each other until further notice.

He flipped through her documentation again, slower this time. It was good work. Clean and comprehensive. She had shaved entire days from the challenge just by offering him such a wealth of information. He slid a sidelong glance her way.

She had not known what might be in the will any more than he or anyone else had, which meant she'd had such numbers at her fingertips all along. She didn't just work here. She appeared to be a phenomenal clerk. No doubt she had made an equally impressive personal advisor to his grandfather.

"Is there anything else I should know about?" he asked.

"I took the liberty of moving your assigned guest quarters to a different bedchamber," she said without looking up from whatever journal she was perusing now.

Given her cool feelings toward him, Benjamin could only assume this meant he had been sent to the mews to sleep with the horses. Whatever surprise she had in store for him, at least it would only be temporary.

He dipped his pen in ink. The wise course of action would be to concentrate on the aviary, not on Noelle.

He dashed off a summons along with an offer of increased wages to each of the names on the list. He would gladly pay double to be done with this farce.

According to Noelle's notes, the aviary required little more than window washers and workers to trim the shrubs. His spirits lightened. The reconstruction would not require a fortnight after all. He could be gone in just a few days.

At the thought, his gaze immediately returned to Noelle. Beautiful brown eyes squinted behind thin spectacles. Plump pink lips pursed to one side as she concentrated on whatever she read. Her slender fingers tucked one of her many errant tendrils behind her ear. His pulse beat faster.

Seeing her before him was like inviting a specter into his heart, whisking him back through time to a different day, a different Christmastide, a different spark in the air.

Five years ago, he'd still believed his grandfather might grow to love him. He would never have dreamed that the old man would steal the locket, much less have to die before returning it to Benjamin.

Back then, his father had still been alive. Benjamin was not yet in the House of Lords, not yet spending every waking moment hunched over a desk or shouting at a podium before his peers.

Back then, Benjamin had been naïve enough to believe he could kiss a pretty girl and maybe it would turn to more. That love was something he could keep.

He had learned differently. Nothing good could stay. The only encounters he was meant to have were with those who wanted little from him except what they could have at that very moment. A favor. A kiss. A moment of his attention. Not a lifetime of it.

The Christmas after he'd left Noelle, Father had died. It

was the last Christmas Benjamin had acknowledged. He refused to celebrate it… or even admit it existed.

Until now. Until *here*. Until her.

Everything about Noelle reminded him of Cressmouth. Everything about Cressmouth was designed to remind and evoke Christmas. Everything about Christmas reminded him of death and loss.

Everyone he had ever cared about had been taken from him. Since childhood, he had lived in terror of losing someone he loved again, until he realized the simple solution. *Don't love.*

Such an ideology might not bring happiness, but nor did it bring despair. In a world where nothing lasted, it was better not to try, not to be disappointed, not to get hurt. He had left her because he had feared being left.

The wise course of action would be to suffer through the next few days with as much distance between them as possible. No matter how pretty she looked in her gold-rimmed spectacles. The more he spent time with Noelle, the harder it would be to go. No sense playing with fire. He should leave their brief connection in the past where it belonged.

But temptation was so hard to fight. She was right *here,* on the other side of the room. A short distance. An eternity this time. When he left Cressmouth, he would not see her again. This was his last chance to gaze upon her face, to hear her voice. To be this close.

He could not bear the silence. But what did they have to talk about, save the shared pain in their past? It would not do at all. He racked his brain for a new topic. A safer topic.

"Did Tiny Tim receive a bequest in the will?" he asked. He had no idea who Tim was, save that the man was rumored to be in want of a duchy.

Noelle stared at him for a long moment, her face devoid of expression. "No. Tiny Tim already embodies the spirit of Christmas. He wants for nothing."

Benjamin could not imagine what that meant. As much as he wished to avoid any conversation that included Christmas, he was more curious about Tiny Tim than ever. Or perhaps it was Noelle who made him curious. The more time he spent with her, the more intriguing she became.

That way lay danger. He should pay attention to the task at hand, not Cressmouth's inhabitants—and definitely not the woman seated across from him.

No matter how tempting he found her.

He forced himself to concentrate on the aviary. "I don't suppose you have a catalogue of all bird purveyors in the region, as well as literature about the ideal feed and habitat conditions of a captured partridge?"

She glanced up. "I can compile it by tomorrow."

Benjamin blinked in surprise. He had been jesting. Noelle clearly was not. He leaned back in his chair. Grandfather might have appointed her to Benjamin's side, but he had no intention of treating her like an employee.

"No need," he assured her. "Partridges are plentiful, and research is unnecessary. It's just a bird."

She lifted her shoulder. "I am a competent clerk. I don't mind dealing with the situation concerning the partridge for you."

"It's not a situation," he said. "I myself am quite competent. If I can help run Parliament, I can acquire a partridge."

"As you wish." Her expression was skeptical at best, but she returned her attention to whatever she had been working on without further commentary.

Benjamin tried not to be offended by her obvious lack of

confidence in him. He might be out of place in Cressmouth, but he was far from helpless. Such a simple project would be completed in no time. He would check the castle cellar for champagne, and stock the aviary with precisely one bird. Easy enough. He did not need her help.

Yet he could not deny his admiration of her organizational skills. The documentation she had prepared on the local workforce had been incredibly thorough. He had no doubt she would be able to deliver just as exhaustive a report on the care and feeding of partridges, the ideal time and place to purchase fowl, and the best ways of encouraging nesting upon arrival. Whatever she thought of him, he did not wish for her to believe a duke might require such molly-coddling. In fact, this was a wonderful opportunity to prove himself.

Due to his estranged relationship with his grandfather, Benjamin had correctly assumed he would neither inherit the castle nor its coin.

Given his grandfather's eccentricities, perhaps Benjamin should not have been surprised to discover the old man had left the castle in trust for the use of the entire village. It belonged to everyone and no one at once; the beating heart of a vibrant community.

Such a philanthropic plan might sound neat and tidy to someone who had never actually had to *manage* a population of any size. Benjamin, however, had spent years dealing with budgets and physical systems and dissenting opinions. Nothing was easy.

No doubt, Grandfather had believed his mad decision to donate the castle to an entire village no more capricious than his decision to squander the Marlowe fortune on the creation of a Christmas village in the first place.

Although Benjamin was unaffected personally by such

whimsy—his title and wealth came from his father's side of the family—he could not walk away without assuring himself that Cressmouth wouldn't flounder before the solicitor could make sense of the accounts.

Benjamin let out a resigned breath. He dealt with books and numbers and policies on a daily basis. The least he could do was look over the journals of record to ensure the castle's affairs were in as much order as possible.

"Where are Mr. Fawkes's notes?" he asked. "While I'm waiting on the aviary renovations, I might as well take a look at the accounts."

Noelle tensed as if the offer had caused offense. Nonetheless, she directed him toward low shelves at the rear of the room. The bookcase was packed with bound volumes with a year engraved on each spine. He frowned. For a short period of time around five to ten years ago, there were two journals for each year.

Curious, he collected the volumes spanning the last dozen years and carried them to his desk.

As Benjamin flipped through the books, Mr. Fawkes's hand slowly and inexorably devolved from clean and precise to an unintelligible scrawl. Numbers were no longer summed, but scribbled. Annotations as to what items were even being referenced began to appear as afterthoughts at best.

Unease churned in his stomach. This wasn't something he could resolve in an afternoon. Organizing this level of chaos, checking the facts, filling the gaps… It would take months to put to rights.

Months Benjamin did not have. Twelfth Night was in eight days.

Heart heavy, he reached for the next journal. This one was

the first duplicate. He let out a deep breath before lifting the cover.

This was a different hand. Bold. Confident. Unerring. He recognized it at once. Its architect was the same woman who had just handed him a fully researched report containing every detail even peripherally related to his grandfather's aviary. His esteem rose even higher.

Noelle had done more than fill in the blanks. She had checked and cross-referenced, trimmed duplicates and made tallies. This wasn't merely a correction to Mr. Fawkes's missteps. It was a masterwork. Its information and presentation more precise and illuminating than any previous volume.

Quickly, Benjamin flipped through the remaining journals. He was not surprised to discover more of the same. Mr. Fawkes's contributions, increasingly incomprehensible. Noelle's, stunningly thorough. He was in awe of the quality. Parliament had voted acts into law that weren't half as elegant and detailed as this.

The year the duplicate journals ceased must have been the year she fully replaced her mentor. Benjamin was astonished Mr. Fawkes had managed to teach her at all with the books in such disarray. Noelle must have taught herself everything she needed to know by performing the painstaking research required to remake Mr. Fawkes's journals into something useful. Good God, she was clever.

Noelle hadn't become Grandfather's "clerk." She had become his savior, and Mr. Fawkes's as well. The counting house—and every account the castle was responsible for collecting or paying—would be in complete disarray without Noelle's timely rescue. Benjamin could not help being impressed at how smart and capable she was.

No wonder she'd had every detail about the aviary at her

fingertips. It wouldn't exist without her. None of Grandfather's projects would.

Had her patrons even realized what a treasure they had? If Grandfather truly cared about his aviary, he would've put Noelle in charge. She would have had it stuffed with partridges in a trice. Two of every bird in England, no doubt.

He frowned. Why *had* Grandfather assigned the task to Benjamin, of all people? He knew the least about Cressmouth of anyone named in the will. Grandfather had to have realized Benjamin wasn't interested in the outcome. He wouldn't be bothering with the partridge and the champagne at all if the fate of his mother's locket didn't hang in the balance.

"You're scowling," Noelle said suddenly. "Do the journals not meet your approval?"

Before he could reply, the door swung open and a woman in a light blue gown and a colorful scarf rushed in.

Splendid. His muscles tensed. Instead of a duke alone in a room with one female, now there were two. He gave the new arrival a closer look. Nearing thirty years of age, at least this one did not appear to be a debutante. Perhaps Noelle had summoned a chaperone after all.

"It is adorable." The woman rushed forward to envelop Noelle in a quick embrace before pointing both index fingers at her throat. "It's perfect."

The scarf, Benjamin realized. Noelle must have presented her friend with a scarf.

"Your Grace, I present Miss Penelope Mitchell." Noelle's laughing eyes were not on him, but her friend. "Penelope, this is His Grace, the Duke of Silkridge."

"Mr. Marlowe's grandson," she breathed, as if that were Benjamin's greatest accomplishment. "How do you do? Isn't this the cleverest scarf you ever saw?"

"It's a thoughtful gift," he teased, "but I don't know about 'clever.' There isn't a colder corner of England."

Miss Mitchell laughed. "Or a more stylish one. I have dozens of scarves. This is the first one that has been personally knitted for me by Miss Pratchett."

His gaze flew to Noelle. Her organizational skills had not only conquered accounting journals, but also colored yarn. She was not just intelligent, but *talented* as well. Full of hidden layers.

Deuce it all, Benjamin had not needed another reason to hold her in high esteem. He had found her unforgettable the last time. Fate was cruel indeed to make her all the more fascinating.

"Of course you would think Cressmouth cold," Noelle told him. "You weren't even wearing your scarf when you arrived."

"I didn't bring one," he admitted. He had not planned on staying long enough for sartorial choices to matter. One night, no complications. And now…

"Miss Pratchett could lend you one," Miss Mitchell suggested. "She has an entire armoire full of scarves she knitted herself."

Noelle's cheeks flushed pink.

"That won't be necessary," Benjamin said quickly to extricate her from obligation. The next time he braved the horrid weather, it would be to climb in his carriage and go home.

Noelle sat on the edge of her desk and faced her friend. "You did not come all the way up here to show me a scarf I knitted myself. Out with it."

"It's a new perfume," Miss Mitchell admitted. She removed a small glass vial from a leather satchel.

Noelle brought the vial to her nose and lifted the stopper. "It smells… pretty?"

"It's supposed to this time. I'm looking for people to test it." From her satchel, she pulled the smallest accordion bellows Benjamin had ever seen. "Individual drops are too inefficient a delivery method. I'm developing a new dispersal system."

"Silkridge volunteers," Noelle said without hesitation.

With a practiced motion, Miss Mitchell squeezed the bellows shut. An immediate cloud of perfume shot from the opening and enveloped Benjamin in a fog of vanilla and lilac.

He coughed into his fist and waved a white handkerchief in the air to dispel the fragrant mist surrounding him. If his gesture of surrender also dispelled the diabolical women giggling to themselves, so much the better.

Noelle stroked her chin. "I believe it's too…"

"Powerful?" Miss Mitchell guessed.

"Feminine," Noelle corrected with a laugh.

"Perfect. This version is for women. The scent is meant to arouse the passions of gentlemen." Miss Mitchell lowered her voice. "I hope the duke isn't attracted to himself all day."

"I'm sure he's used to that," Noelle promised dryly.

Benjamin glared at them both. "You're going to need a smaller bellows."

"She's a scientist, not an engineer," Noelle said. "Her perfumes sell to apothecaries by the drum."

"Although I had hoped…" Miss Mitchell gave her pocket-sized bellows a frown. "Ah, well. I suppose clients can continue applying perfume drop by drop if that's what the public wishes."

"It's a lovely scent," Noelle said firmly. "No matter how one applies it. Where are you off to now?"

"Back to the laboratory." Miss Mitchell returned her items

to the leather satchel. "All that's left is proof of efficacy. A few more trials should do it."

"Be sure to come out of your workshop by tomorrow night," Noelle said. "You won't wish to miss *The Winter's Tale.*"

Miss Mitchell brightened. "I would never."

"*The Winter's Tale,* the Shakespeare play?" Benjamin asked.

Noelle's eyes shone. "Mr. Fawkes adores Shakespeare. He started the tradition."

Of this, Benjamin had no doubt. "I didn't realize Cressmouth had a theater."

"No theater," Miss Mitchell explained. "At least, not the enclosed variety. We've an amphitheater on the other side of the village that we use for plays."

"Are you mad?" He stared at the women in disbelief. "You sit outside for three hours in this weather? On purpose?"

Noelle's eyes laughed at him. "I told you. It's a Christmas tradition."

"Not Christmas*tide,*" Miss Mitchell explained helpfully. "The *town* of Christmas."

"For the last time, it's not—" Benjamin gave up.

"Will you be attending?" Miss Mitchell asked him.

Benjamin gave a theatrical shudder. "Absolutely not. I want nothing to do with Christmas."

Miss Mitchell frowned. "The village or the celebration?"

Benjamin heroically refrained from pointing out that the constant confusion would end if they left the village's original name alone.

"Both," Noelle said. "He'll leave it all behind as soon as he's able."

"When he does, there will be one less duke in Christmas," Miss Mitchell said with a sigh.

Benjamin stared at her. "Not you, too."

Noelle raised her brows. “Not her, what?”

He was starting to believe the entire village had conspired to drive him mad. “At the reading of the will, some woman claimed there were twelve dukes in Cressmouth.”

Noelle exchanged glances with Miss Mitchell.

“The mathematics appear sound,” her friend confirmed.

“Low, if anything.” Noelle tilted her head to one side and pursed her lips as if counting mentally.

“There are not twelve dukes in Cressmouth,” Benjamin burst out in annoyance.

“How would you know?” Noelle asked reasonably. “Can you even name twelve *people* in Cressmouth?”

He folded his arms over his chest. “I challenge you to name all twelve dukes, then.”

“Well, there’s you,” Miss Mitchell began. “Obviously.”

“And the Duke of Azureford,” Noelle continued. “And Olive Harper’s famous stallion.”

“You’re right,” Miss Mitchell said. “Everyone says he’s an excellent stud horse.”

“‘Duke’ the stud horse?” Benjamin said in disbelief. “That’s one of your dukes?”

Noelle raised her brows. “You’ve heard of him?”

“Everyone’s heard of him,” Benjamin said, exasperated. “But he’s a stallion. The literal kind. You can’t count a horse as a duke.”

“Why not?” Noelle asked innocently. “I’ve certainly met dukes who are absolute beasts.”

He bit back a choked laugh. The insult was not even thinly veiled.

“Thank you again, Noelle. I’m off to work on the formula.” Miss Mitchell paused at the door before disappearing into the stairwell. "Don't worry, Your Grace. I'll select a more appropriate subject to test my perfumes in the future."

Surely she didn't mean that to sound so ominous.

"She's a lady perfumer?" he asked Noelle after Miss Mitchell had gone.

"She's a chemist," Noelle answered. "Who sometimes makes perfumes."

He decided against further questions. The answers were unlikely to illuminate the matter. He needed to concentrate on returning to Parliament as quickly as possible.

Benjamin fought a twinge of guilt at being away even this long. He had dedicated himself to prioritizing duty above all else, including his personal happiness. To making himself useful. To proving his life worthwhile.

If he were truly a noble man, his responsibilities to England would take priority over his mother's locket. Above family. Above sharing a madcap morning in a counting house with Noelle.

It was just this one indulgence, he reminded himself. Once the heirloom was back in his possession he would return to the House of Lords, where he was most useful. Being alone with Noelle was a temptation he could ill afford.

He stood up. But before he could leave, a new shadow fell into the counting house.

Mr. Fawkes stood in the doorway, a jovial smile on his ruddy cheeks and the ubiquitous worsted cap clamped over his frizzy white curls.

"I knew I would find you here, my son." Mr. Fawkes beamed at Benjamin with a paternal warmth Grandfather had never shown. "I have come to help."

Benjamin loved Mr. Fawkes like a father. He wished the old man *could* help. He had admired him for so long that seeing the slow deterioration in his journals felt like a vise around his heart.

He gestured to the freshly drafted summons for the aviary workers, who at these prices would have the last details completed by the morrow. "The aviary is sorted for now, but I thank you for the offer. You are most generous."

Mr. Fawkes's jolly face crumbled in obvious disappointment. "I'm no use at all?"

Benjamin's heart twisted. "There is the matter of a partridge…"

"I know an expert on partridges," Noelle said quickly.

He doubted this. Who on earth knew an expert on partridges? Noelle had been right to redo Mr. Fawkes's books, but a man needed to feel helpful. *Order a bird* was an easy task that would ease the old clerk's mind by proving his aid undeniably useful.

Thus decided, Benjamin smiled at Mr. Fawkes. "I put you in charge of ordering the partridge."

Mr. Fawkes gave a sharp nod. "I'm not surprised. Your grandfather appreciated a bowl of hot porridge on a cold day, too."

Benjamin cleared his throat. "Not porridge. *Partridge*."

Noelle gestured toward the ear trumpet in Mr. Fawkes's hand. The older man immediately placed it to his ear.

Benjamin shouted into the opening. "We need a partridge for the aviary."

The old clerk's frown cleared in understanding. "A partridge for the aviary."

Benjamin's tight shoulders sagged in relief. This would work after all. "Yes. A partridge for the aviary. As soon as possible."

Mr. Fawkes straightened his spine with renewed confidence. "You shall have it tomorrow, Your Grace."

He gave a merry click of his heels and marched off.

Benjamin ought to take this opportunity to do the same.

"That's dealt with," he told Noelle gruffly. "I believe I'll retire for the day. Good night."

She nodded without looking up. No doubt she was the one person in Cressmouth who wished him gone as urgently as Benjamin himself.

He carried the stack of summons downstairs to be dispatched at once, and instructed the footmen not only to wait for a reply, but to promise an even greater increase in wages if the answer was anything but yes.

With the restoration of the aviary sorted, Benjamin headed back upstairs toward his guest chamber. At the landing, he belatedly realized he had no idea where he had been transferred. Noelle had mentioned she had taken the liberty of moving him. Had it been a jest?

He caught sight of a passing maid and inquired if he had indeed been assigned to a new room.

"That you have, Your Grace." She gestured down a familiar corridor. "Last door on your left."

His breath caught. Not a guest chamber. His old room. The private quarters that had once belonged to Benjamin himself.

He thanked the maid and made his way quickly down the corridor.

When he pushed open the door, he was not greeted by cobwebs or a stuffy chill, but a bright fire and a silver tray piled with his favorite cakes. He breathed in the warm, familiar scents.

Noelle had done this, he realized. She had brought back a

slice of his past and made a gift of it to him in the present. His heart thumped. She was more than a clerk or personal advisor. This move had given her away.

Whether she wished to admit it or not, a small part of her still cared.

CHAPTER 6

Noelle curved her fingers about the warm teacup in her hands and lowered her face to breathe in the fragrant, familiar aroma. These were her favorite moments of each morning.

Although her friends loved to tease her for her unusual taste in tea, the detour through the glasshouse to pluck fresh mint ensured she started each day with nature and beauty. Then, once she arrived at the castle's dining room, she broke her fast surrounded by hundreds of people she had known and loved her entire life.

What could be better than indulging a favorite ritual among such marvelous company? Until recently, Noelle might have answered *Nothing could be better.*

Today, the minty steam flushing her cheeks did not bring the same simple joy as usual. Instead of joining her friends and neighbors in conversation, her mind was locked on the gentleman least likely to partake of Cressmouth's many charms.

When she'd heard Mr. Marlowe's words for his grandson

at the reading of the will, Noelle had fully expected a man as busy and important as the Duke of Silkridge to laugh off the preposterous terms of his bequest and return to London without any attempt to fulfill the eccentric requirements.

She knew better than to read too much into the fact that Silkridge had stayed. He was not on holiday. He had been coerced into an unexpected delay that very much went against his plans.

But what about Noelle's plans to keep her distance? She, too, had been maneuvered into deviating from her safe, comfortable routine. She had been assigned as helpmate to a man she'd never expected to lay eyes on again. But now that she had…

She set her empty cup onto its saucer and straightened her spine. Just because he was as handsome and maddening and temporary as ever did not mean she could use the dining room as her private refuge.

After all, she was not afraid of falling in love with Silkridge all over again. She knew better this time. Besides, her role as personal advisor meant that every time she helped him fulfill the terms of the will, she was also hurrying him back out of her life. Which was what she wanted. Wasn't it?

Enough stalling. Noelle prided herself on not being the sort to dither, and she wasn't about to start today.

Without further ado, she marched from the dining room to the winding stone staircase leading up to the counting house and mounted the narrowing steps with determination. She was *impervious* to the Duke of Silkridge. She would prove it.

Even before her booted feet crossed the final threshold, Noelle sensed his presence.

He was seated at the oversized mahogany desk that had

once belonged to his grandfather, himself oversized in both body and spirit. Silkridge was dwarfed by neither. His presence seemed to fill the small room.

As always, everything about him was portrait-perfect. His jaw, strong and smooth. His hair, styled just so. The cut of his suit expensive, his waistcoat understated, his cravat a work of art. She swallowed.

He *looked* like a duke. One could tell at a glance. He looked as though he could rise from behind the desk and go directly to address Parliament or bow over his future duchess's hand in a London ballroom. Silkridge did not look like Cressmouth.

He looked like trouble.

There. That should put her spinning heart to rights. Noelle did her best to ignore his proximity as she crossed to her own small desk in the corner.

After taking a seat, her awkwardness did not ease. The duke, however, seemed perfectly at home in a room Noelle had come to think of as hers.

No. This would not do. If this forced togetherness reminded her of all the ways in which they were incompatible, surely politeness dictated that she should return the favor.

"Good morning," she called out cheerily. "Isn't this a lovely Christmas day?"

One could almost see his bubble of practiced calm shatter.

"Christmas is over." He cast her a dark look over a pile of journals.

"Not Christmas the village," she said with an exuberant grin. "Have you ever seen a lovelier place?"

A muscle twitched at his temple. "I don't visit villages."

"Then you agree," she replied at once, her smile even bigger. "This one is the finest you've ever seen."

He was not amused. "The people here are too…"

"Happy?" she suggested helpfully. "Compassionate? Thoughtful?"

"Friendly," he concluded as if there were no greater horror in all the world. "Every one of them insists on conversing with me whenever I pass too close."

Did they? How positively delightful. This time, Noelle's grin was unfeigned.

"You're famous," she pointed out. "And you know how Christmas loves dukes."

"I can't imagine why," he gritted out. "The villagers don't inquire about London or the House of Lords. They wish to complement me on being related to my grandfather."

"He's even more famous," Noelle agreed. "Mr. Marlowe—"

"If you say 'invented Christmas…'" Silkridge interrupted in warning.

Noelle had been about to describe Mr. Marlowe's philanthropy and philosophies, but now that the duke mentioned it…

"No one claims he invented Christmas*tide*," she allowed magnanimously. "But only an imbecile could fail to see Mr. Marlowe's impact on this village. Without your grandfather, it would not be Christmas."

There. Silkridge could not argue the point without invoking the inevitable comparison to an imbecile. Besides, there was nothing to argue. The timeline was stark.

Before Mr. Marlowe's arrival, the village had been doomed. Instead, he had managed to turn it into a place of celebration. A picturesque village on a mountainside, a majestic castle, a plethora of activities, music, food, smiling faces… Cressmouth was truly the happiest place on earth.

For Noelle, anyway. Silkridge appeared unconvinced.

"Why bother?" he asked.

To her surprise, the question sounded sincere rather than sarcastic. As if he acknowledged the possibility that someone might find Cressmouth charming, even if he himself failed to see any attraction.

Noelle had no such difficulty. Without Cressmouth, her life had nothing. The castle gave her a home. Mr. Marlowe had given her hope. More than that. The counting house gave her purpose, but Christmas gave her *meaning*.

"What's not to love?" she said simply.

"All of it," Silkridge answered without hesitation. "It's cold, it's far, it's only relevant once a year..."

"Christmas lives in one's heart, not on one's calendar." She lifted her shoulders. "In my case, it lives all around me."

Nor would she change a single thing. In fact, she resented his disapproval of her village, his dismissal of their joyful way of life. No one was forcing him to paint *I love Christmas* on his top hat. If he didn't see the magic, he was welcome to leave.

"I looked at the journals," he said, changing the subject entirely.

She knew those books like she knew her town. He was right. This was a much safer topic.

"Did you have a question about the contents?" she asked.

"No questions at all," he replied. "That's what's so impressive. Every piece of information one might want is presented within its pages in a clear, easy to follow manner. If one does not wish to peruse the inflow and outflow transaction by transaction, the bold headings and concise summaries quickly communicate the state of accounts at any given moment."

Her pulse skipped. That pretty speech had sounded suspiciously like a compliment. Affirming her position as an essential part of Cressmouth. She stared back at him in silence, almost forgetting to breathe. How long had she yearned to believe it was true?

She had been left on the castle steps as a baby. No note, no explanation, no name. Although the villagers had taken her in without question, although Mr. Marlowe had been a wonderful guardian and mentor, Noelle had never forgotten that she wasn't truly one of them. She had been foisted upon them by parents willing to leave a crying infant in an abandoned basket in the snow rather than keep her. Rather than *love* her.

From the moment she could toddle, Noelle had strived to be an indispensable part of her community. Not just to be needed, to be wanted, but to ensure she would never again be left behind. To convince herself she was right where she belonged.

Whether Silkridge intended to or not, his words had just affirmed she was at least important to the counting house.

"My own man of business doesn't keep books as nice as these," he continued. "I shall have to have a stern conversation with him about increasing his standards."

Noelle blinked. Was that a hint of a smile curving at the corner the duke's lips?

"Send him here," she said when she found her voice. "I shall whip him into shape."

Yes. That was definitely a smile. "You'd more likely stuff him with biscuits and hot chocolate. He would return home the most accomplished man of business in the city, but too portly to fit through my door."

She found herself smiling back. He had deduced the culprit behind the treats in his guest chamber.

The gesture had nothing to do with her feelings toward him. She was simply treating him with the same goodwill all

Cressmouth inhabitants showed one another. Nothing personal.

"Before I forget," he continued, "your report on the aviary was invaluable. Every one of the workers named in your list reported for duty this morning at dawn. With so little left to do, the final touches should be completed by tomorrow." His eyes met hers. "Thank you."

There was no reason for the sudden hollowness in her stomach.

She had *meant* to be useful. Helping people was what she did. He was grateful. Considered her capable and thorough, characteristics she strived to portray. Hastening his departure was a goal they both shared. So why did she feel like she was losing?

"It is my pleasure," she managed, despite the pit in her stomach.

Perhaps she was out of sorts because she had not anticipated being praised for her efforts. Not just because she was a female in a traditionally male role, but because she was simply doing her job. Providing assistance to Silkridge had literally been her mentor's dying wish. This was her post; balancing the accounts, her responsibility.

Yet Silkridge knew all this and complimented her anyway. He'd wanted her to know he appreciated her effort and recognized her talent.

He must be wonderful in the House of Lords, she realized. Demanding and exacting, without question. But also encouraging and fair. As generous with *thank you* as with demands.

"The papers say you are in charge of all of Parliament's committees," she blurted. "That you practically live in the Palace of Westminster."

"It feels that way at times," he admitted. "I lead several

initiatives but can neither take credit nor full responsibility. The committees work together toward a common goal. Every one of us wishes to make England a safer, healthier, more prosperous home for all its people."

Noelle was not at all convinced that every lord was like Silkridge. The fact that he guided his life by such a principle caused a crack in her armor. They were not as dissimilar as she wished to believe. She cared about others. He cared about others. They both put the community first. Hers was Cressmouth. His was all of England. He was as needed in the House of Lords as she was in this counting house.

The realization that they shared similar perspectives made her traitorous heart like him all the more. Her pulse skittered. She could not stay in this room another minute.

She leapt to her feet.

He jumped to his. "What is it?"

It was the obvious concern in his magnetic blue eyes. The way he strode toward her as if to rescue her from any evil, even the demons in her own mind. It was the familiar shape of the mouth she had twice kissed but never would again. It was her erratic heart, slapping its wings against her ribs as if only by allowing it to escape could she once again fly.

"I..." The word was too soft, a breath, a plea. She knew what she wanted but dared not voice it, for fear he might give it to her.

His hand touched the side of her face. It was all she could do not to nuzzle her cheek into his palm. His hand was warm, his body too close and yet not close enough.

"I'm trying as hard as I can," he whispered huskily, "not to kiss you."

She did not move away.

Neither did he. "I beg you to slap me before I lose the battle."

She could not break away. If she lifted her hand it would be to place it against his own, or perhaps to throw herself into his arms.

This was madness. He said as much himself. Yet if he was relying on her to stop him from indulging in a kiss they both knew far too dangerous to allow...

"Help!" called a footman from the stairwell. "Miss Pratchett, come quick! It's Tiny Tim!"

She and Silkridge burst apart as if galvanized.

Noelle spun toward the open door.

Silkridge was already rushing over the threshold and down the stairs. "Where is he? His sickbed? The infirmary?"

"The menagerie," the footman responded. "He lives there."

The duke paused. "Lives there?"

"He's our Christmas goat." Noelle sidestepped the befuddled duke to follow the footman down the stairs.

"What?" The duke called down to her. "Wait, *what?*"

She did not elucidate until they had reached the foot of the stairs.

"Your grandfather brought a pygmy goat back from Africa," she explained, "and declared—"

"That it was the town's official Christmas goat?" the duke asked in disbelief.

"—that he should be called... Tim." Noelle motioned for him to hurry. "This way to the menagerie."

The duke was perhaps understandably hesitant. "What other beasts are in the menagerie? Bruce, the puma? Horatio, the puffin?"

"Just Tim," she said as the footman swept open the door.

"We didn't feel it safe to introduce other animals. Tim jumps onto everything."

"Rather, he doesn't anymore," the footman put in. "Tiny Tim arrived full of vim and vigor not a week before Mr. Marlowe took ill. At first we thought his weakened spirits were due to mourning his master."

"You thought a goat was in mourning?" Silkridge repeated, incredulous. "Over a man he'd known less than a week?"

"Mr. Marlowe had a way of getting into one's heart from the very first," the footman said staunchly.

Noelle stepped between them. "What's happening now?"

"Nothing's happening." The footman gestured at the small, white-and-black spotted goat lying listlessly in a shadowed corner. "He's been doing this for a sennight."

The duke frowned. "Why summon Miss Pratchett? She was my grandfather's clerk, not his animal trainer."

"She was his personal advisor. One of them, anyway." The footman gave Noelle a commiserating glance. "We could have called Miss Underwood, but…"

"I understand," she assured him. This was not the moment for Virginia's eccentric aphorisms. This was the time for action.

She stared at the motionless goat.

"Has he been eating?" the duke demanded.

The footman shook his head. "Appetite is always the first to go when one suffers a depression of the spirits."

Silkridge looked as though he might throttle the man.

"Has anyone else been summoned?" she asked. "An expert on goats?"

With an exasperated sigh, the duke stalked over to where Tim lay, and placed the back of his hand to the goat's furry forehead as if checking the temperature of a child. "How much has he been drinking?"

Noelle stared at the goat dubiously. At times like this, she wouldn't mind a drink herself.

"Not a drop," the footman assured him. "Of anything. We have even been adding bits of ice to his bucket to keep the water nice and cool."

"Take it out," the duke said at once. "Goats require fresh, lukewarm water or they won't drink."

The footman turned wide eyes to Noelle. "Is that true?"

She had no idea, but it was as good a plan as any.

"His Grace has no reason to dissemble," she told the footman. "Please fetch a fresh pail of water. Mind that it is not too cool."

The footman nodded. "At once."

The moment he was gone, she turned to Silkridge. "Is it true?"

"Of course it's true," he said. "I've better things to do than invent fake facts about pygmy goats. Nonetheless, you should have the footman send for an expert."

"It sounds like you are one," she admitted. "How else would you know Tim's preferred temperature for drinking water?"

"One of my properties has goats," Silkridge said dismissively, as if every land owner exhaustively researched all flora and fauna upon his property.

No wonder he was phenomenal when it came to crafting laws. He was likely the only member of the House of Lords that truly understood whatever subject they were discussing.

The footman not only returned with a pail of fresh water, but with three more footmen all bearing the same.

Silkridge raised his brows. "What's this?"

"Wasn't certain how lukewarm 'lukewarm' ought to be," the footman admitted. "Brought four different varieties to ensure Tiny Tim received his preference."

To her surprise, Silkridge did not scoff at this notion. Instead, he knelt next to the goat and offered water from first one pail, then another, until at last Tiny Tim's parched tongue lapped up more than a few drops.

"He did it," the footman breathed. "Tim's cured!"

"I suspect it will take several days to recover from severe dehydration," said the duke. "You should send for a proper veterinarian all the same."

But he scratched behind Tiny Tim's ears, rather than leaping to his feet and dusting the goat hair from his ducal breeches.

Noelle's heart thumped. Silkridge was *softhearted,* of all things.

Perhaps that was why she had almost kissed him. Not because he was arrogant and bullheaded and about to disappear from her life before she would get another chance. But because he constantly surprised her with proof that he was so much *more.*

She knew not to trust romantic emotions. Being kind to a goat, being nice to her, did not mean the duke was capable of falling in love with Cressmouth or anyone in it.

Even if he could, it wouldn't be enough. Noelle was never enough. Her own parents had left her. Was it any wonder a London lord would do the same?

She knew this deep into her bones. Had sworn to never again put herself in a position to be abandoned. The very last person she should be gazing at with calf's eyes was the Duke of Silkridge. He was destined to leave her. Danger incarnate.

And yet she couldn't look away as he held a water pail to

the lips of an exhausted goat and stroked its bristly hair in comfort.

The same skills he used to command Parliament were on display before her eyes. Clever and decisive, capable and compassionate. Silkridge's ability to adapt to the moment was second to none. Anyone who chanced upon the duke engaged in such a selfless activity could be forgiven for believing him incapable of inflicting pain.

He looked up at her. "You were somehow responsible for my grandfather, Mr. Fawkes, the counting house, the castle's welcome biscuits, *and* a Christmas goat?"

"I don't mind," she stammered. "Cressmouth needs me."

It had never seemed like a lot before. Or if it had, all the better. The more the village needed her, the less likely she would find herself alone.

"You deserve a period of rest," the duke said firmly. "A holiday from this endless 'celebration.'"

She shook her head. "I would never leave Cressmouth."

He snorted. Of course he felt the opposite. He couldn't wait to leave.

His inevitable departure ought to fill her with relief, not emptiness.

She knew better than to wish he would stay. It was impossible. He was a duke. He belonged in London. She was nobody. She belonged here.

Yet she could not help but wish she could change his mind. About Cressmouth. About Christmas. About her.

If he of all people admitted Christmas was magic, it might do more than prove her right.

It could make him want to stay.

CHAPTER 7

By the third morning, the counting house was starting to feel less like a tiny chamber atop a tall, solitary tower, and more like a shared retreat high above the rest of the castle. Noelle no longer feared Silkridge might be present. She secretly hoped he was.

Her disappointment at finding the room empty was quickly eclipsed by her surprise at finding it changed.

Mr. Marlowe's side of the chamber was the same. Hers now boasted new sconces in addition to daylight from the tower window, and a cushioned chair designed for the comfort of someone of her height. The area looked positively inviting.

She stepped around her desk to the new chair and eased onto the plush cushion. Firm, but not too firm. Comfortable. Not so high that her feet could not reach the floor, not so low that the desk was out of proportion. It was perfect.

She grinned to herself as she rose to fetch the next journal in her quest to improve each one chronologically. She was almost finished with the task. With the new chair and the sunnier lighting, it would be a joy to work in the counting house today.

As she turned from the bookshelf, the scent of mint reached her nostrils.

A footman stood in the doorway bearing a teapot, toasted bread, and cheese on a silver tray. "Shall I place this on your desk?"

She nodded in wonder. The tower was too tall for bellpulls, so Mr. Marlowe had never had one installed. As king of the castle, servants brought any repast or libation he might wish throughout the day.

As junior clerk, Noelle was expected to take her meals in the communal dining rooms with the rest of the castle.

The arrangement was more than generous. Mr. Marlowe did not charge his staff or his neighbors a penny for partaking in refreshments. It had become part of her routine. Waking at dawn, walking to the glasshouse for fresh mint, stopping by the breakfast room for a bit of toast and cheese before heading up the long winding staircase to the counting room.

She had never wanted or expected more. She was still proving herself.

Yesterday, Silkridge had casually mentioned the workers had been renovating the aviary since dawn. He had been there to oversee them. Noelle had not. Her absence had not been intentional. With both Mr. Fawkes and Mr. Marlowe, she was used to being the first to her desk in the mornings. Silkridge's dedication was a surprise. In order to beat him to the counting house today, she had skipped her morning routine.

He had anticipated far more than her early arrival.

Instead of attempting to spoil her with plates heaping with meat and eggs and the finest tea in the kingdom, he had sent a tray bearing the items she actually preferred.

But how? She hadn't seen him in the breakfast room before. Noelle doubted herself capable of missing him. Whenever he was close, her skin tingled as if charged with electricity.

Which meant the duke had been forced to actively go find out what she might want. Perhaps he remembered her love of mint tea from their youth, but her breakfast habits had changed after becoming clerk. Silkridge hadn't relied on half-remembered memories. He had investigated to ensure he presented something she desired.

And *oh*, did she desire! A shiver tingled along her skin. Try as she might to deny it, the kiss they had almost shared, the one they had no business indulging, was all she could think about.

And now, blast him, every time she sipped her favorite tea she would think of him as well.

Just as she lifted the steaming cup, he strode through the door.

She did not tease him with *Happy Christmas*. It would break his heart to realize his many acts of kindness were very much in line with the Cressmouth spirit.

"Good morning." The low caress of his voice heated her more than the tea in her hands.

She blushed. "Good morning."

He took his seat behind his grandfather's grand desk as if he belonged there. As if they both did.

"How goes the aviary?" she inquired.

His blue eyes lit with satisfaction. "Almost finished."

Her stomach twisted. His achievement should make her happy. Bidding him a final farewell was what she wanted. Wasn't it?

He leaned back in his chair, his manner confident. "Shan't

be long now. The only missing piece is a ceremonial bird and a broken bottle of wine."

Noelle had never felt less like drinking champagne.

"Thank you for the tea," she said. "And the chair."

He shrugged this away as if such gifts were an everyday part of any man's morning routine. "You are good at your post. You might as well be comfortable while doing it."

The sentiment was bittersweet. As she was helping him leave, he was helping her stay. Nothing had changed.

"What are you working on?" he asked.

She held up one of Mr. Fawkes's old journals. "Deciphering this."

"Can I help?" Silkridge asked.

She nearly dropped the book in surprise. "There's only one left to do after this. It's the last volume on the right. You'll find fresh journals on the row beneath."

Without delay, he retrieved the old volume and its new replacement and returned to the desk to work.

Noelle watched in silence for a long moment. Soon, she couldn't keep the words back any longer. "Don't you have more important things to do?"

"Yes." His clear voice was matter-of-fact. "But all the things I should be working on are hundreds of miles away. As soon as I return home, I will devote myself to catching up on all my responsibilities. Until then, why not be of service to you? After all, it's just one more day."

Just one more day.

The words were icy balls of bitter hail, pelting into her with each cold syllable.

She tried to calm the erratic beating of her heart. Why now? Why like this?

The distance between them had been so much easier when

she could despise him. Now that she knew him better, she realized she had hated a version of him that had perhaps never existed.

It wasn't that Silkridge didn't care about her. It was that he cared about everyone else more. The House of Lords. England, the collective. His duty to every one of this country's noble citizens. His responsibilities to his dukedom. Noelle could never compete with that. She was an orphan, a clerk, a nobody. Their destinies could never entwine.

But with every moment she spent with him, the more she wished for a future she could never have.

Despite having no interest in Christmas or his grandfather's castle, Silkridge was seated behind the old man's desk performing the duties of a common clerk. Not because it would aid the castle, but because it would help *her*.

That was only the latest in a long string of surprises. From the first, Silkridge had made no disparaging comments about finding a female at the helm of the counting house. The opposite. Rather than try to talk Noelle out of her choices, he respected them. Had gone out of his way to make the small room in which she spent the majority of her time into a cozier place. He was doing his best to make her life better.

She would miss him all the worse.

Her fingers trembled as she toyed with her plume. "Do you like London?"

He looked up. "Have you ever been to the city?"

She shook her head.

"Then you don't know what you're missing. It's definitely not…" He glanced about the cold stone tower. "…*this*."

Noelle winced at the reminder that even if Silkridge weren't expected in Parliament, he still would have no interest in staying here. But even if her village was all wrong for him, she wanted him to understand why it was so special to her.

"I know you hate that Cressmouth is as far from London as possible whilst still being in England, but that's what I like about it," she said. "I live in a castle. I work on a snow-dusted mountain. I, a woman, can be a clerk."

"You say that like it's a good thing," he said drolly. "Wouldn't the social whirl of a debutante be more fun than the drudgery of a clerk?"

"I don't consider it drudgery," she explained. "I have no particular love for mathematics, but I adore putting things to rights. Creating order. Organizing people and events. It does not matter to me whether I'm arranging welcome biscuits in the common rooms or the transactions that pass through this counting house. The point is helping. I would much rather be useful than useless."

A startled laugh burst from him. "Are debutantes useless?"

"Not by choice," she said. "They certainly don't grow up to be clerks. They aren't in charge of their lives at all."

He raised his brows. "Pray tell, who is in charge of debutantes' lives?"

She could not tell whether he was mocking her or genuinely curious. Perhaps he had never considered a female perspective. Now would be a fine time to start.

"First, the wet nurse and then the governess," she said slowly. "That covers the first sixteen or so years. After the come-out, the ruling parties become the sponsor and the chaperone. Once a courtship has begun, it changes again. Only her father has the power to accept a suitor's request. And after that, her husband. The end."

He frowned. "Hardly the *end*. Any debutante who follows that path never has to work a day in her life. Once she's secured heirs, she's free to devote herself to fashion and parties and social calls. A life of leisure, by any estimation."

Noelle ran a finger down the spines of the journals she'd worked so hard on these past four years. "Perhaps that's not what I want."

"You are opposed to a life filled with pleasures?"

"I'm opposed to an *empty* life," she clarified. "I would not wish for idleness to define me. Work and play are not mutually exclusive. I may be up here in this tower six days a week, but seven days a week, I am out and about in the village with my friends and neighbors. We are all useful. And we all like having fun."

The corner of his mouth twitched. "Fun as in the annual house party with one of your many dukes?"

She narrowed her gaze at him. That tradition had begun well after his last visit. "How do you know about the annual house party?"

She could swear his cheekbones deepened with color.

"*Cressmouth Chronicle*," he admitted.

It was her turn to burst into laughter. "You subscribe to the Cressmouth gazette?"

"Of course not," he protested quickly. "My grandfather insisted upon the quarterly journal being delivered to my home, quite against my wishes. I have never been able to cancel the subscription no matter how many letters I send."

She giggled at the thought of him responding to each circular with an angry letter for having successfully received it. "You should read the articles. They're quite dreadful."

"I know," he admitted. "Why do you think I wrote so many demands for my subscription to be annulled? Whenever the deuced rag arrived, I could not prevent myself from reading it cover to cover."

"All is well," she assured him. "I have heard there are worse guilty pleasures a gentleman could have."

"Like building places to launch dirigibles?" he said wryly. "Or stocking a menagerie with precisely one malnourished pygmy goat?"

She could just imagine the duke's incredulous expression as he read each article. "Was there no mention of Tim in the latest gazette?"

"There was no latest gazette," he said. "At first I thought delivery was a little late, then shockingly late, then began to fear my requests to cancel had been answered after all. As it happened, Grandfather had fallen ill, and the quarterly fell by the wayside."

Noelle's breath caught. Silkridge was right. All the villagers' attention had been on Mr. Marlowe's rapidly worsening condition. In a matter of weeks, their founder had gone from a robust, jovial man to a resting place in the castle mausoleum. She froze.

Had anyone thought to inform his grandson? Was the only information he ever received about his own grandfather the snippets he gleaned from a nonsense quarterly journal? Worse, was the real reason Silkridge had not been present for his grandfather's final days because he had not known anything was amiss until the summons arrived for the reading of the will? Horror gripped her.

"You didn't know," she whispered.

His expression shuttered, but he did not pretend to misunderstand. "I would not have come anyway."

A week ago, she would have believed that. Today, she was not so sure. Silkridge's strong sense of duty would have won out over past slights. Mr. Marlowe had to know that. Her heart clenched.

The oversight was no accident. A man who would force the *Cressmouth Chronicle* on his grandson and mention every villager by name in his will would not have left a task as obvious as informing his grandson of his ill health to chance.

Whatever rift had come between them, she could no longer presume Silkridge shouldered the blame. If the duke had not been informed of his grandfather's condition, it was because Mr. Marlowe had planned it that way. Despite how his grandson might feel.

She swallowed. "Your grandfather should have—"

"He's gone," the duke interrupted. "Let's neither beatify nor vilify him. We know what kind of man he was."

Noelle was no longer certain she knew what kind of man Mr. Marlowe had been.

This village had been home for to her, if not from the moment of her birth than at least ever since her basket was discovered on the castle steps. Silkridge could not say the same. The town had not been a home for him any more than his own grandfather had been a parental figure. An eight-page circular four times a year was not the same as having a family.

She suddenly wished she could change that for him. Undo years of estrangement and give him not only a grandfather but an entire village. If he could understand why she felt as she did about Cressmouth, perhaps he would have learned to feel the same.

But that ship had sailed.

No. It had never existed. The past was immutable. Perhaps the duke had strong reasons not to wish to stay here in the present. She straightened her shoulders. All she could do was keep her distance. Protect her heart however she could.

Footsteps sounded on the landing.

She and Silkridge broke their silent gaze and turned their heads toward the open doorway.

"Begging your pardon, Your Grace." A footman stood at the ready. "The aviary is complete. Mr. Fawkes sent me to inform you that the item you requested has been placed inside, per your wishes."

Noelle's stomach sank. The aviary was completed; the partridge delivered. There was nothing left to detain the duke from leaving. He could be gone within the hour.

"Just a moment." Silkridge turned to Noelle, his expression inscrutable. "Since you love to organize events, can you arrange for a bottle of champagne and as many witnesses as necessary to be present outside the aviary at noon tomorrow?"

Tomorrow. He was giving her twenty-four hours to accomplish a task that could be completed in less than one. She swallowed. Perhaps the extra day was for them.

"As you please," she said quickly. "How many witnesses? The will specified a minimum of four."

His gaze lowered for a moment before he responded. "The entire village is welcome to attend."

She glanced up sharply from the notes she was writing. "You're making the official opening something for all?"

He raised a brow. "Did you think I would not?"

"I was positive you would not," she admitted. "Your grandfather's will and testament specifically stated that you are not required to do so. You've no particular affinity for the project. I would have assumed you'd rather finish the task with as little fuss as possible in order to be on your way more swiftly."

"And you would be right," he said. "But the village would prefer to be present. The aviary does not belong to me, but to

Cressmouth. Perhaps I'll even get a mention in the next circular."

The corner of his mouth gave a self-deprecating quirk.

Noelle did not smile. She couldn't. Her heart was beating too rapidly at the sweetness of the gesture. He was doing the opposite of what he wished to do for the benefit of her village. Or possibly… for her.

"Very well," Silkridge said to the footman. "That will be all."

"Wait." Noelle winced. Had she just contradicted a duke in front of a servant? She would apologize later. She put the finishing touches on the announcement she had been drafting and ran over to the footman. "Please see that this gets copied and posted throughout town by the end of the day. Put it next to the bills for tonight's play."

The footman accepted the papers and headed off with alacrity.

She glanced over her shoulder toward the duke's desk and nearly jumped out of her skin to discover he was right behind her. Her pulse quickened.

He offered her his elbow. "Shall we visit the recently renovated aviary?"

"As you wish," she stammered and somehow managed to curl her shaking fingers about his arm. She did her best to ignore how good the warm strength of his muscles felt beneath her palm.

Silkridge led her down the stairs and through the castle not as if they were en route to visit a partridge, but rather off to attend the finest ball in all the land.

Noelle could not help but wonder what it would be like if that were really true. If at the end of the stroll they did not enter an aviary, but an enormous ballroom filled with dancers and chandeliers and musicians. It would be magical.

Cressmouth had no shortage of assemblies, where someone or other would take a turn at the harpsichord, but it must be nothing like London.

Nothing like arriving on the arm of the Duke of Silkridge.

Even if it would only be for one night.

The thought caused her heart to contract. If she could have one night with him, a night of joy and love and magic where anything at all was possible, would she take it? Even if she knew it would all disappear by morning? Knowing she could have him no other way would make it very, very tempting. Who could blame her for seizing onto a moment's happiness, especially if a single moment was all she could get?

She tightened her grip on his arm and thanked the heavens that she would not be put to such a test. One stolen kiss would have to be enough.

When they reached the aviary, Mr. Fawkes stood at the entrance to greet them with flushed cheeks and the triumphant smile. "The finishing touch has just been delivered."

He swept open the door.

The aviary was as gorgeous as Noelle remembered. Tall and arching, paneled with angular glass windows that the workers had done a wonderful job of cleaning. Every surface shined to perfection.

Growing up through the earth floor were dozens of bushes and trees, selected to correspond with the various types of birds Mr. Marlowe had outlined in his notes. They had been watered and trimmed into a true sight to behold.

All that was missing was the bird.

She frowned. Although she knew the aviary contained

nothing more than a single partridge, the vast space seemed inordinately quiet and still.

"Do you see it?" she whispered, searching branches for a hint of feathers.

"No. I had no idea partridges were so good at the art of disguise," the duke murmured back. He turned around. "Mr. Fawkes, where is the partridge?"

"Your Grace walked right past it," Mr. Fawkes chortled. He pointed to a small tree that had not yet been planted.

A tree containing no birds at all.

The uneasy feeling in Noelle's stomach matched the expression on Silkridge's face.

He stepped forward. "That's not a bird."

"Of course not." Mr. Fawkes puffed up his chest proudly. "It's a pear tree, just like you asked."

"Not 'pear tree.'" The duke reached for Mr. Fawkes's ear trumpet. "I said…"

Rather than place the horn to Mr. Fawkes's ear, the duke handed it back to the old clerk without another word and turned to face Noelle with a desperate expression.

"Pear trees are… tastier than porridge?" she offered weakly.

Silkridge threw up his hands in exasperation. "I shall never escape this place."

His words were a knife in her gut. The duke might want to kiss her, but he didn't want to stay.

"Is something wrong?" Mr. Fawkes asked nervously.

"Thank you for your service," Silkridge shouted into the old clerk's ear trumpet. "The castle wouldn't be the same without you."

Mr. Fawkes beamed at the duke and patted him on the

shoulder. "Anytime you need me, lad. I am at your beck and call."

The duke managed to wait until Mr. Fawkes exited the aviary before letting out a long slow breath.

Noelle felt for him. The old clerk's ruined hearing had failed the duke not once but twice. Both times, Silkridge had been a remarkably good sport. She doubted his grandfather would have handled the situation with such grace. Silkridge was a good man.

She, on the other hand, was far less noble. A tiny part of her was glad that Mr. Fawkes had failed to come up with the goods as promised. His mistake had given her a reprieve from the duke's inevitable departure. She could keep him a little while longer. This was a blessing.

The duke swung his frustrated gaze from the pear tree to her. "Stop the announcements before they're posted. We will have to cancel the christening."

"Or," she said gently. "You could let me deal with this."

He stared glumly at the spindly branches devoid of fruit before him. "By tomorrow?"

Her stomach twisted. She might have considered the mix-up a dream come true, but to Silkridge it was a nightmare. He would rather be anywhere else but Cressmouth. He would leave within the hour if he could. She would do well not to forget that.

"I told you," she reminded him. "I know an expert on partridges."

He slid her a look out of the corner of his eye. "Why would any village have an expert on partridges?"

"Bird expert," Noelle amended. "Virginia loves animals. She can solve this puzzle."

"Can she?" His voice was doubtful. "Doesn't her cat love birds?"

"Not one whit," Noelle answered with forced cheer. "Don't worry. Virginia keeps everything in its place. She'll know right where to find a spare partridge."

He nodded. "Thank you."

Noelle could not quite bring herself to say *it's my pleasure*. She was ushering Silkridge out the door when all she wanted was for him to stay.

For the first time in her life, she wished she weren't so deuced efficient.

"This is our last night," the duke said as if reading her mind.

She swallowed. "Yes."

He nodded slowly. "Then I accept your help under one condition."

She frowned. Surely he wouldn't ask her to move the event up even sooner. "What condition?"

His voice grew husky. "Allow me to escort you to tonight's play."

She stared at him, her voice faint even to her own ears. "Tonight's play?"

"*The Winter's Tale*," he said. "Didn't you say it was your favorite?"

"I said it was in an amphitheater," she reminded him. "The outdoor kind."

"It will be worth it," he said softly, his blue eyes locked on hers.

Her heart leapt. Perhaps he was changing his mind about her. Perhaps she could even change his mind about Cressmouth.

"On one condition," she said, and bit her lip.

His eyebrows shot up. "Name it."

"Let me give you a tour of the village first," she said impulsively. "Show you everything the *Cressmouth Chronicle* cannot begin to cover."

He glanced over his shoulder as the wind whistled against the aviary's many panes of glass. "At this very moment?"

"One couldn't ask for a bluer sky," she said. "We can take a picnic lunch. Fruit and meats and cheeses."

His expression was skeptical. "A picnic lunch in the back of a carriage?"

"In the back of a sleigh," she corrected. "Cressmouth is made for traveling thus. Besides, how can you see the town if you keep yourself sequestered inside somewhere?"

His gaze was unreadable. She had asked for too much. He was going to say no.

"I hope it's a sleigh with a roof," he muttered.

"No roof," she chirped. "I need to fetch my coat from my chamber."

He proffered his elbow. "Shall I summon a maid?"

"No," she said quickly. "It's faster if I do it myself."

He led her toward the stairs. "Then I shall do the same. My room is down the corridor."

She knew. It was all she could think about. But how did *he* know? Her heart pumped faster. Did he lie awake at night thinking of her doing the same at the other end of the corridor?

"I won't be but a moment," he promised as he left her by her door to go and fetch his own great coat and top hat.

She hurried into her room and slid on her warmest pelisse, her kid gloves, her prettiest scarf, her thickest muff, her winter bonnet. After a moment's hesitation, she also retrieved a second scarf. One she had just finished last evening.

When she stepped out in the hall, the duke was already outside her door. She waited until they were outside in the back of the horse-drawn sleigh with a picnic basket between them before handing him the scarf.

"Put this on," she ordered. "Cressmouth won't seem nearly as cold if you are properly dressed."

"It never seems cold when I'm near you," he replied softly.

The back of her neck heated with pleasure.

He wound the scarf about his neck and opened the picnic basket. "Tell me absolutely everything about this ghastly village while I gorge myself on fruit and cheese and pretend that I'm listening."

She looked over at him sharply, but his eyes were full of laughter.

"Beast," she chastised him. She motioned for the driver to begin a sedate pace.

She and Silkridge enjoyed a leisurely picnic as they traveled through the snow-covered streets. The sky was clear, the breeze pleasantly crisp. It was a glorious Cressmouth winter day, perfect for snuggling. Thank heavens there was a picnic basket between them.

Laughing with Silkridge in the back of a sleigh was far more perilous than Noelle had anticipated. She had cared for him once before. Her heart remembered the sensation like putting on warm woolen mittens. If she did not guard herself…

"And there's the smithy," she announced breathlessly, forcing herself to concentrate on the promised tour and not to give over to emotion. "The French family who owns it knows everything about blacksmithing and carriages. The Duke of Azureford swears by their craftsmanship."

"He would," Silkridge said. "Azureford is always nattering on about winning phaeton races."

Noelle grinned as they rounded another corner. "All this open land belongs to Olive Harper, who breeds racehorses. She has several phenomenal stallions absolutely everyone is after, and won't sell no matter how high an offer she receives."

"I know," Silkridge said. "Her family's stud farm is infamous throughout England. If I have to sit through one more aside in the House of Lords for peers of the realm to discuss horseflesh instead of policy..."

"Do you want to listen to the tour or to give it?" she teased him. But she enjoyed hearing stories about Cressmouth's influence on London, rather than the other way around.

He waved his hand. "Continue, continue."

Over the next hour and a half, she managed to point out the majority of the town's sights and people. That was, between nibbles of food, and giggles at the duke's constant interruptions.

Everyone they passed called out cheery greetings, and although the duke made certain to mutter *humbug* under his breath each time, Noelle was increasingly convinced he did so for her benefit rather than his.

By the time they arrived at the amphitheater, being with him felt as natural as the afternoon sun. When they took a seat near the center facing the stage, it was all she could do not to nestle her head on his shoulder and curl into his warmth.

The heated glances he had been sending when he thought she didn't notice indicated he was feeling much the same.

"Is being a counting house clerk what you want from your life?" he asked suddenly, his eyes searching.

"I'm good at it," she said simply. "It's important."

"To you or to Cressmouth?" he asked.

She frowned. "It's the same thing."

"It is not the same." His expression was intense. "You should not concentrate on Cressmouth to the exclusion of your own life."

"I don't mind," she assured him. Cressmouth was her family, her home. She wouldn't abandon their needs in favor of her own. "I don't need both."

The duke's gaze did not waver. "I think you should be able to have it all."

He made her *want* it all.

In that moment, Noelle realized the horrible truth. It was too late for shields. Allowing him back into her heart wasn't the problem.

He had never left.

CHAPTER 8

A fortnight ago, Benjamin would have laughed at anyone who suggested he would one day voluntarily spend several hours outside in the winter cold away from all his responsibilities, away from London. Even this afternoon when he had offered to escort Noelle to the play, he hadn't known it would become one of the most enjoyable days of his life.

How he wished he could wrap his arm about her and pull her close. Unfortunately, just like the ride in the open sleigh, they were much too visible.

Although they had arrived at the amphitheater an hour early, eager spectators had already begun to fill the long, curved rows. Snow had been cleared from the stone benches and the sky was a brilliant blue. He could not deny it. If one were to be forced to watch an outdoor play, in the middle of winter, one could not ask for finer weather.

The breeze had given Noelle's cheeks a rosy glow. Despite the protective barrier of a winter bonnet, a few golden tendrils had managed to come loose and bounced becomingly against the side of her face.

He forced himself to tear his gaze from her beautiful profile before he gave himself away. The amphitheater was growing full.

The couples amongst the audience were easy to spot. The touch of a hand, an intimate glance, two bodies seated so close as to become one. His chest tightened.

Once upon a time, Benjamin would have scoffed at romantical fancy. That way lay inevitable sadness. He was too strong to be taken by such a naive emotion. His heart, too well protected.

But now when he glimpsed couples in love, he no longer experienced a sense of satisfaction at having managed to keep such ill-fated folly from his life. Instead, a strange loneliness entered his chest. A yearning to expand his heart rather than hide it. If only for a moment.

He brushed the back of Noelle's fingers with his own. "Thank you for letting me borrow a scarf," he murmured.

She gave a quick shake of her head. "It's yours."

And there was that melancholy again. Hope warring with emptiness. He shook his head. "I shall not rob a lady of her scarf."

"It's not mine," she said shyly. "I made it for you."

Those five words warmed him all the way to his heart.

Even though he had hurt her once before, even though he could not stay, she had still knitted him something to keep him warm. It worked. With her, he felt invincible.

He couldn't recall the last time anyone had done something just because they thought he would like it. Not until her. She had managed to do something thoughtful every day.

Starting with arranging for him to have his old bedchamber back.

They now slept on the same floor. In the same wing. Down the same corridor. His blood heated. Perhaps *slept* was too ambitious a word. He had barely caught any rest at all from lying awake each night thinking about her.

She smiled up at him from beneath her bonnet. "Thank you for agreeing to a sleigh ride."

Absolutely his pleasure. "I cannot imagine a better tour guide."

"Did you like the village a little better than you imagined?"

"It isn't terrible," he admitted. "Given its unfortunate location."

"High praise," she said, her eyes twinkling. "Perhaps you should become a Cressmouth tour guide yourself."

Of course she was teasing. He was the last man for the job. Noelle, on the other hand, was perfect here. Everyone they passed clearly adored her. And why wouldn't they? She was selfless and friendly, cheerful and outgoing...

Benjamin's complete opposite.

"You're not coming back, are you?" she asked, her voice quiet. "When you leave."

He shook his head. "I have no family here. Why do *you* stay?"

"Because I do have family here," she gestured around the crowded amphitheater. "Everyone you see is my family."

"You know what I mean."

"I don't think you know what I mean," she returned, her dark gaze intense. "Family isn't limited to blood. It's who you make it. Family is a *choice*." Her voice cracked. "*Home* is a choice."

"I am sure this village is perfect for those who have chosen to make it their home," he admitted grudgingly. "I cannot be one of them. I am needed in the House of Lords and on my own properties. The aviary needs to open as soon as possible."

"We have an appointment with the expert on partridges in the morning," she said, her eyes on the empty stage rather than on him. "Will you be leaving as soon as the bottle breaks?"

He swallowed the words he wished he could say and forced himself to be practical. "Almost. I'm not leaving without my mother's locket."

Her gaze snapped to his. "It is very important?"

"The most important thing in my life." He cleared his throat. "Next to my country, of course."

"Of course," she murmured.

But he didn't expect her to understand. Noelle still believed his grandfather a maker of miracles, not a breaker of dreams. She didn't know the whole truth.

Benjamin wasn't even convinced playing the fool's game with the wine and the partridge would result in success. For all he knew, Grandfather might have been buried with the locket. If only the solicitor had been willing to tell Benjamin where to find it! Just to prove to himself that he wasn't fighting for nothing. That all his years of anger and hurt and waiting had not been in vain.

Noelle's voice softened. "What's wrong?"

An idea caught him. His heart raced. In this town, Noelle knew everything and everyone. She had perhaps entered the fee for guarding the locket into one of her journals.

His words tumbled out faster than he meant. "Do you know where the items inventoried as part of my grandfather's estate are deposited?"

"Your locket, specifically?" she asked.

"*My* locket, specifically," he agreed with more emotion than he intended.

She nodded. "All jewelry is being held by Angelica Parker."

Of course. The artist of the jewel-encrusted tiaras. Thanks to the tour he just witnessed, Benjamin knew exactly where to find her.

It was all he could do not to leap up from the stone bench, tear off through the crowd, and keep running until he arrived out of breath at the jeweler's door. He needed to see the locket. To ensure it still existed, to verify the condition it had been kept in, to feast his eyes on the beloved portrait.

He forced himself to remain seated. Not for the impending play or even the scandal such a departure would cause, but for Noelle. This play meant something special to her. He wanted this evening to be special for both of them.

It was all they would have. He would not ruin it.

"Silkridge, as I live and breathe!" shouted a jolly male voice from right behind him.

Benjamin twisted in his seat and stared in disbelief at two dapper London gentlemen that looked for all the world as if they had been dropped into the most delightful soirée they'd ever seen.

"Do you know them?" Noelle whispered.

Did he ever. They were his first cousins and heirs presumptive. No doubt intending to play the angel and the devil on Benjamin's shoulders. He could not help but return their grins. Incorrigible beasts, both of them.

"Miss Pratchett, may I introduce Nicholas and Christopher Pringle." He held out a palm. "Cousins, this is Miss Pratchett."

"You must call me Christopher," his younger cousin

gushed without hesitation. "Two Mr. Pringles are impossible to remember."

"I can be memorable," said his elder cousin with a wolfish smile. "Some call me Saint Nicholas."

"Because he is absolutely wicked," Christopher stage-whispered. "Don't worry, my dear. You are safe with me."

"She is safer with *me*," Benjamin said, more forcefully than he had intended. "Why are you here?"

Before the words were out of Benjamin's mouth, Nicholas had already been distracted by a pretty face across the crowd and took off in immediate pursuit.

Christopher sat down next to him with a wide smile. "Once we heard you were still here, we had to see for ourselves. I can't recall the last time you took a holiday." He winked at Noelle. "Although, now I understand the attraction."

"Miss Pratchett lives here in Cressmouth and has been kind enough to show me her village," Benjamin said quickly. He did not want to imply that there was any more to it than that. There could never *be* anything more to it than that. Best to change the subject. "I cannot believe you followed me here. I did not mean to encourage a trend."

"Don't worry," Christopher assured him. "It was a trend long before your visit." He glanced about in obvious pleasure. "I have never seen such a charming place in all my life. Who wouldn't wish for Yuletide year-round? I could live here forever."

"It's not—" Benjamin began, but Christopher was already off and running, bubbling over with all the wonderful ways Cressmouth was superior to any other village he had ever seen.

"*He* should be the tour guide," Noelle whispered in Benjamin's ear.

He sighed. Men like his cousins flocked here for a distraction, which was a luxury Benjamin could not afford. He ought to concentrate on his responsibilities. Return to the real world.

"No wonder it is now such a point of pride to have a cottage in Christmas," Christopher was saying. "I've been here all of two hours and I vow I've made a hundred friends for life. Have you ever been so charmed, Silkridge?"

Benjamin tightened his jaw. "It's not called—"

"Maybe I should stay," Christopher said suddenly. "Or at least take an annual holiday here. Is that a strange thing to do?"

Noelle answered before Benjamin could. "Many have dual residences. Anyone with a title, of course, and several others who have family elsewhere but also consider us their home. I am not at all surprised you've made fast friends of my neighbors. That's the Christmas spirit."

"I like that," Christopher exclaimed. "I shall work on my Christmas spirit."

Benjamin heroically refrained from dropping his face into his palm.

Before his eyes, Noelle and his cousin engaged each other in an animated conversation about all the wintry fun that could be had within the village walls. Sledding, wassailing, roasting chestnuts on an open fire.

If they noticed Benjamin sitting stoically between them, they gave no sign. It was what he deserved, he supposed. His retribution for lack of Christmas spirit. Or punishment for his intense desire to keep all other men away from Noelle.

As much as he longed to sweep her into his arms and carry

her out of this amphitheater into the first private corner where they could be alone, he recognized such thoughts for the fantasy they were. A woman like her would not seek his money or title, but his entire heart. She wouldn't settle for a compromise. She would expect him to make room in his priorities for a holiday he had sworn off entirely. She wouldn't increase his solitary family by one but rather by an entire village.

Noelle would never leave Cressmouth. It would be like ripping her heart from her body. And he could not stay. Every mention of Christmas was a knife through his chest, a constant reminder of all that he had lost, the pain that he had been through, the suffering his grandfather inflicted even now.

This village would never be his home. It was a living nightmare.

"What is the most famous aspect about Cressmouth?" Christopher asked. "Has it a particular claim to fame?"

Noelle thought it over. "I suppose the twelve Dukes of Christmas."

Benjamin could not stay silent anymore. "Horses do not count. There are currently thirty odd dukes in all of England. I cannot possibly believe that a third of them choose to holiday in this ice house."

"You're the odd one," Christopher said with a laugh.

Noelle nodded up at him solemnly. "Christmas is for believing."

"It's not called—" Benjamin burst out laughing despite himself. "You're doing it on purpose now, aren't you?"

"I cannot imagine what you mean." She blinked at him innocently. "I must say your cousin is quite charming."

Yes, Benjamin supposed he was.

If coming face-to-face with Noelle after all these years had reminded Benjamin of Christmases past, then Christopher was the very embodiment of present-day Christmas.

It was more than a matter of living in the moment. It was as though Christopher was living the life Benjamin would be living if he had made different choices. Christopher was gregarious and easy-going. As comfortable in small gatherings as in a crowd. He loved bobbing for apples and singing carols and he likely wouldn't leave Cressmouth without purchasing a sleigh. He was carefree in a way that Benjamin never had been, even as a child. How could he be?

Benjamin's life had begun with tragedy. His mother had not died during childbirth, but rather from complications that had plagued her thereafter. She lived just long enough to pose for a miniature portrait with him in her arms, and then was taken from him. Taken from them all.

Grandfather had blamed Benjamin ever since.

Father had been his only ally, but he too had been ripped from Benjamin before his time. When Grandfather stole the locket, withheld the last link to family…

If it had not been for those formative events, would Benjamin be like Christopher today? Might he be cheerfully milling through a crowd of strangers, turning them into life-long friends one by one?

He was jealous, he realized in surprise. Not of his cousin's carefree life, but of his easy connection with the villagers. Over the last few days, he had realized that the people of Cressmouth weren't being so nice and solicitous to him because of his title, or even his connection to the village's founder.

They were just *nice*.

Benjamin hadn't been experiencing the spirit of Christmas. He was experiencing the spirit of *Cressmouth.*

The villagers had become more important to Benjamin than any other shire in England, perhaps because they weren't nameless and faceless like the rest of the population. He no longer cared about their welfare on a policy level, but a personal one.

"Wherein our entertainment shall shame us, we will be justified in our loves," shouted an actor. "For indeed..."

The Winter's Tale had finally begun. Unlike the good people of Cressmouth, Benjamin had not seen this play before. Or any play, to be honest. He kept himself far too busy. Although he could not imagine sitting through the exact same play year after year, the audience was rapt with attention.

He leaned back slightly for a better view. He was watching Noelle rather than the play. He couldn't help it. She was far more interesting and a lot less easy to read. Every time he looked at her, his thoughts jumbled. He wished he had kissed her. He was relieved he had not. All his thoughts of her were contradictions. She made him want to stay. She made him want to flee. She made him... *want.*

His arms felt empty without her in them. He yearned to know what it might be like to wrap them about her, to feel her body pressed against his. To claim her mouth with a kiss.

Only her mouth, of course. He could claim nothing else, and he should not even be thinking of that much. It did not matter that she consumed his every thought, his every desire. It did not matter that she somehow made him feel at home no matter whether they found themselves in an amphitheater, on a sleigh, in a counting house, an aviary staring at a pear tree.

No matter how fond he might be of Noelle, she was not of his status. He could not have her. She was his grandfather's clerk. This was not his home. He had to try to remember.

"My prettiest Perdita!" called Prince Florizel from onstage. "But, oh, the thorns we stand upon..."

Noelle's breath caught.

He touched his fingers to hers in question.

"Prince Florizel allows nothing to stand in his way," she whispered, her eyes shining as she gazed down at the stage.

The pieces clicked together. Although Perdita was abandoned as a baby, Florizel fell in love with her anyway. *Chose* her anyway. No wonder Noelle loved this part. Benjamin's chest clenched in regret.

He could not be her Prince Florizel. There was no magic spell to save them in the end. No running off to Sicily together.

Regardless of any wild fancies in Benjamin's heart, he was not in a position to take a wife outside his class. Not when thumbing his nose at Society's conventions could lose him political allies and impede his ability to make a difference in the House of Lords. Too many people were counting on him.

"Sure the gods do this year connive at us," said Autolycus on stage, "and we may do anything..."

Benjamin understood the sentiment. He knew all too well what it was like to feel as though the fates had conspired against him. Being with Noelle made him wish he *could* do anything. Watching her laugh at lines she had heard countless times and tear up at melodrama she already knew would occur was the most endearing thing he had ever seen.

She was not tired of this place, this play, this eternal Christmastide. She loved it. She looked forward to every aspect with anticipation and allowed herself to feel it all so deeply it was as if every line were experienced anew.

For so long, Benjamin had wondered why a woman as intelligent as Noelle wasn't more like him, and now he could not help but wonder the opposite. While he could not foresee any future for himself that did not involve utmost dedication to duty and responsibility, he was intensely grateful she had been spared the same fate.

The pleasure she took from life was infectious. She was a force impossible to deny. He had visited the bedside of a goat, for God's sake. Was willingly sitting in the open air in the middle of the winter with a warm woolen scarf wrapped tight about his neck. A scarf Noelle had knitted for him, not knowing if she would ever witness him using it.

"I am ashamed," said Leontes onstage. "Does not the stone rebuke me, for being more stone than it?"

Benjamin was glad they had spent time together outside the counting house. The sleigh, the picnic, the play. He could not recall a happier day. She could even make a snowy evening seem warm and inviting. He would remember this forever.

He tried not to think about the moment he would have to say goodbye. Surely she understood why he couldn't stay. He did not choose to be a duke, to have a seat in the House of Lords, but it was not a responsibility one could shirk.

His throat tightened as he realized he hoped for her approbation. Her acknowledgment that he had no choice, that of course England must be his priority in all things, would perhaps ease the pain of having to walk away.

"Oh, peace, Paulina! Thou shouldst a husband take by my consent," said Leontes onstage. "This is your son-in-law, and son unto the king, who, heavens directing, is troth-plight to your daughter. Hastily lead away."

The audience erupted into applause.

Benjamin blinked. It was over?

He got to his feet with the others, unable to believe he had spent the entire play casting surreptitious glances at Noelle.

Her friends suddenly surrounded them.

"That was wonderful," exclaimed one. "I love it when the bear chases Antigonus off the stage."

"The best year yet," Noelle agreed with a smile. She glanced up at Benjamin. "Did you enjoy the evening?"

"Even more than I anticipated," he admitted.

"Let's go caroling," bubbled another of Noelle's friends. "It's a Christmas tradition!"

Benjamin had no idea if "Christmas" in this case referred to the incorrect name of the place or the festive period, but he couldn't summon the urge to correct them. It was their village. They could do as they liked. He wouldn't spoil their fun.

But he couldn't join them.

Noelle smiled up at him, her eyes sparkling. "Do say you'll come. Carols are ever so much jollier after a bowl or two of mulled wine."

Looking at her, he was tempted. She lived and loved so openly and freely. Who wouldn't wish to share in her joy?

"I can't," he said honestly. This was his opportunity to visit the jeweler holding his mother's locket and find out what condition it was in. "Do have fun with your friends. Where shall I meet you tomorrow?"

"How about half ten, in the glasshouse? I am meeting Miss Mitchell to give my opinion on her newest scent."

He narrowed his eyes. "You don't mean to ambush me with perfume again, do you?"

"One must take risks," she admonished him with a twinkle in her eye.

"I shall take that under advisement," he said gravely.

Before her friends could renew their efforts to include him in their fun, he edged away from the crowd and picked his way down the snow-packed lanes toward the jeweler's shop.

His heart beat faster and faster in trepidation the closer he came to the jeweler. It was a moment of truth. Either Grandfather had finally been true to his word, or the old man had taken the locket to his grave.

Hands shaking, he rapped upon the jeweler's door.

No answer came. His frenzied knocks received no answer.

The play. Of course. He clenched his chapped fists in frustration. The entire village had filled the amphitheater. Perhaps even now, the jeweler was off wassailing and would not return for hours.

He stared doubtfully at the rustic cottage. It was clear that the jeweler worked on one side of the building and lived on the other. Less clear was whether finding a duke encamped upon her front doorstep would be enough to convince her to answer his questions.

He might have to wait until morning. His shoulders sagged. What was one more sleepless night?

Just as he turned to go, a pink-cheeked woman with a brisk step turned onto the front path.

His heart thumped. "Miss Parker, my apologies for calling so late and unannounced."

"I am never too busy for a social call," she said cheerfully. "And the sun has not fully set. May I invite you in for a cup of tea, Your Grace?"

He cleared his throat. "I'm afraid this is not a social call."

She tossed a merry look over her shoulder as she unlocked the door. "Is Your Grace in the market for a tiara?"

"Tiaras tend to clash with my hats," he said solemnly. "Else I would be your best customer."

"I shall design one to fit your top hat," she replied with a glint in her eyes so wicked he feared her words were true.

"I've come about my mother's locket," he said quickly. "The heirloom mentioned in my grandfather's will. I have been told you are the keeper of all named jewelry."

"Indeed." She beckoned him inside and into an impressive workman's chamber, with all manner of tools hanging from the walls and behind the counters.

"Do you mind showing me the locket?" he asked, hoping years of rage and hope and grief didn't appear on his face.

She hesitated. "I cannot let you take it."

"I won't," he promised. "I am a man of my word and I will fulfill my grandfather's wishes, no matter what I think of them. I want to confirm that his word is just as trustworthy. I have not seen the locket in five years. I need to ensure it is indeed the one I am after."

"Very well." From about her neck, she lifted a long chain bearing an intricate key. "If Your Grace would give me a moment?"

He nodded jerkily. He was so close now. Another moment was nothing. Soon he would know the truth.

She stepped into an adjoining room and out of sight. "Will you be in Cressmouth long?"

"I'm not here on holiday," he said, his voice as light as he could muster. "I will stay only as long as it takes to retrieve that locket."

Muffled sounds came from the other room. His heart pounded. She must be opening the safe.

"Are you looking forward to the christening party for the aviary?"

"I won't be attending." He tried not to grit his teeth. Being forced to make small talk was excruciating. He just needed to see his mother's face. "Cressmouth will have to celebrate without me."

She emerged from the adjoining room with an expression of surprise. "You're leaving immediately after tomorrow's ceremony?"

"I shall pick up the locket, jump into my carriage, and never look back." The words were brutally honest.

Retrieving the locket and escaping Cressmouth, Christmas, and his grandfather's clutches for good had always been the plan. That single-minded goal had consumed him since the day his grandfather had first stolen the locket.

Yet the idea of never seeing Noelle again suddenly made his chest feel hollow.

Without further questions, the jeweler held out her palm. "Is this the one?"

Heat stung the back of Benjamin's eyes. It *was* the locket. Exactly as he remembered it. A perfect oval, trimmed in gold lace and embossed on the front with the silhouette of an angel.

He reached for it with trembling fingers.

"May I?" The words came out too scratchy to be understood, but the jeweler nodded anyway.

He lifted the small oval in his hands. It felt weightless. Empty. As if it no longer contained his mother's soul. The gold chain dangled through his fingers, brushing between them like a strand of hair. Not that he remembered what his mother's hair had been like. All he had was the image on the inside of this locket.

If it was still there.

He undid the clasp with reverence and eased open the locket. On the left side was nothing. That space had been reserved for a future portrait that had never come to pass.

On the right side was his mother. His heart thumped in relief, and grief, and sorrow.

There she was. Smiling. Happy. Gazing at the baby in her arms with an expression of such love it took Benjamin's breath away. This was his mother. All that was left of her.

"Is it as Your Grace remembered?" the jeweler asked softly.

He feared his throat too tight for words, so he gave a short nod instead.

"These last few years, Mr. Marlowe never let it out of his sight," the jeweler murmured. "He said it was the last portrait of his daughter."

Fury, hot and sharp, bubbled inside him. "It was the only likeness of her I ever had."

Grandfather's constant refusal to return the heirloom had been like being denied his family all over again.

Why could they not have shared her? Benjamin had offered to compromise. It would have cost so little to commission an artist to create a copy of the portrait. Grandfather had dismissed the plea out of hand. Once he'd gained possession of the locket, he'd ceased acknowledging Benjamin altogether. His fingers shook at the injustice and rejection. Why did he have to lose so that his grandfather could win? Why could they not have been family to each other?

His vision blurred as he gazed down at his smiling mother. She had loved him, his father had loved him, unconditionally, then they'd been stolen first by God and then by a grandfather who loved to *play* God with others.

Love was dangerous. It was out of one's control. The more one cared about another person the more likely they were to be ripped from one's side. The only way to protect himself from hurt was to concentrate on the things he could control.

Leave Cressmouth. Encase himself in ice. Dedicate himself to his country, not love.

There was no need to fear the title dying out. Thanks to his cousins, he already had two heirs presumptive. If he kept his mind on nothing but Parliament, there would be no need to fear anything at all.

Love only led to hurt. The only way to ensure he would never again lose someone he cared about was to do his best not to care.

"If you're satisfied…" The jeweler held out her hand.

His heart clenched. He was not satisfied. He wanted things he could not have. He wanted the emptiness inside to go away.

But he forced himself to hand back the locket. "How soon after the ceremony may I have it?"

"Immediately after the bottle breaks," she said. "Shall I prepare a cushioned jewelry box for travelling?"

Benjamin shook his head. "I'll wear it home."

He was never losing contact with his family again.

CHAPTER 9

Benjamin awoke long before dawn. Confirming the locket's existence had only caused the hours to stretch out that much longer. This was Twelfth Night. His last day in Cressmouth. His last day with Noelle.

His appointment with her wasn't for two more hours. He'd broken his fast, dashed off a handful of letters and responses, and was now far too restless to stay cooped up in his old bedchamber. A place he would be leaving behind for good this time.

Perhaps one last walk about the castle would put the strange sensation in his chest to rest.

He stepped out into the corridor just in time to glimpse his cousin Nicholas arriving at the landing.

Nicholas leaned against the balustrade and waited for Benjamin to approach.

"So that's where they stuffed you," Nicholas said. He gestured down the opposite corridor. "Mine's that way. Stunning view from the mountaintop. Have you seen the horizon at dawn?"

Benjamin lifted his brows. "You are just getting back to the castle?"

"I'm just returning to my guest chamber," Nicholas clarified with a wicked smile.

"'Saint Nick,'" Benjamin muttered. "A rake to the core."

Nicholas's smile only widened. "It may be cold outside, but inside..."

"No wonder you're enamored with Cressmouth," Benjamin said.

"It has many, many charms," Nicholas assured him. "I see why so many come here for distraction."

"I don't think 'Christmas spirit' means seducing pretty maidens," Benjamin said dryly.

"I have never seduced a maiden," Nicholas said, his expression hurt. "I allow myself to be seduced by those who aren't maidenly in the least. They know exactly what they're getting. That's why they want me."

Benjamin raised a brow. "One night to slake their lust?"

"Mutual slaking," Nicholas agreed. "A rakish gentleman simply provides requested entertainment. A pleasurable evening for both parties without any promises or strings. Everybody wins."

"Perhaps that's true if no strings and no promises are indeed what both parties are after," Benjamin agreed. "I should expect it gets complicated when one party wants more than the other."

Nicholas shook his head. "That is the easiest situation to resolve. Stay away from those who want more than your body or more than one night."

"Easy," Benjamin echoed. He had spent a lifetime doing just that. "But doesn't it get... lonely?"

A dark shadow flickered across the blue of Nicholas's eyes,

and just as quickly it was gone. "It's impossible to be lonely when there's always someone new to meet."

Benjamin stared at his cousin as if seeing a ghost. He had always considered Saint Nicholas his opposite in all things. It was disconcerting to have to revise that opinion.

Although the two lived unquestionably different lives, the consequence was the same. Each morning, they woke up alone. There was no one there who had shared dreams and hurts, who had been by one's side for months or years or decades. No one who could answer *yes* to *remember the time when?* No one whose touch was familiar, whose kiss felt like coming home.

Although Nicholas had chosen a different route, Benjamin now suspected they were both on the path to a very lonely future. If something didn't change, his future Christmases would be as empty as all the rest. He frowned.

Wasn't that what he wanted? He couldn't get hurt if he didn't open himself up to love.

Nick clapped him on the shoulder. "I'm off to my chamber. Where are you heading?"

"Menagerie," Benjamin answered. "I want to visit a goat."

"I've changed my mind. I'm coming with you," Nicholas said immediately. "I had no idea there was a goat."

When they entered the menagerie, a footman was keeping an eye over the invalid.

Benjamin hurried closer. "How's Tiny Tim?"

"Tiny Tim?" Nicholas asked.

Benjamin gestured. "Pygmy goat."

Nicholas nodded. "I see."

"Much improved, Your Grace," the footman said with obvious relief. "We are ever so grateful."

"Grateful to Silkridge?" Nicholas asked. "Did you bring the castle a pygmy goat as some sort of Christmas gift?"

"I did not," Benjamin replied. "I have made a personal resolution to deliver fewer goats as gifts this season."

"His Grace's knowledge about the beast's constitution brought Tiny Tim back from the brink of death," the footman said proudly. "It was nothing short of a miracle."

"Silkridge performed a Christmas miracle," Nicholas repeated, his expression baffled. "*You*?"

"I may have relayed a few suggestions based on my research into caprine physiology due to the livestock present on my own properties," Benjamin said humbly.

"And His Grace summoned his personal physician all the way from London," the footman continued with pride.

Nicholas blinked slowly. "You summoned your personal physician for a goat?"

"It's not just any goat," said the footman. "It's Tiny Tim."

Nicholas stared at Benjamin in disbelief.

"Not *my* physician," he explained. "A veterinarian."

Slowly, Nicholas shook his head. "You're a different man."

Benjamin wondered if that were true. If he *was* capable of changing.

If either of them was.

Just like his cousin, he had put walls up around his heart to keep others from getting in. Unlike his cousin, part of Benjamin now wished it didn't have to be that way.

The opening ceremony for the aviary was in just a couple hours. This would be Benjamin's last opportunity to spend time with Noelle before collecting his mother's locket and putting Cressmouth behind him. A strange emptiness filled his chest. Leaving Noelle would be harder than ever. He pushed the thought away.

Just because he could not be here for her physically did not erase a sudden need to provide for her in his absence. He doubted she would agree. Noelle did not need Benjamin's help to survive. She was smart and strong and independent. But to him, she was so much more than that. She had turned her entire town into a family. If he could give her anything at all, it would be more time to enjoy that family while she had it.

He left his cousin in the menagerie and made his way down to the temporary office the solicitor had set up in the castle in order to oversee Grandfather's last will and testament.

"Your Grace!" The solicitor leapt up from his chair. "How may I be of service?"

Benjamin took a seat across from the desk. "I would like to employ an assistant clerk for the counting house."

The solicitor's eyes widened. "You wish to replace Miss Pratchett?"

"No. I wish to employ an assistant for her," Benjamin said. "She has taken on far more responsibility than her predecessors realized, and should not be worked to death. Miss Pratchett deserves recreational time with which to do as she pleases."

"An assistant." The solicitor shuffled through the papers on his desk. "I was one of Mr. Marlowe's most trusted men of business, yet he left no notes about creating such a post. I will investigate to see if the budget—"

"*I* wish to employ," Benjamin repeated. "I will also pay whatever wages are required for the research and recruitment of potential employees. The appropriate individual must ease Miss Pratchett's load, not create additional concerns."

The solicitor nodded in comprehension. "Consider it

done. I presume Your Grace wishes to have final say, once we have whittled down the options."

"Miss Pratchett shall have the only say," Benjamin said firmly. "She may employ as many assistants as she requires, at her complete and total discretion."

The solicitor noted quickly. "Understood, Your Grace. I shall see to it immediately."

Benjamin glanced at his pocket watch and rose to his feet. He did not wish to be late for his meeting with Noelle.

In his eagerness to see her, Benjamin strode into the glasshouse a full quarter of an hour before they were due to meet.

She was there among the flowers on the other side of the vast conservatory, speaking to Miss Penelope Mitchell, her perfumer friend.

Benjamin did not care a fig about colognes, or the rows of spices for the kitchen, or the profusion of local and exotic flowers for the gardens. None of their fragrances or colors could compare to Noelle.

She was captivating. The morning light caught the sparkle in her eyes, the golden shine in her hair. Her happy, upturned face was so animated and enthusiastic he felt himself smiling from across the glasshouse without even hearing her words.

Noelle always had that effect on him. She caused him to smile when he didn't mean to, when he couldn't explain his exuberance even to himself. Being with her gave him such a profound sense of contentment it almost made him wonder if he'd ever truly been happy before he met her. Noelle *was* his glasshouse; his color, his light, his warmth. Even when winter raged out-of-doors, she made his soul feel like summertime.

He wished he could keep a ray of her sunlight with him for the rest of his days.

Although he had been careful not to make a sound, her head turned sharply as if she had sensed him watching her from afar. A wide smile spread across her face. His lips curved in an answering smile. He couldn't help it. Her pull was as powerful as the sun.

He started walking toward her.

She bid good-day to her friend and hurried forward to greet him. They met in the middle of the glasshouse, surrounded by the scent of spring and a cornucopia of wild beauty.

If only he could stay here, or steal her away when he left. But he belonged to London and she to Cressmouth. More insurmountable, she was an orphan and he was a duke. Homes could be changed, but heritage could not. Society's position on the matter was clear.

Not that Benjamin was in the market for a wife, he reminded himself. Soon enough, he'd be too busy with Parliament to have time for distractions of any kind. This was his last one.

"Did you solve your friend's problems?" he asked gruffly.

She grinned up at him, brown eyes sparkling behind gold-rimmed spectacles. "I am arranging an event to celebrate her latest success."

"Complete with an enormous bellows to spray the entire crowd?" He gave a little shudder.

"Not this time," she said with a laugh. "Customers must make do with glass vials."

"I am certain the event will be a success," he said in seriousness. "With your eye for detail, I've no doubt you are a phenomenal hostess no matter what the event."

"It's a calling," she said with a grin. "There's nothing I cannot organize."

He stared at her in silence for a moment. She *would* make a phenomenal hostess. The sort that might make an equally phenomenal duchess. If such were an option.

"Would you ever leave Cressmouth?" he asked suddenly.

"Leave?" Her eyes widened with obvious alarm. "Why would I wish to?"

"What if it wasn't a permanent change?" he pressed. "Would you not even go on holiday somewhere, once in a while?"

She shook her head. "I wouldn't like to be far away. Cressmouth has everything I need."

"It cannot compete with London," he said a bit more defensively than he intended.

London was where his mother and father had lived. The now-empty Silkridge residence contained the few happy family memories he'd ever had. It was the only place that had ever felt like home.

"*London?*" she stammered with the same level of terror as if he had said *snake pit*. "I wouldn't feel comfortable. Everything I've ever heard makes it sound like the opposite of Cressmouth. It's so big, so far away, so overwhelming…"

He could not fault her there. The city was indeed the opposite in many ways. Some of its characteristics negative, some of them marvelous. But his question had been answered, and the answer was no. His home would make her miserable. He would much rather keep her happy.

"How about you?" she asked. "Will you return to holiday in Cressmouth someday?"

Return to a place that contained her, only to have to leave her behind over and over again? A village that symbolized everything he could not have, now more than ever? He would not survive such a nightmare.

"I'm afraid not," he said quietly.

Noelle bit her lip as if swallowing words she wanted to say. She cast her gaze downward.

"What is it?" he demanded.

With a sigh, she lifted her eyes to his. "I know why you're leaving this time. You're a duke. You have a duty to Parliament."

He gave a curt nod.

Her next words were a whisper. "Why did you leave last time?"

"Because I wanted to stay." The hoarse admission wrested from his throat.

Her eyes widened. "You wanted to stay… with me?"

Before he spilled any more unintended confessions, he pulled her close and slanted his mouth over hers.

She yielded to him immediately, grasping his shoulders as though she feared he would pull away.

He never wished to stop. This was what he needed. The woman he missed every minute they were apart.

He had left her before due to the same sensation she instilled in his heart even now: *fear*. Fear that if he let himself be vulnerable again, he still couldn't keep her. It was not a risk he wished to take. Not a heartbreak he wished to live through. Yet each kiss only made him want to claim more than her mouth. He wanted to taste her skin, to know her body, to meld as one.

If a single kiss could make him feel as if their souls had cleaved together, how much harder would it be to bear a lifetime without her if he risked sharing more than that?

"The eagle can fly over a hundred miles to be with its mate," mused a female voice right behind them.

Benjamin ripped his mouth from Noelle's and tried to calm his galloping heart. The avian expert had arrived.

"Virginia," Noelle said, her cheeks flushed and her voice breathless. "You're early."

"I'm half an hour late." Without demanding further explanation, Miss Underwood turned abruptly and began striding away. "This way to the partridge."

He offered her his arm, so they could hurry after her retreating friend.

Noelle gave him a shy smile that melted his heart.

"Come along," Miss Underwood called. "I've installed the partridge in the closest outbuilding in order to give you the honor of carrying him into the aviary."

He slanted a startled glance toward Noelle.

"That means you," she said quickly. "I seek no honor."

Benjamin gazed down at her. He had never met anyone more honorable.

Regardless of how she might have felt in the beginning, she was not helping him now because she wished to be rid of him, but rather despite the fact that she did not. His spirits sank.

He had never been less enthusiastic about getting his way.

CHAPTER 10

For the first time, Cressmouth's endless winter felt less charming and more simply...cold.

Noelle tried to keep her shaking fingers from gripping too hard as she looped her arm through Silkridge's and allowed him to escort her—and the partridge—to the aviary.

The bird was cozily ensconced in a covered wicker basket hanging from the duke's other arm. Noelle felt significantly less stable. Of the two, her fluttering heart seemed more likely to fly from her chest than the bird from the basket.

It was a quarter to twelve. Within the next half hour, Silkridge would deposit the bird in the aviary, break the bottle of champagne, and be gone.

"Are you ready?" she whispered.

She wished she hadn't spoken. She already knew the answer.

"Yes," he said with a quick glance to ensure the safety of the bird inside the basket.

Noelle was not ready. She doubted she would ever be. All she could think about was the incredible kiss they had just shared. It had transported her out of the glasshouse, out of the castle, into a world of fantasy where nothing could keep them apart.

She supposed she could have delayed him artificially. He did not know her bosom friend was an expert on birds. He had not asked for her help. If anything, he had seemed perturbed that his grandfather's will had thrown them together in such a fashion. At first.

Now she was uncertain what to think.

She had no doubt that he desired her. His ardent kisses had proven that. Nor could she doubt that he liked her. He had agreed to a sleigh ride, attended a seasonal play, wore her scarf about his neck. But such moments were far from enough.

His kisses made her want *more*. To keep Cressmouth, to keep him, to have it all.

She wanted him to want to stay. To choose *her*. Having him be part of her life, part of her home, a part of her heart…

For a moment, when he had captured her in his arms, she had thought it possible. That their connection was unbreakable. That perhaps she could keep him.

But of course she could not.

Her lips twisted at the irony. A debutante would rejoice if the gentleman she fancied was a duke. For a title-less orphan like Noelle, it meant she and Silkridge were more than star-crossed. Their futures were predetermined. This forbidden spark between them might lead to a bedchamber, but never to the altar.

His was a world of power and riches and political alliances. He could not marry her if he wished to. Besides, was that even a life she would want? Noelle would never be accepted amongst those of his class. Here in Cressmouth, she was more than accepted. She was part of a family.

A distant roar of voices met their ears before the source came into sight.

He slanted her a startled look. "Is there a disturbance?"

"There's a party." Noelle did not feel like celebrating. She forced herself to smile anyway. "I had bills posted across the village, remember?"

His expression was dubious. "How many people would choose to attend the grand opening of a one-bird aviary?"

"All of them." She pointed as the queue came into view.

A long line of laughing, wind-flushed faces snaked over every inch of the snow-covered garden and down the street.

"This crowd could fill Vauxhall," he said with a chuckle.

The thought caused a pain in Noelle's chest. She had never seen Vauxhall. Never wanted to before. But she suddenly could not put the thought of being there with Silkridge out of her mind. Or the thought of him being there with someone else.

He paused just before they came into full view of the crowd and turned to face her.

"Our time is almost over," he said softly.

It always was. They were never granted more than stolen moments. She swallowed hard. "Do you remember what happened five years ago?"

"Our first kiss?" His warm gaze was intent on hers. "I've never forgotten."

Neither would she. This was torture.

"Why do you hate Christmas?" she whispered.

It was not the real question she meant, but much easier to ask than *why do you keep leaving me?*

His expression closed. "I don't wish to discuss it."

Her voice trembled. "Was it because we—"

He grabbed her hand and placed it to his chest.

"It has nothing to do with you," he said roughly. "My father and I had a reason to despise Christmas time since the year I was born. Losing him just gave me another reason. My grandfather's castle, this picturesque holiday village… You are the best thing in it."

She drew in a shuddering breath and dared to hope.

"Could you stay?" she whispered. "If there was a reason?"

As she gazed up at him, church bells began to ring the hour. Her stomach twisted. Noon. The magic was over.

He took her hand from his chest and placed it back on his elbow. "I cannot stay, no matter how many reasons I find. I belong in London, in the House of Lords. My duty is to Parliament."

She nodded dumbly. She could not hope to compete against a love of country.

She had just hoped there might be room for her, too.

CHAPTER 11

Benjamin stood before the entrance to the aviary and faced a crowd of hundreds.

He had given any number of addresses to Parliament that ought to carry much more weight and import. But for the first time, he felt as though he stood at the crossroads of his own life.

At last, he was seconds away from washing his hands of his grandfather's final manipulation. Minutes away from once more having in his possession an heirloom he had feared lost to him forever. An hour away from being back in his carriage with which he could finally put all things Cressmouth and Christmas behind him for good.

So why hadn't he begun the proceedings?

He tried not to send another glance toward Noelle, but the temptation was impossible to resist. If he had yearned for her before, his addiction had only increased. It was as if his eyes wished to drink her up, to commit every eyelash, every wrinkle of her nose, every curve of her lips to memory.

But he was too close to having done with his grandfather's final manipulation. He could let nothing stand in its way. Especially not his own emotions.

"Welcome to the Castle Aviary Grand Opening," he called out, feeling absolutely ridiculous using such terminology to describe a single brown game bird nestled in a wicker basket.

The crowd let out a thundering cheer, as if he had announced the war with France was finally over and that he had personally defeated Napoleon Bonaparte armed with nothing more than a partridge.

They could not possibly be serious. He slid an incredulous glance toward Noelle.

"We like parties," she said with a grin. "And Mr. Marlowe. And Cressmouth. There's really no way this could go wrong."

Benjamin hoped not. Nonetheless, he lifted a corner of the blanket covering the basket to ensure he carried a partridge, not porridge, and that nothing else could go awry. The bird lay in the center, one wing covering its head as if to block out the roar from the crowd.

"My sincere apologies," Benjamin whispered. "Soon you can hide in a tree where you belong."

With a flourish, he opened the door to the aviary and whipped the blanket from the basket to allow the bird to fly inside.

The partridge did not move.

He gave the basket a little jiggle. Had the bird expired in the hundred yards from outbuilding to aviary? God help him.

The partridge opened one baleful eye and glared sullenly at Benjamin.

His shoulders relaxed. The creature hadn't died. It just hated him.

"Behold the partridge!" Benjamin shouted and shoved the uncovered basket over the threshold and into the aviary.

Nothing happened. No chirps. Not so much as a flutter.

Benjamin ignored the bird. It was inside the aviary. That was all that mattered. The terms were complete. A thousand people could file indoors to gather around a basket if they so wished. He had fulfilled his part of the bargain.

"Champagne," murmured Noelle and gestured toward a footman.

Almost fulfilled. One last step, and his mother's locket would finally return home. Benjamin's heart was racing so fast it had become difficult to think. He accepted a ceremonial saber from one footman as another held the bottle of champagne aloft.

Benjamin did not feel like Napoleon conquering new lands. He felt... like part of the town.

He motioned everyone to back up a safe distance from the entrance and lifted the saber. "I dedicate this building to—"

"Mr. Marlowe!" the crowd screamed in unison.

Their deafening roar drowned out Benjamin's words as he met Noelle's eyes. "To the indomitable Miss Pratchett."

With a swipe of the saber, the neck's seam began to crack. A loud *pop* filled the air as the cork went flying. Foamy champagne sprayed upon the wooden doorframe and Benjamin's black boots.

His heart leaped. He'd done it!

Two footmen rushed forward to relinquish him of the saber before the stampeding crowd overtook them.

Benjamin glanced inside the aviary at the bird in the basket.

It was empty.

"Where's the partridge?" he whispered to Noelle.

"I didn't see it move," she whispered back, frowning into the interior. "It cannot have disappeared."

Benjamin gritted his teeth. He had no wish to actually enter the aviary. He did not want to be caught by the tidal wave of the crowd.

Worse, however, would be for the solicitor to cry foul and claim he had not executed his grandfather's bequest as promised. Benjamin had not come all this way to fail now.

He stalked through the entrance, scouring atop branches and behind decorative shrubs in search of the elusive bird.

The crowd poured in behind him.

Rather than follow Benjamin along the carefully curated path through the aviary's painstakingly pruned flora, they streamed to an empty corner on the opposite side of the aviary containing nothing but a plain, spindly sapling listing on its own in a bucket of dirt.

Benjamin frowned. *Had* his grandfather's will said "pear tree?"

"It's a brilliant partridge!" a voice called out.

"She looks perfectly at home," called another. "Placing her on a pear tree is a right lovely touch."

His body flooded with relief. The partridge had been spotted. The ordeal was over. He had christened the one-bird aviary with all the pomp and circumstance required of him, and was free at last to reunite with his family. The locket and its portrait could finally return home. He could be hours away by nightfall.

Benjamin darted desperate glances around the aviary in search of Noelle, but it was no use. The entire village was attempting to cram itself inside.

He would say goodbye after he retrieved the locket. Perhaps that was better anyway. Poetic. She would be the last thing he saw before he left. The only memory of this place he wished to keep.

He squeezed his way through the crowd to the exit. Once his Hessians touched the ground out-of-doors, he took off running without a backward glance. If the queueing villagers found it odd to spy a duke loping away from his own celebration, Benjamin did not care.

Only one thing mattered.

The winter chill stole the air from his lungs and the snow-covered streets slid beneath his boots. In mere moments, he arrived at the jeweler's out of breath and triumphant.

She was waiting for him behind the counter of her jewelry room.

His heart was pounding. "The aviary is open."

Miss Parker's eyes crinkled. "I heard."

Even from several blocks away, the crowd's excitement was audible.

He stepped forward. "May I—"

"Here." She retrieved a thin silk pouch from a hidden nook.

He held out his hands, surprised they were not trembling. He had prevailed. He had *won*.

Miss Parker upended the pouch and dropped its contents into Benjamin's outstretched palm.

He had promised himself he would immediately clasp the locket about his neck for safekeeping, but he needed to gaze upon his mother's face once more. The hollowness he'd carried inside all these years would fill with love once more. With family. He unlocked the clasp and opened the locket.

There. Faded with time, but finally back in his hands. His pulse slowed. He should be full of warmth, of victory. The emptiness should have receded. He had everything he always wanted.

And yet the hollowness remained.

"Is something amiss?" asked the jeweler with concern.

He snapped the locket closed. "Nothing. Thank you for giving me my family back. I will take good care of them."

Before she could ask any more questions, Benjamin strode out of her workroom and back out onto the front stoop. The blustery wind blew over the village and through his chest.

He lifted the chain to his throat and clasped it about his neck.

No. This would not do.

He unwound the scarf, untied his cravat, and slid the gold oval underneath his shirt until it nestled against his heart. He frowned.

The locket's return should warm him more than any scarf, than any cravat, and any amount of wool or cozy fire. Instead, he felt cold. Every gust of wind seemed icier than the one before, penetrating his great coat and his waistcoat and his linen shirt until it sliced all the way through his soul.

He curled his hands into fists and glared up at the relentless blue sky. Why hadn't the return of the locket given him all the things he had hoped it would bring? He had his family back. He had his mother right next to his heart.

But the portrait's return failed to vanquish the loneliness and emptiness and resentfulness. The locket bore a permanent place about his neck, but failed to fill the hole in his chest. The heirloom was a memento he would always cherish, but still just a *thing*.

His breath shuddered. Now that he had the locket back, he realized the awful truth. A portrait was just paint, no matter how much he might like to believe otherwise. It didn't erase the pain. His mother's likeness could not replicate the real person. The happy family in the miniature would never exist again. What it represented was long gone, just like both his parents.

His chest clenched. What was better, to cleave to a faded likeness or to keep loved ones close while one still had them? The answer was clear.

He wrapped the scarf Noelle had made him back around his neck and cut through the wind toward the castle. She was the one person he could rely on. He was not yet ready for goodbye.

When he drew close, the aviary was still bursting at the seams. Villagers spilled across its threshold and milled about the garden. Benjamin doubted Noelle was among the revelers. She was one of the few who hadn't been looking forward to the aviary's opening.

He circled around the bustling crowd and entered the vacant castle. Nothing but silence greeted him. Benjamin's footfalls echoed as he raced up six flights of steps to Noelle's chamber.

When she opened the door, he pulled her into his arms and kissed her. He couldn't have stopped himself if he wanted to. The heat of her mouth was the only warmth he required. Her embrace, more than enough protection from the cold. Nothing else mattered but holding her tight.

At last, he forced himself to lift his head. "May I come in?"

"Please do." With a blush, she shut the door behind him and gestured toward a receiving area before the fire.

His nerves were far too raw for sitting down, but he followed her anyway. He was not ready to let her out of his sight.

Her eyes were full of questions. He no longer believed he had any answers.

"Silkridge…" she began.

"Benjamin," he said firmly. "I've no wish to stand on formalities with you of all people."

"What do you want?" she said quietly.

You.

Happiness.

A new life. A different world. One where they could be together. Anything but this.

He tossed his hat onto the closest chair and shoved a hand through his hair.

Noelle gazed up at him uncertainly from behind her spectacles. "I thought you went to fetch the locket."

"I did."

The words sounded as cold and hollow as the yawning cavern in his chest. Nothing about today had gone as planned. Now that he was here, what could he expect but more heartache?

Her fingertips brushed against the back of his hand. "What happened?"

"It's what didn't happen," he said at last. "I thought…"

Her gaze softened. "Start at the beginning."

"I can't remember the beginning," he said bitterly. But he forced the words out anyway. "My mother died shortly after giving birth to me. That was my first Christmastide. The only one where I had a family. The last time my father celebrated anything at all."

Her eyes widened in understanding. "You never had a Christmas."

"Not one I'd wish to repeat. I lost my father during the same time of year, and just as suddenly." He let out a shaky breath. "Everyone I have ever loved has been taken from me before I could say goodbye."

"Is that why…" she began hesitantly. "…the locket means so much?"

"It's more than a locket."

He lay his great coat and scarf over the back of an armchair and tossed his cravat atop the seat.

His neck felt bare. Exposed. But he was about to expose even more. He lifted the locket from beneath the linen of his shirt and allowed it to fall back against his chest.

"It's beautiful." She lifted her hands as if to touch the gold frame then let them fall without doing so. Her eyes met his.

"Open it," he said. "You can meet my mother."

Gently, she slid her hand between the locket and his chest and undid the clasp.

He held his breath.

From this angle, he could not see the portrait inside, but he had committed it to memory. At this moment, he was not looking at the locket. He was looking at Noelle.

"You look like your mother," she murmured. "You have her eyes."

His throat grew tight. They wouldn't recognize him now. "I suppose I've grown a bit since that portrait was painted."

A soft smile curved her lips. "You'll have to hang this next to your most recent likeness in your hall of portraits."

He didn't answer.

Her brow furrowed. "You haven't a hall of portraits? I thought all titled families…"

"There aren't any of me," he said. Just the thought gave him chills. "After my mother died, my father never posed for another portrait. Neither did I."

Her eyes widened, and she returned her reverent gaze to

the locket. "This miniature truly is beautiful. I hope it has brought you the peace that you sought."

"It didn't." Somehow, he kept his voice from cracking.

She glanced up sharply. "It wasn't as you remembered it?"

"It was exactly as I remembered," he said. "And nothing more. I thought… I was certain…"

She touched the locket's delicate frame. "How did you lose it?"

"What I lost was my family. The locket was *stolen* from me. My grandfather felt he had more claim to his daughter than a child did of his own mother."

She drew in her breath. "That's why you hated him."

"I didn't hate him. He hated me." Benjamin took a deep breath. "Mother died of complications caused by my birth. She barely lasted a month. That was my fault."

"It was *not* your fault," Noelle said sharply, her eyes fierce.

"Tell that to Grandfather," he said with a curl of his lip. "I always thought if I could get the locket back, I could get my family back. Part of them, anyway. This was the one piece I had. The only tangible thing I could hold onto."

"Until he took it," she murmured quietly. "That must have hurt deeply."

It had been devastating. This was the first time Benjamin had ever spoken about how it had felt. His pulse felt wild and uneven.

"I should have expected it," he admitted. "Grandfather despised me from the moment of my birth. He blamed my father, too. I was a child. I didn't understand. All I knew was that my mother was gone, but I still had a grandfather. My letters went unanswered, he was suddenly too busy to be disturbed any time Father brought me for a visit. As I got older, I realized he had no interest in getting to know me. He wished I hadn't been born."

Noelle gasped. "Surely he would never wish—"

"He said so to my face," Benjamin said flatly. "That was my mistake, too. When he invited me five years ago, I should have suspected a trap. It turned out, he'd learned of the locket. I was so eager to finally make peace, of course I handed it over when he asked for a closer look. That was the last time I saw it. Grandfather threw me out of the castle—"

"Threw out his own grandson?" she said in shock. "A duke?"

"I wasn't a duke yet, and he didn't give two figs about his grandson. He had what he wanted, and it wasn't me."

"That was… the day after our kiss?" she asked.

Benjamin nodded. "I never came back."

"You weren't allowed back." Her eyes flashed. "Your grandfather wouldn't let you."

He lifted a shoulder. "Either way, I've come to regret it."

She tilted her head. "You think things would have worked out differently if you had tried to visit your grandfather again?"

"Not him." Benjamin stepped closer. "I regret all those years without seeing you. At the very least, we deserved a chance to say goodbye."

"You didn't get to say goodbye to your grandfather, either," she said quietly.

"I've never got to say goodbye to anyone I care about." His chest tightened at the barrage of memories. "I can't let it happen again."

She lowered her gaze. "That's why you're here."

"Not the only reason." He couldn't stay away. That was the problem.

He was not used to making confessions of any kind. Had insulated himself on purpose so that he would not ever be in a position where he was expected to slice open his heart and bare what he kept inside.

With her, he felt even more vulnerable. But she was different. Noelle did not judge him or shower him with platitudes. She simply listened and understood.

He had never known how powerful such a simple act could be.

His heart thumped wildly against the back of her hand where she held the locket. The miniature inside was his most prized possession. Its protective gold housing symbolized not just family, but love.

The blank spots on the other side of his mother's face had been meant for a new portrait. His own, perhaps. It was now destined to remain empty. He had vowed to never again risk his heart on something so fleeting as love or family, but if he ever were to do so…

He reached behind his neck and unclasped the chain.

The locket pooled into Noelle's open palm and she glanced up at him, startled. "I didn't mean for you to—"

Her words cut off as Benjamin reached behind her neck and reaffixed the clasp.

Now the locket lay not against his heart, but hers.

"Don't give up on having a family," she whispered.

"I'm not," he answered and pulled her into his arms.

This kiss was different from all the others. Neither a claiming nor a submission, but a flaying open, a laying bare. This kiss was who he was. His hopes, his fears, his grief, his desire. He hoped he could make her understand.

Benjamin had not given up on his family. His grandfather had closed himself off. His parents had been stolen away to heaven. That was it. There was no one left to give up on. No reason for hope at all.

Noelle's kisses had made him yearn for a happy ending. That a wish could come true, that vulnerability could bring joy instead of grief. That love did not merely have to be a symbol, but rather something real and true and lasting.

But he knew better.

When he broke the kiss, it was as if a piece of his heart broke with it. He had to get out of Cressmouth. Away from the false hope of endless Christmas. Everything about it reminded him of anger and loss. Everything except her.

He did not agree with Society's view that an orphan like Noelle was beneath him and unworthy. But his feelings didn't matter. As a duke, he was forced to operate within that society. To make deals and alliances. To uphold conventions and expectations.

He could promise her nothing but heartbreak.

"I can't stay," he whispered hoarsely.

She nodded. "I know. I've always known."

"I never wanted to leave you," he said hoarsely, lest she doubt the demons that drove him. "I had to leave this town. I still do. It reminds me…"

She reached up to caress his cheek.

He leaned into her warmth. "I have no good Christmas memories."

"Until now." She wrapped her hands around his neck. "Let's make some new ones."

His heart thumped and he crushed his mouth to hers.

Perhaps she was right. The past was the past. It was time to make new memories. Time to risk lowering his guard, if only for a moment.

Tonight was all they could ever have.

His blood raced. What would it be like to let go of all the old fear, all the shame and anger, and give himself over to the moment completely? Could exposing his heart bring more joy than he'd ever believed possible?

Or would making himself vulnerable to intimacy cut even deeper?

CHAPTER 12

Noelle swayed as her runaway pulse pounded through her veins. She wrapped her arms about Benjamin and held on tight, the locket about her neck now sheltered between two hearts instead of one. Perhaps then they could be whole.

She did not blame him for the estranged relationship with his grandfather. Nor could she blame him for the resulting distaste for all things Cressmouth and Christmas.

Her heart dipped in sympathy. They had both lost their parents. It was not an easy thing to get over.

Noelle had never had a family portrait before, or any relic of her parents whatsoever. Had she possessed such a priceless heirloom, she would have cherished it above all others. No wonder Benjamin had done the same.

By entrusting his most treasured possession to her keeping, it was as though he was sharing his family with her. As if she too were deserving of such love. As if Noelle held equal weight in his heart.

How could she help but love him?

Her pulse skipped in warning. It was no longer a suspicion in the back of her mind. She was hopelessly, madly, deeply in love with a man who would leave her behind. Abandon her, just as her own parents had done.

No. Not as her parents had done. They had left no sign, no word, no token of affection. Benjamin was *here*. His lips pressed to hers, his tongue hot and demanding. From any other man, a locket would be nothing more than a piece of jewelry. In Benjamin's case, he had given her his heart.

At least, as much as he was willing to part with.

Could she not do the same? She yearned to reveal herself to him, body and soul. The thought of such a risk terrified her now more than ever, but this was their last opportunity.

"I thought you didn't want me," she whispered against his mouth.

He raised his head sharply, his gaze intense. "I pushed you away not because I don't want you, but because I cannot keep you. Yet I long for you like a sapling longs for rain. Although I know I cannot stay, I long to touch you, to taste you, to feel you against my skin."

Noelle's lungs caught. She had known he would not offer empty promises. Those words were simultaneously the most romantic and the most devastating thing he could have said to her.

The golden locket about her neck was the reason he had returned to Cressmouth. The locket was the reason he was here in her arms right now. It was his heart, divided into halves. One side contained the past. The other side was for the future.

They had both seen that the future was empty. But today did not have to be.

She wanted Benjamin more than anything under the sun. Their differences might be irreconcilable, but she wouldn't let that stop her from enjoying him for as long as she could.

"I never stopped thinking of you," she confessed between kisses. "Night after night, replaying your touch in my mind. Your kiss. Wondering what else we might have shared if we'd had time."

His dark gaze was tortured. "It isn't just time that divides us. If it weren't for everything that lies outside these walls, I would make love to you all night."

A delicious shiver slid down her spine. She sank her fingers into his hair to pull him close. "Then why don't you?"

His mouth claimed hers, his hands cupping her bottom to pull her tight against him. "Because you deserve so much more than I can give."

He was trying to scare her away. It wouldn't work. Noelle already knew the end of the story and was choosing him anyway. If her heart was destined to break, she would take every bit of pleasure while she still could.

"Give what you can," she whispered. "Take what you please."

His breath was ragged. "Noelle—"

"One night," she said as she tasted his lips. "Unless you aren't interested."

"*All* I want is you," he growled. "But if I cannot offer marriage, I certainly cannot rob you of your virginity."

"You cannot steal what is freely given," she reminded him.

"It's not honorable," he said, want and indecision warring in his eyes. "A gentleman wouldn't—"

"—say 'no' to a lady. Especially not if it's what he wants, too." She cupped his cheek. "If there won't be a second chance, shouldn't we take the one we have?"

He kissed the inside of her palm, her wrist, her lips. "Being with you is the one thing that makes me happy."

She wrapped her arms about his neck. "Don't we deserve one night of happiness together?"

"One night. Just for us." He lifted her in his strong arms.

She held on tight. "A night to remember."

In a few swift strides, they reached the bedchamber and tumbled atop the bed.

She pushed all thought of losing him out of her head and immersed herself in the current moment. The soft down of her bed. The hard muscle in his body. The bright crackle of the fire. The matching flame deep inside her.

Her heart soared higher with each kiss. She had dreamed of this, dreamed of him. The weight of his body pressed against her. She thrilled at the sensation, at the knowledge that soon she would know him more intimately than she had ever dreamed.

When he slid to one side, separating from her, she tried to break the kiss to complain about the loss. Before she could do so, his hand lifted her breast from its bodice and words failed her completely. She felt beautiful. Cherished.

Her fingers dug into the mattress with pleasure as he toyed with her bosom. Each touch of her nipple sent waves of desire through her body. This was what she had longed for. True connection.

When he moved his mouth down to her exposed breasts, she flung her arms up over her head and arched into him. She gave her body to him and in return he aroused her more than she had believed possible. It was all she could do not to claw the clothes from their bodies.

As he teased her bosom with his mouth, he tugged the

hems of her skirts from her ankles to her hips. She gasped at the sensation of cool air against her exposed skin, of his hot mouth over her nipple. When his hand cupped between her legs and dipped in teasing circles, her body responded at once. She gripped his shoulders, digging her fingernails into the material to ensure he did not cease his ministrations.

A tightness was uncurling deep inside her. A fullness, a wanting. Every lick of his tongue, every flick and dip of his finger brought her closer and closer to the edge. Every time he gave, she wanted more. It was heaven and torture twisted into one. Her body pulsed with need. Something was happening. Something like…

All at once, she could withstand the delicious pressure no longer and shattered against his fingers.

"More," she gasped when she finally caught her breath. "Not your hand. I want *you*."

He covered her mouth with his as he unbuttoned the fall of his breeches. At once, the weight of his shaft fell against her, hot and heavy, nestled perfectly against the juncture of her thighs. He reached between them, as if making certain she was ready for him.

She was more than ready. She was impatient. She wanted to give him the same pleasure he had given her. She wanted to find an even greater peak together.

As he eased into her, inch by inch, she wrapped her legs about him and brought him closer, deeper. Not just into her body, but into her heart. Into her soul.

The sharp stab of pain as he entered her was quickly replaced by renewed desire. Her pulse raced as she lost herself in his kiss.

Joining with him was more than she dreamed. But when

he rocked his hips and started to move… She held on tight, allowing the sensations to run through her, opening herself to him completely, taking everything he had been trying so hard not to give. In return, she would share everything she had.

If only for one night.

CHAPTER 13

Noelle awoke alone. When she stretched her arm out toward Benjamin, there was nothing beside her but cold linen and an empty bed. Her breath shuddered.

The wind outside whistled through cracks between the windowpanes, indicating the weather outside was as turbulent as her heart. She pushed her leaden feet off the edge of the bed and forced herself to the window. The glass was almost covered in frost. Snow was falling too deep and fast for any tracks to be visible in the streets below. There was no sign of Benjamin.

Perhaps he was halfway to London. Perhaps he was just down the corridor in his chamber, arranging for his trunk to be loaded into his carriage. Preparing to abandon her a second time. Her fingers shook with panic.

She forced her gaze from the window and sucked in a deep breath. Benjamin was incapable of abandoning her. Only someone who had made a commitment to stay could abandon another person. They had both been careful to make no such statements. There had been no promises. Benjamin was behaving exactly as he had warned from the start. If she didn't want her heart broken, it had been up to her to prevent it from becoming involved.

Besides, his departure today had nothing to do with last night, she reminded herself. A duke like Benjamin had duties, responsibilities, all sorts of things that were more important than her. Noelle's stomach twisted. Who knew? Maybe her parents had also had better things to do. More important priorities than keeping an unwanted daughter. She should be used to being alone by now. Of course Benjamin must return to his real life.

A life that didn't include her.

She touched her trembling fingers to her chest. The golden locket did not feel cold, but warm. Heated from her flesh, her dreams, this nightmare. It seemed to pulse against her skin as if it had a heartbeat of its own.

By giving her the locket, Benjamin had given up the thing that he loved most. Surely she was strong enough to do the same. No matter how it hurt. After all, that was the deal she had made. One night. Nothing more.

With listless movements, she cleaned her face at the basin and put on a day gown. She did not feel like freshening up or going anywhere at all. But what she wanted even less was a protracted goodbye with the man she loved.

Having to stand before him as he made his rejection official would be more than she could bear. Even if she'd known to expect it all along.

She wrapped herself in her warmest pelisse and fled from her bedchamber, from the castle, from anywhere she might spy Benjamin leaving her for good. That was the only defense she had left.

If they did not say goodbye, if the words were never spoken, perhaps it would be as though their parting had never happened. As if their story was not yet over. As if she could hold onto a small part of last night, a small part of *him* forever.

Even if it was all a lie.

CHAPTER 14

Benjamin was desperate.

He had searched everywhere in the castle for Noelle and couldn't find her anywhere. After he had slipped out to order her favorite breakfast, she was no longer in the bedchamber where he'd left her. Nor was she up in the counting house working on journals. She wasn't in the breakfast room, the glasshouse, the aviary…

She had vanished without a trace.

"Your Grace?" a footman murmured. "Your carriage is ready."

Of course his coach was ready. Benjamin had summoned it two hours ago, when he had believed Noelle was awaiting him in her chambers. But she was not there, she was not anywhere, and he was standing at the castle exit with his heart bleeding out of his chest. He *had* to say goodbye.

Yet he could not dally any longer. He should not even have stayed last night. At this point, he would have to race south, stopping for fresh horses as often as possible, to have a prayer of reaching London in time to be in his seat when the current session of Parliament began.

"Your Grace?" the footman tried again, his voice hesitant. "Should we have your driver return the coach to—"

"No. I'm going now." Benjamin whirled away from the empty receiving hall and strode outside into blinding sunlight.

Some might consider Cressmouth at its most picturesque with a fine layer of snow dusting every surface and even more snowflakes drifting lazily from the skies. Benjamin was not fooled by its beauty. This morning's high winds had been warning enough. He needed to get off this mountain and back to a main road as quickly as possible. Even if it meant leaving without seeing Noelle.

He climbed up into his coach and took his place against the plush squab. His hands should not be shaking. He had known this moment would come. Had been looking forward to leaving Cressmouth behind.

Now it felt as though he was leaving the most important part of himself behind with it.

He swung his gaze from the empty heavens to the castle. There lay another hard truth. Grandfather might have kept the locket from him all these years, but the old man had never possessed the power to deprive Benjamin of loved ones.

That was something he had been achieving on his own.

He signaled his driver and the horses started off down the snow-packed lanes. Soon Benjamin would be home. His chest should not feel this empty. He had known attachments could not last. His mother's gold locket had proven love was only a symbol, not something he was destined to keep. Just like Noelle. He was glad he had given her the locket. She was just as dear to him as the people inside. And destined to remain far out of reach.

The wind picked up force. He ignored it. No matter how low the temperature dropped, it was far colder in his heart. A wise man would lower his shields for no one, but Benjamin feared it was too late for that. The drawbridge had already been breached. Noelle was inside.

Any more time with her, and the damage would be irreversible. His soul would be inextricably linked to hers. Retreating while he still could was the only way to protect his heart.

If there were any pieces left unbroken.

The castle slipped from view. He tried not to feel the loss. There was no room in his life for sentimentality. He was expected to speak on a new law within a week. To meet with a half dozen committees dedicated to improving the lives of people all over England. That was his priority. His *duty*. How could a man in his position possibly choose one person over many, no matter how much he loved her?

He almost slid out of his seat in shock. *He loved her.*

Bloody hell. It was too late for defensive measures. He had not fortified his shields in time. Precisely as he had feared, his soul was bound to hers—and he still had to leave.

He tightened his fists in his lap. This desperation clawing through his chest proved the point. If he married Noelle, he would want to spend every moment of his time with her, wherever she might be. That wasn't a choice. Such a union would either mean shirking his duties to Parliament or his commitment to his wife.

Neither outcome was acceptable. He could not force Noelle to London only to leave her in an empty home while he spent all his time in the Palace of Westminster, embroiled in endless committees. Besides, she had no wish to leave Cressmouth. He had asked her. She had been clear.

The carriage clopped by a merry red sign partially dusted with snow:

Thank you for visiting Christmas!

His gut twisted in revulsion. Was it any wonder he hated the holiday festive season? All it had ever brought him was loss.

This time, he had caused the loss himself.

Driving away and leaving Noelle behind wasn't allowing him to return to his old life. It was destroying an alternate one. A better life he couldn't have.

His heart clenched with longing as he thought of how sweet she had looked in the morning light, sleeping softly by his side. She was an angel.

A sudden drop of ice pierced him inside at the realization of what he had done.

He had hurt her so badly the first time he had left, never to return. Now he was doing it all over again. No wonder she was avoiding him, as though he didn't exist. As if the passion they had shared was meaningless. Soon, it would be.

All that would be left was the imprint each had left behind.

CHAPTER 15

The further Benjamin got from Cressmouth, the emptier he felt inside. The long empty path ahead seemed both physical and metaphorical. How he hated that he hadn't been able to find Noelle before he left! One more separation without a goodbye in a long, sad history of regret.

The snow swirling all around him evoked the sleigh ride they had shared. The frosted tips of the evergreens lining the road reminded him of how warm it had been in that glasshouse when he'd finally given into temptation and kissed her. He was a long way from home and the distance was getting further with every mile.

At that thought, his chest tightened. When he had clasped the locket about Noelle's neck, he wasn't giving her his heart. *She* was his heart. The locket was now just an object, but she was everything. And he had been forced to leave her behind.

The horses slowed as they pulled the carriage over a narrow bridge. It felt as though he were crossing not just a stream, but from one life to another. From laughter to loneliness. From Noelle… to nothing.

His stomach twisted. Returning to London should not feel like a part of him was dying. He was being responsible. He was performing his duty.

Yet all he could think about was Noelle. Watching her giggle and tear up at a play she had seen a dozen times. The mirth on her face when they realized Mr. Fawkes had delivered a pear tree instead of a partridge. The way she had teased him about goats and birds and perfume. How brilliant she was. The counting house, how helpful she was to her friends, how quickly she had arranged the opening ceremony for the aviary. His breath grew shallow.

Every moment of the northern holiday he had never wished to take, Noelle had stood by his side. She had done much more than make it bearable. Whether they were laughing together, working together, or making love together, she filled his heart with joy. He was his happiest when he was with her. *She* was the missing piece he had been looking for all along.

And now she was gone. His heart banged against his chest in protest.

The driver picked up speed. This far from Cressmouth, the snow had disappeared. The ground was no longer frozen. The steeds carried them further, faster. No matter what Benjamin's heart might want. He rubbed his face.

The only person he could blame for leaving Noelle behind was himself. This morning, he had chosen to summon his horses, climb in his carriage, return to London. But he'd put up his walls long before that. Years ago when they'd shared their first kiss, he had already become cold and inaccessible.

This time was worse. He had shut her out of his heart when all he wanted was to let her inside. She made him a better person. Her willingness and ability to force him out from where he was most comfortable had been good for him. Good for them. She enriched his life.

And she didn't even *know*.

He slumped back against the squab. He had been a fool to leave without telling her. Without explaining how much she meant. Even if he returned for occasional visits… it would be far less than she deserved. Far less than he wanted.

He touched the scarf about his neck. The one Noelle had knitted for him, even before he had given her a reason to forgive him, much less trust him. All he'd given her in return were more reasons to lose faith in him all over again. All in the name of England.

The road widened as the carriage exited the forest and clattered out between wide swaths of farmland. At this pace, they would make it to the first posting-house in no time. Be in London earlier than expected. One more face amongst the many. An automaton serving the House of Lords and nothing more.

Was this who he wished to be? Cold, dutiful, emotionless? He was not that man anymore, if he ever truly had been. He would have to do better. Noelle deserved so much more than he'd been able to give.

Sharp, familiar fear pricked the edges of his mind. The terrible conviction that if he opened himself up, if he let himself love, if he admitted the truth out loud, he would lose her anyway. He drew in a shallow breath.

Weren't some things worth everything? Wasn't Noelle worth the risk?

For so long, Benjamin had believed he would be worth nothing as a gentleman if he did not give his all to the House of Lords. He now suspected the lowlier man would be the featherwit who let the chance of the love of a lifetime slip away yet again.

What use was being the hero of Parliament, if he could not be a hero to the woman he loved most?

With a sudden movement, he signaled the driver to stop the coach at once.

The horses halted obediently. It was Benjamin's heartbeat that ran amok.

Carefully, the horses turned the carriage about in the slippery lane and headed back in the direction they had come. He urged the driver to make haste.

Winning Noelle back wouldn't be easy. Perhaps he was already too late. He had left her twice. She might be unwilling to try a third time. But it didn't matter. He had to try. She was worth any risk at any price. *Love* was worth it.

The horses raced back up the narrow path curving around the mountain. There would be no return toward London today. By the time the beasts would arrive at the castle, they would be too exhausted to continue on.

Benjamin didn't *want* to continue on. Not alone. He wanted Noelle. He needed her to know how much he loved her. How much he regretted every moment without her. How he hoped never to part again. He had to get to her. Snow sprayed from the wheels of the carriage as he took curve after curve.

Mr. Fawkes was right. It *was* better to have loved and lost than never to have loved at all... But it was even better to get his imbecilic arse back to Cressmouth posthaste and do his damnedest not to lose Noelle.

He knew how much she loved her mountain village, how much a part of her it was. She had no reason to trust him. She might not wish to share her life with him even if she believed his heart was true.

Perhaps the issues weren't insurmountable. He would beg her hand and find a way. Although he couldn't promise himself solely to Cressmouth, he could promise himself to her. Even if he turned out not to be enough, Noelle was worth fighting for.

He had to try.

CHAPTER 16

Noelle sat at Penelope's dining nook with one elbow propped upon the table and her chin in her hand. Although her dear friend did her best to distract her with impassioned scientific explanations about the chemical compounds in her newest perfume, nothing could keep Noelle's mind from Benjamin. No quantity of piping hot tea could chase away the endless chill inside her heart.

The moment she let her guard down, her worst fear came true. She had been seated right here at Penelope's breakfast table when the coach with his ducal crest had rolled by.

He had left her, exactly as her parents had done. Just like she had expected. She had known not to believe it could be different this time. It was not his fault.

She could not accuse him of raising false hopes. Making love had been her idea. More than an idea, it had been an intimacy she had yearned to share with him for so long. If she was feeling melancholy because she hadn't been strong enough to say goodbye, it was no one's fault but hers.

Her lungs froze in sudden horror.

Was lack of goodbye not the precise situation that had hurt Benjamin the most, time and again? The very reason the locket about her neck was so precious to him was because everyone he ever cared about had been ripped from him before he had a chance to say goodbye.

His family had not meant to leave him so abruptly.

Noelle had done it by design.

She lowered her face into her hands.

"Are you all right?" Penelope asked softly.

Noelle pushed to her feet. "I have to go."

She could not impose on Penelope any longer.

In minutes, Noelle was bundled against the cold and trudging back toward the castle, back toward the empty counting house and her lonely bedchamber, back toward the rest of her life. One without Benjamin.

Perhaps loneliness was her destiny. It was no one's fault Benjamin had been born heir to a dukedom. No one's fault his primary seat was miles away. No one's fault his duty was to the House of Lords. If she wished to be angry, it might as well be with the stars above.

From the moment he'd come back, she'd known she could expect nothing from him.

And yet he'd managed to surprise her anyway.

The comfortable chair and better lighting in the counting house. His repeated kindnesses with Mr. Fawkes, no matter how many misunderstandings. The way Benjamin had made Tiny Tim's health his personal responsibility. How he'd let her shove him into a sleigh and sit through a festive play despite all the pain Christmas had brought him.

He'd done it all for Noelle. Because he wanted to be with her, while it was possible.

She strode through the castle entrance and headed toward

the counting house stairs. Perhaps journals and accounts would keep her mind from Benjamin better than tea with a well-meaning friend. At least she could make herself useful.

"Miss Pratchett," a male voice called just as she reached the winding staircase.

She turned around to find Mr. Marlowe's solicitor smiling at her. "May I help you?"

"I should say so." He nodded with satisfaction. "We've no less than eight candidates for your review. I've taken the liberty of inquiring into their references for you."

She stared at him blankly. "Candidates for what?"

"The apprenticeship, of course. One moment, miss." The solicitor fetched a stack of papers from his office. "Here we are. His Grace arranged for you to have an assistant. As I've stated—"

"What if I don't want an assistant?" she stammered.

"Then don't pick one," the solicitor replied. "His Grace was quite clear on the matter. You alone have the authority to select as few or as many apprentices as you deem fit for the counting house."

"*I* have the authority," she repeated. "*Me*."

The solicitor nodded. "Every decision left to your sole and complete discretion, miss. If you'd like me to search for different candidates—"

"I'll take the list," she said quickly and stepped forward to accept the documents.

Her pulse pounded. Benjamin had recognized how much work it had taken to clear up the old records and put them to rights. He had warned her not to spend so much time in the counting house that there was no room left in her days for life.

This was his way of letting her have everything she

wanted. A position of acknowledged importance as well as the freedom to take time for herself. She held the papers to her chest. With the right staff in place, the counting house would function whether Noelle was absent for an afternoon or an extended holiday.

The corner of her mouth curved. Whether he liked Christmas or not, Benjamin had managed to provide both for Noelle and for the villagers. He had ensured less work for her and created new positions for others. He had left Cressmouth a better place.

"How is Tiny Tim?" she asked suddenly.

The solicitor didn't blink at the sudden change in topic. "As neat as ninepence, miss. Jumping all over everything again. A new lease on life, I'd say."

Noelle took a deep breath. The pygmy goat wasn't the only one who felt like leaping for joy. It was time for her to change as well.

As long as she only viewed herself as a function of Cressmouth, there was no room in her overextended life for anyone else. Not even Benjamin. She was equally responsible for pushing him away. For not making room. For being a fool.

Cressmouth would be right here all year round… but Noelle didn't have to be.

If she was willing to try.

Her hands shook as she pointed out a pair of names to the solicitor. "These two look promising. How soon can they start?"

"They're here now, miss." He gestured toward his makeshift office. "Both have years of experience with accounting. Shall I send them up to familiarize themselves with ours?"

"Send Mr. Fawkes up, too. He'll enjoy sharing the castle's history as he acquaints them with the accounts."

"As you please, miss. Should I tell them you'll be up shortly?"

"No," she said slowly, her resolve strengthening. "I don't think I will be."

When Benjamin had asked if she would be willing to visit London, she had dismissed the idea out of hand. But he hadn't been trying to take something away from her. He was trying to offer her something *more*.

She had been wrong to judge her self-worth on her loyalty to her village. Leaving its borders for a time wouldn't mean she loved it any less. He had come here, to a place filled with ghosts and bad memories. Surely she could survive a trip south to an unfamiliar city.

Her heart pounded. She didn't want to let go of Benjamin. She wanted to hold on tight. Only together would they be whole.

She shoved the documents into the solicitor's hands and spun back toward the castle exit.

He stepped aside and clasped the papers to his chest in bafflement. "Where are you going, miss?"

To Benjamin. There was no time to waste.

"I need to see a lady about a horse," she called over her shoulder and ran out the door.

Outside, the weather was just as cold as before, but no longer felt so bleak. This time it seemed the winds of change, a breeze of possibility hurrying her along her way.

Her pulse raced with urgency.

Noelle had no carriage of her own and Cressmouth was too small a village to have a plethora of hackneys one could hire in order to chase after a lost love. She would have to make do on horseback.

She slipped on a patch of ice and caught herself on a wooden pillar as she skidded off the street and onto the famous Harper stud farm.

Olive was in the barn tightening a leather tack when Noelle arrived.

"Horse," Noelle panted. "Please."

Olive looked at her doubtfully. "I've just saddled up Earl. He won't be a sedate ride. He's been restless all day and—"

"Perfect," Noelle said quickly, grateful Olive was the sort of friend who didn't ask questions. "I'll have him back by nightfall."

Probably.

"Earl is a full-grown pony. He hasn't an assigned bedtime," Olive said with a smile as she pushed a mounting block beside him. "Good luck."

Noelle glanced at her friend sharply, then launched herself into the sidesaddle. Perhaps the real reason Olive hadn't asked any questions was because she had already surmised the answers.

"Thank you," she said and meant it. "For everything."

Olive moved the mounting block out of the way and gestured toward the open road. "Go and get him."

Noelle turned into the wind and gave Earl his head.

Benjamin might have had a two-hour head start, but he was also pulling a heavy coach. A single rider on a fast pony ought to be able to make up the same distance in half the time.

Noelle blinked falling snowflakes from her eyelashes and held on tight. She had to do more than merely catch up with Benjamin. She had to let him know how much he meant. How much she would love to stay together. How she was even willing to give him a proper goodbye, if that was what he preferred.

Just as she began to suspect her limbs had frozen to the back of the pony, she caught sight of a distant carriage ahead, a coal-black smudge in a world filled with white.

It wasn't the coach she was searching for, however. This carriage wasn't leaving Cressmouth. It was heading right toward her at breakneck speed.

She coaxed Earl to the side of the road to allow the carriage to pass.

When the driver drew close, he halted the horses and a well-dressed gentleman leapt out of the coach right before her eyes.

Benjamin. Her heart soared. He had come back for her!

"I love you," he said before she could open her mouth. "I didn't tell you when I could, so I'm telling you now. I love you, Noelle Pratchett. I'll never tire of saying so."

All the cold and numbness left her legs as she gazed down at him speechlessly.

"Tell me one thing." He stared up at her, his eyes beseeching. "Why did you hide from me?"

"Goodbye was too final," she said, her voice cracking. "I loved you and you left me anyway. I didn't want it to be over. I couldn't… I can't… You weren't…"

"I'm right here." He held out his arms and she slid down into them. "I came back. I don't want to go anywhere without you."

"Neither do I," she whispered.

He wrapped his scarf around them both, holding on tight. "You love me?"

"Of course I do, you dreadful beast." She snuggled her cheek into his warm chest.

He lifted her chin and forced her to meet his eyes.

"Come with me," he said urgently. "Let me show you a different kind of season. We can fill up the coach with anything you want to bring, and I'll arrange everything else."

"Leave Cressmouth?" Her voice might wobble, but her heart was sure. She would go anywhere to be with him. All he had to do was ask.

"As my wife," he said quickly. "Come as my duchess. Let me be your husband."

"I will never fit in with the beau monde," she stammered. "I'm an orphan…"

"So am I," he said with a crooked smile. "And who cares what they think? I don't want to fit in with the *ton*. I want to fit together with you. To marry *you*. When we start our family, we'll raise our children to know they are loved."

"And Christmas?" she asked, her heart pounding with joy.

"A lovely village," he answered without hesitation. "We can spend half the year here, and half the year in London. What do you think?" His eyes were beseeching. "Mightn't it be the best of both worlds?"

"No." She wound her arms about his neck to give him a kiss. "It'll be the best of both seasons."

He grinned. "That means yes?"

"It means I'll go anywhere, as long as I'm with you." She kissed the tip of his nose. "After all, why have one home when we could have two?"

CHAPTER 17

Three months later
London, England

Noelle sat as still as she could. She was sharing a beautiful stone bench in the middle of Vauxhall Gardens with her new husband.

Benjamin lowered the arm he had curved protectively about her waist to just below her hip in order to give her derrière a surreptitious squeeze before returning to position.

Noelle tried her best not to squeeze him back.

The portrait artist poked his head out from behind the easel then returned his focus to his canvases.

He was making two records of this moment. A large likeness of Benjamin and Noelle for the hall of portraits in the primary Silkridge residence, and a miniature of Benjamin to fit the other half of the gold locket she wore next to her heart.

She risked a brief glance up at Benjamin from beneath her eyelashes.

He caught her in the act, and swooped in to steal a quick kiss.

"Not in front of the artist," she scolded him under her breath as her cheeks flushed with heat.

Benjamin's voice lowered huskily. "He's too busy working."

"What of the other people?" she reminded him, darting a glance over her shoulder at the hundreds of Londoners enjoying the beautiful weather and equally gorgeous flowers.

"Do face forward, Your Grace," Benjamin said with mock severity. "A professional artist is attempting to paint our portrait."

Noelle pinched his thigh. "Beast."

She had never been happier.

London was even larger than she had anticipated, and full of many more pleasures. She had made countless new friends, joined book clubs and charitable societies. And every moment that Parliament was not in session, Benjamin was by her side.

Last night, they had spent an exhilarating evening in his brand new opera box at the Royal Theatre. The night before, a soirée at the Ormondton residence. She and Benjamin had spent so much time waltzing in each other's arms these past few months, Noelle was once again in need of new dancing slippers.

The very best problem to have.

She received weekly reports from her apprentices in the counting house. The competent new team had the accounts well in hand. It felt like a miracle.

Noelle could *enjoy* her Season in London, and then enjoy the holiday season in Cressmouth. She leaned her head into

Benjamin's shoulder and smiled contentedly. Where they were on the map didn't matter.

Anywhere they could be together was home.

EPILOGUE

The following December
Christmas, England

"I want a ride to the play!" called a lad bundled in so much winter clothing his face was barely visible.

With a practiced hand, Benjamin guided his sleigh to the side of the road. "Climb aboard. I believe there is an inch or two of room left."

His wife unsuccessfully stifled a giggle as the village children behind them jostled each other like a box of puppies to make room for the new arrival.

Although *The Winter's Tale* would not begin for another hour, this was their fifth trip through the village. Benjamin was starting to suspect that the children fled the amphitheater as soon as they arrived in order to sneak a sleigh ride again and again. Not that he minded.

Although his life was now split evenly between two worlds, his heart belonged wholly with the woman at his side.

Some high-in-the-instep aristocrats looked down their

snobbish noses at a duke making a love match, but Benjamin had no regrets whatsoever. Indeed, their united efforts toward making a difference in others' lives had made them something of a favorite in many circles.

Noelle had quickly become the perfect wife and partner. Over the past year, they shared intimate discussions about politics over matching cups of mint tea, and then spent blissful hours in the London whirl enjoying concerts and soirées and fireworks in the gardens. Her innate grace and sweetness had won plenty of new friends.

Life together in Cressmouth was just as delightful. He and Noelle had decided to build a private cottage rather than reside in the castle, and Benjamin could not be happier with that decision. He had come to love the sound of blustery winter wind outside while he and his wife heated up the evenings inside. He loved *Noelle.*

He lifted the brim of her bonnet to plant a quick kiss on one of her rosy cheeks.

"No kissing!" cried a chorus of young voices in the back from the sleigh.

A pelting of snowballs to the back of Benjamin's greatcoat immediately followed.

He scooped up whatever snow he could and tossed it back over his shoulder as he had done every other time he had temporarily "forgotten" the children's no kissing rule.

They screamed with delight as the loosely packed snow rained down on them in flutters of snowflakes.

"Here we are," Benjamin called out as he pulled the sleigh before the amphitheater. "Out you go. Find the best seats in the house!"

The children tumbled out of the sleigh and streamed toward the stage, but Benjamin had no doubt half a dozen would find their way back onto his path in the next quarter hour. Benjamin loved it. Moments like these were how holiday traditions were born.

"Happy Christmas to all!" Noelle laughingly called toward the children's retreating backs.

Benjamin nuzzled the curve of her neck. "And to us… a sizzling night."

His favorite tradition of all.

KISS OF A DUKE

12 DUKES OF CHRISTMAS #2

CRESSMOUTH GAZETTE

Welcome to Christmas!

Our picturesque village is nestled around Marlowe Castle, high atop the gorgeous mountain we call home. Cressmouth is best known for our year-round Yuletide cheer. Here, we're family.

The legend of our twelve dukes? Absolutely true! But perhaps not always who—or *what*—one might expect...

CHAPTER 1

Marlowe Castle
Christmas, England

"To the *Duke!*" yelled a half-sotted voice in the middle of the packed ballroom.

"To Penelope Mitchell!" the crowd shouted back, raising their goblets of spiced wine in unison.

Clinks of crystal glasses and peals of merry laughter filled the high-ceilinged assembly room as the spectators' cheers warmed the nutmeg-scented air.

Despite this being the third such toast in the past half hour, Miss Penelope Mitchell still couldn't quite credit that the entirety of her mountaintop village had crowded into the castle's largest chamber to celebrate something other than the year-round Christmastide their town was primarily known for.

As a lady chemist, she couldn't be prouder.

Her satisfaction wasn't solely because the townsfolk had gathered to celebrate the accomplishments of a woman, or even because the accomplishment in question was a perfume she had invented herself.

As far as Penelope was concerned, she and one thousand of her neighbors had gathered to celebrate a breakthrough in *science.*

Unlike more well-known natural philosophers, Penelope's primary field of study was neither plant life nor the animal kingdom. The majority of her observations and chemical experiments took place in the custom-built laboratory next to her kitchen. An unobtrusive metal firewall separated both rooms from the rest of the house in case of accidental fire or explosion.

Today, it was Penelope's soaring heart that felt close to detonation.

"Congratulations!" shouted her bosom friend Miss Gloria Godwin over the joyous din of the crowd.

Although Gloria directed her passions toward the infinite expanse of the heavens whilst Penelope preferred to focus on glass vials of chemicals she could hold in her hands, the two had been inseparable since childhood.

"Thank you," Penelope said, as soon as she edged close enough not to have to shout. The party had been underway less than an hour, and already she feared losing her voice before morning. "I cannot believe *Duke* is this successful."

"It isn't," Gloria said matter-of-factly. "The party isn't for your perfume. The celebration is for *you*. We're proud all of England has recognized your talent."

Penelope gave her a crooked grin. "Who knew our town's resident lady chemist would become a champion not only of science, but of fashion?"

"I did," Gloria said without hesitation.

Penelope's cheeks heated. "You're a good friend."

"And you're mad as a hatter," Gloria replied with a flash of her dimples. "But it seems so is everyone else. There's nothing England likes better than to copy whatever barmy antics appear in the scandal sheets. I ask you, what sort of man would douse himself with animal secretions in an attempt to attract a woman?"

"A wise man who understands science," Penelope protested. "It's chemistry, not madness. A natural reaction. When the olfactory glands of certain mammals are exposed to the—"

"Stop right there." Gloria covered her ears and pretended not to hear. "This is a party, not the annual gathering of the Natural Philosophers Society." She frowned. "*Is* there a Natural Philosophers Society?"

Penelope opened her mouth to answer.

"No, don't tell me. Don't tell anyone," Gloria said quickly. "That's not why we're here, darling. No one cares *how* your perfume works. They just love that it *does*. All those articles and caricatures and gossip columns with stories of previously unrakish men being practically trampled by eligible females within minutes of applying your *eau de toilette*... You're a genius."

Penelope swallowed an uncomfortable lump in her throat at the praise. "It's not genius. Experiment after experiment has proven that the properly proportioned secretions of both musk whales and civets—"

"No, no, no." Gloria grabbed a fresh glass of mulled wine from a passing footman and shoved it into Penelope's hands. "Do *not* explain how it works. To anyone. That ruins the magic."

With a sigh of frustration, Penelope lowered her nose to smell the steam of her spiced wine. Of course "how it works" was the important bit. Chemists, natural philosophers, and alchemists alike dedicated their lives to trying to decipher the workings of nature. Being able to turn an undesirable element into a desirable one was the entire point.

"Then what *is* the 'magic?'" she asked.

Gloria raised her brows in surprise. "*Prinney* wears your perfume, because none other than Beau Brummell told him true gentlemen shan't leave their dressing rooms without it. The Prince Regent! In your perfume! *That's* the magic. Now that you're famous—"

"I'm not famous," Penelope reminded her. "A specific combination of painstakingly researched olfactory elements is famous."

"—our town is more renowned, too," Gloria continued, brown eyes shining. "I shouldn't be surprised if we have twice as many visitors this year, from those wishing to see the birthplace of *Duke*."

"My laboratory?" Penelope reared back in horror. "I allow no one inside. In order to keep the pristine environment unadulterated with—"

"Not your laboratory," Gloria assured her. "They want to see the beautiful Christmas village that inspires you. Who wouldn't want to visit a snow-topped mountain and return home inspired, too?"

Penelope tightened her lips, lest the truth spill out. She wasn't inspired by a snow-dusted mountaintop village, no matter how picturesque. She was driven by molecules and vials and complex chemical compositions. The irony was remarkable.

She hadn't intended to turn London's fashionable set on their ears. She had been competing in a nationwide quest to determine causal factors in the mating habits of certain nocturnal mammals. Her intent had been to prove that lady natural philosophers were just as competent at investigation as their male counterparts.

That her research should result in the discovery of a chemical compound just as potent when applied to humans had been incidental to her cause. When she'd packaged it as *Duke* and sold it on a lark, she hadn't anticipated how quickly the new scent would take over local shops, then regional distributors, then national magazines, then end up as part of the morning toilette of the most influential man in England.

Or that Brummel would convince Prinney, too.

She grinned at Gloria. Progress had been made. The Natural Philosophers Guild had refused to allow a lady chemist's research into their precious contest, but England had taken notice nonetheless. What did it matter that their fellow villagers had come to celebrate scents rather than science? Her smile dipped.

"Where's Penelope?" boomed a voice from across the tumultuous chamber.

"Speech!" shouted another.

Penelope ducked her head to hide her face before she could be spotted. She was used to spending weeks at a time in the privacy of her laboratory. Not pontificating on stage in front of her neighbors. If she stayed near the back, they wouldn't find her.

"Speech, speech!" the crowd echoed in raptures.

"Go on, you brilliant woman." Gloria tried to nudge her in the direction of the grand dais on the other side of the ballroom. "Your people await."

Penelope sent a dubious glance in the direction of the dais. She couldn't even see it behind all the people. "What do they expect me to say?"

"You gave them what we all want," Gloria explained with a smile. "A tool to help them find love. What could be purer?"

"That's not what I did at all," Penelope said in surprise.

"Speech, speech!" cried the crowd.

"I didn't say you personally acted as matchmaker," Gloria chided her gently. "But you created a perfume that enables two previously unknown people to come together and perhaps discover love."

"I created a chemical solution that enabled two previously unconnected *compounds* to come together," Penelope stammered. "It has nothing to do with love."

"Everything has to do with love," Gloria said.

Penelope shook her head. "There is no love. It's an illusion. A romantic fantasy invented to explain chemical reactions as old as nature itself."

Gloria's mouth fell open. "How can you say that? You camped in tents for months and witnessed the effects of your compounds firsthand. If your perfumes can make rodents fall in love, you cannot deny that—"

"Civets are Viverridae, more similar to primitive felines than rodents," Penelope interrupted. "And they don't *fall in love*. Their females go *in heat*. In fact, as Samuel Williams wrote in his *Natural and Civil History of Vermont*—"

"What do American natural philosophers know about love?" Gloria spluttered.

"That it doesn't exist," Penelope blurted out.

"Speech, speech!" screamed the crowd.

"Love is a fictional construct invented to make natural biological urges sound more palatable in Polite Society," Penelope explained earnestly. "Animals excrete scents. Humans are animals. If we're in love with anything, it's our own excretions."

"Good God." Gloria stared at her in disbelief. "That is the least romantic—"

"Romance is an arbitrarily prescribed set of unnatural behaviors and absurd superstitions created to explain and engender a mythical emotion we invented whole cloth. All because we believe ourselves to be superior to other animals."

Gloria spluttered in disbelief. "Surely you agree modern society is superior to the lives of rodents and primitive cats!"

Penelope sniffed. "Male civets don't douse themselves with the glandular excretions of other, more popular civets in order to attract the attention of voluptuous female civets at local assemblies."

"They would if they could," Gloria muttered beneath her breath. "All males are optimists."

"Speech, speech!" roared the crowd.

"Someone fetch Penelope Mitchell!" shouted a man near the dais.

"I see her!" a woman shrieked. "She's with Miss Godwin!"

Penelope rolled back her shoulders. "Very well. I don't know anything about love—"

"*Obviously*," Gloria muttered, louder this time.

"—but science has proven that olfactory information can incite sexual arousal in both genders of many animals, causing the mating instinct to demand immediate and natural carnal satisfaction. I can talk about that. I've personally observed many instances of—"

Gloria grabbed Penelope's arm and turned her away from the stage.

"No speech!" she shouted over her shoulder. "Miss Mitchell is much too shy and… er… ladylike. She appreciates your support. Enjoy the party! And the wine! Talk amongst yourselves!"

"Furthermore," Penelope continued thoughtfully as her best friend tugged her a safer distance from the dais, "I'm *glad* I'm in no danger of 'falling in love.' I like being a chemist and I like being a spinster. There's no reason to fuss with the permanency of a husband if all a woman wishes to do is satisfy the occasional natural urge."

Gloria wrinkled her nose. "But what about all the other women?"

Penelope tilted her head. "What other women?"

"The ladies who *do* wish to fuss with the permanency of a husband. You might not have a biological or financial or romantical need for marriage, but I daresay most women do not have that luxury. They *have* to marry." Gloria's voice faltered. "And we like to believe in love."

Penelope's heart twisted in remorse. Gloria was right. Penelope might be too rational for romance, but that was no reason to ruin the experience for anyone else. In fact, Penelope was in a unique position to actually do something about it.

"You've inspired me," she announced.

"I-I've inspired you?" Gloria stammered in obvious concern. "To do what?"

"To help," Penelope said. She gave a sharp nod.

Gloria blinked. "Help how?"

"With science." Penelope tapped her chin. "What did *Duke* do?"

"Make an obscene amount of money?" Gloria guessed. "Revolutionize modern perfumes?"

"*Men's* perfumes," Penelope corrected with chagrin. "An easy market, and a mistake. The world doesn't need more dandies and rakes."

"What does it need?" Gloria asked suspiciously.

"Empowered women," Penelope replied without hesitation. "I cannot control Society, but I *do* control what I research in my laboratory. *Duke* was just the beginning. I have more research. The next product I launch will be *Duchess*." She straightened her shoulders in determination. "For women."

Gloria clasped her hands to her chest. "You could make a perfume to help women find husbands?"

Penelope nodded. "Or become female rakes. Ladies' choice. Once you attract a man, it's up to you if you want to keep him."

Gloria burst out laughing. "There's no such thing as lady rakes."

"There should be." Penelope gave her a wicked grin. "Why should men have all the fun?"

"Speaking of rakes..." Gloria grabbed Penelope's arm and bounced on her toes. "Don't look now, but Nicholas Pringle just walked into the ballroom. Nicholas Pringle! Here, in this very ballroom."

Penelope shrugged. "Who?"

"Only the most fawned-over rake to ever grace the Society pages. I recognize him from the caricatures alone. He once—Is that his *brother*?" Gloria let out an appreciative whistle beneath her breath. "It must be a brother. He looks just like him. Don't look! They'll know we're talking about them. My heart is pounding. I can't believe this is happening."

"I can't believe you're overreacting." Penelope gave an exaggerated yawn. "How handsome can two men be?"

"I'm not overreacting," Gloria promised. "I'm just the first to—"

Audible female gasps rippled through the crowd, followed by several dramatic swoons.

"—the first to notice," Gloria finished smugly. "They call

him 'Saint Nick' because he's as wicked as they come. One look and you're smitten."

Penelope raised a brow.

Gloria fluttered her eyelashes. "At least I didn't swoon."

"No, but you bruised my arm." Penelope wrenched out of Gloria's grasp and angled her head toward the open ballroom doors. "Where are they?"

Gloria fanned her throat. "Saint Nick is the gentleman with—"

"Found him." The strangled words barely escaped Penelope's suddenly dry throat. Gloria was right.

From a biological perspective, he was the finest male specimen Penelope had ever seen. And as a living, breathing woman… Good heavens.

Features: symmetrical. Jawline: chiseled. Visage: arresting. Light brown hair tumbled over a perfectly shaped head. His cravat was as white as chemists' talcum, a subtle explosion of sharp points and soft folds designed to add elegance without distracting from the rest of the package.

And Saint Nick made one tempting package.

The hard curves of his muscled arms and wide shoulders were shown to advantage in a dashing coat of black superfine that begged to be touched. His waistcoat was the shimmery silver of magnesium, an element oft-combined with iron. She wondered if his will was just as strong.

Coal-black boots, tight-fitting buckskins, kid gloves… All he'd need to do was jingle a bell and every woman present would clamor to be his.

Every woman but Penelope.

Yes, his looks were the very definition of all that was virile and desirable in a gentleman. But his approach to life made him the last man who could hold her interest. He was an accomplished rake. A man who relied on *romance* to woo silly women.

The urge to spread one's seed might be a natural male directive, but Penelope would never fawn over a man with nothing to recommend him beyond symmetrical features and pretty words. She had better things to do. Her mind preferred the comfort and excitement of her laboratory to pointless strolls down moonlit paths with a man who couldn't hold a meaningful conversation.

Penelope cared about facts, about science, about logic. A natural philosopher would never select a mating partner based on external beauty alone.

"Uninterested," she said abruptly. "Shall we find the dessert buffet?"

"We should find someone to introduce us," Gloria breathed. "I had no idea Saint Nick had a younger brother. I'm very, very interested."

Penelope frowned. "If you had no idea he existed, how do you know he's the younger brother?"

"Because Nicholas Pringle is first in line to a dukedom," Gloria replied with a cheeky grin. "Scoff at Society papers all you like. Some of us use them for important research."

Penelope gave an affectionate roll of her eyes. "I wouldn't want a husband who must mind a dukedom."

"Low probability," Gloria answered promptly. "He's heir presumptive to the Duke of Silkridge, whose first banns were announced last Sunday. The Pringle brothers are his cousins. They've no other titles, which means they visit London for social reasons, rather than to attend the House of Lords. I presume their country piles are elsewhere."

Penelope burst out laughing. "You *have* done a lot of research."

Gloria gave an angelic smile. "What else am I to do? Spinsters like me have to wait around for your new perfume in order to have a chance. Unless opportunity knocks. Let's go introduce ourselves to the Pringle brothers."

"Absolutely not."

Gloria's brows arched in surprise. "Because Saint Nick is a rake? Since when do you care about propriety?"

Penelope shook her head. "Because you're right. I should be working on the new perfume. I started a female version at the same time as the male version, but *Duke* was easier. I halted the other project when I learned the Natural Philosophers Guild was seeking applicants to research practical applications of John Dalton's atomic theory."

Gloria's mouth fell open. "You mean… it's almost done and you abandoned it? The magical *eau de toilette* that could have viscounts and earls swooning at my feet?"

"It's close," Penelope hedged. "I'm not yet in a position to declare with empirical certainty that *Duchess* will outperform *Duke*, but I intend to lock myself in my laboratory until it's ready for trials."

"All the more reason to introduce ourselves to the Pringle brothers while they're still here." Gloria narrowed her eyes. "A month from now, after I bathe myself in reptile excretions—or whatever ungodly concoction you plan to create—when I next meet him in a crowded ballroom, I can say, 'Why, Mr. Pringle, I haven't seen you since the Christmas soirée!' And he'll say, 'Mmrrgle blrrrgmmph' as he falls at my feet in a manly, yet glorious, swoon."

Penelope shook her finger in mock reprimand. "If you apply more than the recommended dosage, *all* the men in the ballroom will say 'Mmrrgle blrrrgmmph' in unison as they crumple gracelessly to your feet."

"Even better," Gloria said with delight. "Nothing starts a conversation quite like regaining consciousness among a dizzy heap of equally smitten gentlemen."

"Once the new perfume is ready, women needn't bother *talking* to prospective gentlemen anymore," Penelope promised. "Chemistry will take over and the subsequent natural urges will guide them straight into your arms."

Gloria pushed her lips into a pout. "What about those of us who *enjoy* talking to men?"

"Ninnies, all of you." Penelope linked her arm with Gloria's. "I'd rather hold a conversation with a *bain marie* than some empty-headed rake."

"Even one as wicked and handsome as Saint Nick?"

"Especially not him," Penelope replied firmly. "Now, where was that dessert buffet?"

CHAPTER 2

Mr. Nicholas Pringle came to an abrupt halt inside the doorway of an enormous ballroom. He had no choice. The extravagant, high-vaulted chamber was packed elbow-to-elbow with what appeared to be every resident—and guest—of the small mountaintop village known as Christmas.

Ladies in fine frocks and gentlemen in tailored waistcoats. Ordinary men and women who looked as though they'd strolled into the castle straight from their farm, shop, or garden. A fair number of children not yet old enough to be presented at court squeezed through the bustling crowd to pilfer treats from an extensive buffet that an army of cooks would struggle to keep replenished.

Nicholas turned to his brother in disbelief. "This is your idea of a small, intimate gathering to get to know our temporary neighbors?"

Chris tossed him an unrepentant grin. "It's even better than I had hoped."

"What did you hope?" Nicholas asked suspiciously.

"The posted bills invited townsfolk to celebrate the success of a local perfumer," his brother admitted. "I didn't mention the details because it sounded…"

"Boring?" Nicholas put in dryly.

"As you can see, it is not! We are in luck." Chris's brow creased. "That is, if we can edge ourselves inside the ballroom."

"Allow me," Nicholas said magnanimously and rose to his full height in order to cast a practiced smile at the ladies most likely to recognize him.

His brother reached for his arm. "No! Don't—"

It was too late. The curve of Nicholas's "sensuous mouth" (as reported by the scandal columns) and the glint of wicked promise in his "sapphire irises" (never described as mere cerulean) had already wrought their magic.

A river of breathless gasps rippled through the female portion of the crowd, in many cases accompanied by the clutch of dainty hands to suddenly heaving breasts or the flurry of a painted fan aimed at an overheated décolletage.

"Six," Chris said in disgust. "One half-smile from you and half a dozen perfectly healthy ladies swoon to their feet."

"Nonsense. This crush is packed far too dense for anyone to fall down." Nicholas yanked his brother forward. "You go first. They're making way."

After the briefest of baleful glares, his brother led the way deeper into the crowd.

Nicholas allowed himself a small grin. He and his brother were both here for the same reason: women. But there the similarity ended.

Chris sought a gentle young lady of good breeding and pretty manners with whom he could fall in love and marry.

Together they would fill a large nursery with spoiled, happy children.

Nicholas could not imagine a worse fate. His tastes ran to women who preferred a quick tumble over boring talk. Those who measured their liaisons in hours, not lifetimes.

His recent fame in the caricatures had only deepened his rakish reputation. The women who chased him sought conquest, not courtship. Nicholas didn't mind. The last thing he needed was to entangle himself with a marriageable woman. He would gladly hand all of those to his brother.

"Speech, speech!" came a shout from the other side of the ballroom.

The crowd roared its agreement.

"Are you certain this party is about perfume?" Nicholas asked. "What can possibly be said about toilet water that we don't already know?"

"This is the birthplace of *Duke*," his brother answered with reverence. "The inventor is somewhere in this room."

A flood of irritation washed away Nicholas's buoyant good humor.

"Where?" He curled his hands into fists. "I'll throttle the cretin right now."

"It'll ruin your image," Christopher chided him. "And mine. No throttling."

"That horrid perfume is a plague upon London," Nicholas growled. "It's ruining my life."

"I like how it smells." Chris shrugged. "So does everyone else."

Nicholas scowled at him. "That's what's horrid about it."

"That it works?"

"Yes." Nicholas said with feeling. "It shouldn't exist. A rake is a noble calling—"

"What's noble about it?" his brother cut in skeptically.

"—in which a man utilizes his mind—"

"His body, you mean." Christopher smirked. "The primary criteria for 'rakedom' seems to be nothing more than a handsome face and a hard—"

"—in order to engage a willing female participant in a few hours of mutual satisfaction." Nicholas narrowed his eyes. "This pox of a perfume has every dandy, greenhorn, and featherwit in London dousing himself in *eau de toilette* and believing himself a dashing conqueror of women."

Chris lifted a shoulder. "The ladies do seem to like it."

"It's cheating," Nicholas said firmly.

"So is having a handsome face," his brother countered. "See how well you do with a flour sack wrapped about your head."

Nicholas sent him a flat stare. "My face is real. This accursed perfume is false. It must be stopped."

"Don't wear it," Chris suggested.

"I would never," Nicholas said in outrage. "One shouldn't need to smell like a duke in order to find a woman."

"I wonder if it smells like any dukes we know," his brother mused.

"It smells like all the dukes we know," Nicholas gritted out. "And the earls and the viscounts and the footmen and the furriers and the bakers and the butchers and the—"

"Everyone's wearing it. I know," Chris interrupted with a grin. "That's the point of this party. *Duke* works. I've heard no less than a dozen gentlemen swear it was their key to securing a bride."

"No man should use a parlor trick to attract women," Nicholas snapped. "Whether it's to take them to bed or to the altar. Deception is dishonorable."

"I concede the point," his brother said after a moment's

thought. "I would never wed a woman whose interest in me was anything other than genuine. But we have different goals. You are not interested in marriage. Or have things changed?"

"*Never.*"

A chill slid down Nicholas's spine at the very idea. It wasn't just the thought of forever that gave him pause. Wives were alarmingly unpredictable. He preferred knowing exactly what each day would bring.

As a rake, the lines were clearly drawn. One night. One time. Nothing more. Everyone knew what to expect. The women he dallied with sought the same things. They lived in the same world, comported themselves by the same rules. Courtesans, widows, women of independent means who either did not have a reputation to protect or were well-practiced in secrecy.

Nicholas was here for a holiday. This northern village of eternal Christmastide had already given more gifts than anticipated. His brother was welcome to woo any doe-eyed virgin or proper young lady he might wish. The fallen women were the only ones Nicholas was interested in. They wanted a good time; he could provide it.

Chris glanced over his shoulder as if hearing his thoughts. "Aren't you getting a little too old to pursue the life of a rake?"

"How old is too old for pleasure?" Nicholas countered. A preposterous notion. What else was the point of life?

"At least admit we are getting too old for debutantes," his brother insisted.

"I've never wanted one," Nicholas said with a shiver. Ghastly thought.

"What *do* you want?" his brother asked softly. "Do you know?"

Nicholas considered the question. At six-and-thirty, he much preferred ladies close to his age.

Over the years, he had been propositioned by every kind. Married, widowed, fallen. They weren't after romance, but distraction. Nicholas was happy to provide it. None of them were looking for love. It wasn't a service he provided, or even a concept he believed in.

His brother, on the other hand… Nicholas arched his brows. "I suppose you believe your future bride is elbowing her way through this crush, guided by Fate itself into your open, willing arms?"

"I hope so," Chris said fervently. "Isn't that what we all want?"

Nicholas stared at him. "I cannot imagine wanting to wake up to the same woman day after day."

Nor would they wish that with him. For ladies seeking husbands, he was a terrible choice. For those seeking one night of pleasure, however… He was exactly the right man.

His brother leaned forward earnestly. "Haven't you ever had an evening so perfect that you wished every day going forward would be just like it?"

"Not once."

Nicholas didn't even have to think it over. He had never even wished to spend a week with the same woman.

"There she is!" His brother tilted his head excitedly in the approximate direction of three hundred celebrating villagers.

"There who is?" Nicholas craned his neck. "Your future bride?"

"The inventor of *Duke*." Chris explained, his eyes shining. "The reason everyone's here."

"Wait. The evil perfumer turning every idiot in London

into a self-professed rake is a woman?" Nicholas said in disbelief.

Chris raised his brows. "Are you interested now?"

"Very interested," Nicholas replied. But not for the reason his brother expected.

He wanted a private audience with the lady perfumer for something else entirely.

CHAPTER 3

Nicholas hid the flower he'd purchased from the castle greenhouse behind his back and turned up the snow-dusted walk leading to the perfumer's front door. No matter how hard he tried, life was full of surprises.

Instead of visiting comely ladies of ill repute, today's target was some bluestocking lady chemist whose naïve oversight had spawned chaos in London's previously stable social order. The only way to stem the explosion of faux rakelings was to halt production of *Duke*.

At least the errand should only take a moment. Not because Nicholas expected his reputation to do the work. By all accounts, Miss Mitchell was as awkward and science-obsessed and reclusive as the most fervent of her male counterparts. The lady was unlikely to have heard of him.

In this case, one could not count on so-called sapphire irises or the curve of his smile to sway her. The rose in his hand was just for insurance. Nicholas intended to appeal to her logic. As a natural philosopher, she was no doubt already immersed in some new project. He would encourage her to give up *Duke* and focus on that instead.

His knock upon the door was answered by neither a maid nor a butler, but the lady chemist herself. Miss Mitchell wore thick leather mitts with strange burn marks, a stiff gray smock dusted in white powder, and a beleaguered expression. "What?"

Nicholas thrust the flower forward out of reflex.

The prevailing wisdom was that roses could dissolve any disagreement between a lady and a gentleman. Because he had never returned for a second day's company with the same woman, Nicholas had never had to test the theory. He hoped his brother was right.

It did not appear so.

Rather than coo or simper or whatever female reaction single red roses were meant to elicit, Miss Mitchell glanced over her shoulder as if she had left something far more interesting in another room before returning her irritated gaze to Nicholas. "Did you want something?"

What was the best opening gambit?

Her eyes were neither cobalt nor emerald nor turquoise, but brown: a color rarely waxed poetic upon by romantic fools. Clearly, they had never glimpsed Miss Mitchell's eyes. Hers were not a dull brown, or a forgettable brown, or even a plain, serviceable brown. Not even the brown of coffee or cinnamon or chocolate.

Hers were different from all the other brown eyes Nicholas had ever seen. Deeper. Sharper. More dangerous. These were eyes that did not merely look, but *saw*. He would need to be careful.

"Forgive me for not waiting for a formal introduction," he

said pleasantly, lifting the perfect rose a little higher so she could not miss it. "My name is—"

"'Saint Nick', the infamous London rake." She pursed her lips. "I've heard."

Well. That explained the frosty welcome.

"My calling card phrases it a bit differently," he said, and tried again. "I am Mr. Nicholas Pringle of London, and I am pleased to make your acquaintance."

"That makes one of us." She sent another impatient glance over her shoulder. "I'm not interested in you or your services. Is that all?"

"I'm not offering myself to you," Nicholas stammered. There was nothing to purchase. He wasn't a cicisbeo. Good God. How had he lost control of what was meant to be an easy conversation? "I was merely hoping for a brief tête-à-tête."

She arched a brow. "Then why bring a flower?"

Excellent point, blast it. He'd known her eyes would see too much. He chucked the rose onto a snow bank. "Now may I come inside?"

A sudden, deafening din rent the air like the chaos of a hundred woodpeckers drilling their beaks in unison against a sea of clattering pots.

"Very well," Miss Mitchell said and disappeared.

At least, Nicholas presumed she'd said *very well* aloud. He could hear nothing over the ungodly racket. The last thing he wanted to do was inch closer to it.

He stepped over the threshold anyway. If he came back some other time, the chemist might not allow him inside. This was his chance. The perfect, golden opportunity to… to… Good God, how could anyone think with that brain-splitting clamor rattling the walls?

"Miss Mitchell?" he shouted. Or hoped he shouted. He could not hear himself over the infernal noise. "Do you need help with—"

All sound abruptly stopped. A heavy silence filled the air so thick and so absolute it was almost more deafening than the cacophony had been.

His ears felt as though they were underwater. He couldn't hear anything. Not the wind, not the ticking of a clock, not the noise from the street outside. Only the sound of his own startled intake of breath assured him he hadn't been struck deaf.

Miss Mitchell appeared from around the corner, wiping a fresh dusting of white powder from her smock as if nothing of interest had occurred. "You were saying?"

Nicholas cleared his throat. "Might I ask the origin of that fascinating sound?"

"My kitchen alarm," she said with all the same import one might give a comment upon the weather. "When I reinforced the walls to inhibit distribution of sound, I had to counteract my own efforts by inventing an alarm with even greater capabilities in order to discern its call when the sound barriers are engaged."

The explanation engendered a dozen new questions. Why had she felt the need to cut off all sound? How had she achieved it? Why create the world's most deafening alarm instead of leaving her door ajar? And most importantly—

"What are you cooking?" he asked.

"Baking," she said. "My maid does the cooking. Baking is chemistry. I never pass up an opportunity for chemistry."

Nicholas hesitated. From any other woman, a rake could correctly assume any oblique comment referencing "chemistry" to be an invitation to create some… all night long.

He was used to women coming to him entranced by tales of his prowess in a bedchamber. Sexual desire was something he understood, something he appreciated, something he enjoyed exploiting with someone who felt the same.

Miss Mitchell clearly was not that woman.

She was singularly unimpressed with his rakish reputation, and thus far remained unswayed by his looks or charm. And yet she had let him in. He straightened. Perhaps she was more open than she seemed.

He gave her a winning smile. "I would like to talk to you about *Duke*."

"You have eight minutes until my biscuits are done."

His stomach immediately growled. "What kind of biscuits?"

She glanced around the corner. "Seven and a half minutes."

"Can we move within sight of the clock?" He flinched. "It won't ring the same alarm again, will it?"

"Yes." Miss Mitchell motioned for him to follow. "This way."

She led him through a thick metal door into the cleanest kitchen he had ever seen.

Although he himself did not bake, as a lad he had learned that befriending the staff of any kitchen was the easiest way to be slipped extra treats. Over the years, he had enjoyed countless jam tartlets, fig pudding, crème brûlée…

But his favorite dessert of all remained fresh-baked biscuits. Crisp on the outside, gooey on the inside. Crumbly and sweet and delicious. Perhaps a sip of cold milk to wash it down.

"Seven minutes," Miss Mitchell said as she hoisted herself on a tall stool near the fire.

He did the same. "I'll cut to the chase. *Duke* is cheating. It must be stopped."

She inclined her head. "Cheating how?"

He considered where to begin. "You accused me of being a rake."

"It was no accusation. You do more than simply dabble in occasional carnal activities. You are an accomplished rake with a well-deserved reputation."

"Exactly." He leaned back. Although the picture she painted wasn't ideal, she had just proven his point. "I deserve my reputation. I earned it through my actions. I did not dump it on from a bottle."

"Yes, the dumping is problematic," she mused. "I am investigating airborne diffusion methods. My theory is that a fine overall mist will prove far superior than concentrated doses applied to limited pulse points."

"You have to stop," he broke in.

She glanced up. "Because you don't think it works?"

"Because it does work. A man shouldn't win a woman because he purchased cologne water."

"Do tell." The corner of Miss Mitchell's mouth twitched. "How *should* a man win a woman?"

Nicholas immediately recognized his mistake.

"No one should win anyone else," he said quickly. "Love isn't a game. It's something that happens naturally."

By some miracle, lightning did not strike him where he stood.

"*Duke* doesn't promise love," she pointed out with a laugh. "It promises easier access to women."

Nicholas gazed at her in disbelief. Clearly, he had misjudged the situation.

"It delivers on that promise," he agreed carefully. "Therein lies the problem. We should be upholding the standards for love, not lowering female inhibitions."

She arched her brows. "Should we?"

What kind of question was that?

He started over. "You believe in love, don't you?"

"No." She chuckled. "Do you?"

"I… haven't experienced it directly," he hedged. She didn't believe in love?

"But you're searching for it?" she pressed.

"This isn't about me," he said. "I'm not your customer."

She lifted a shoulder. "Then why should I care about your opinion?"

"It's not even *my* opinion," he blurted. "Don't you know other people who believe in love?"

She cocked her head in thought. "Gloria does."

He had no idea who Gloria was, but he was glad the lady believed in fantasies.

"There you have it," he said with relief. "Gloria believes in love. Don't you think she should find it? What if you discovered her in the arms of the wrong man, all because he hoodwinked her delicate senses with some five-quid manipulative odor?"

Miss Mitchell stared at him. "That is literally the entire reason men are dumping it on by the bucket. They want to be the wrong arms that hapless women tumble into."

"And you wish to be a party to that?" he burst out in disbelief.

"It cannot happen," she said simply. "Women aren't 'hapless.' That is a fiction men choose to believe. Be logical. A manufactured scent may capture a lady's attention, but no perfume melts away clothing. Women make *choices*." She glanced over his shoulder. "Five minutes."

Nicholas ground his jaw. Miss Mitchell was impossible. How could he make her understand? She had thus far been unmoved by appeals to love or emotion. He needed another tack. Which left the most universal motivator of all: money.

He sighed. "I'll buy it from you."

"Five pounds," she said immediately. "You can find a bottle at any chemist's shop."

"No." He leaned forward. "I mean the whole thing. *Duke*. I want full and exclusive rights over production and distribution."

"You want to produce *Duke* yourself?" she asked doubtfully.

Not exactly. He planned to cease production altogether. Once distribution was up to his discretion, he would simply stop providing it. Situation solved.

He gave her his most charming smile. "Name your price."

CHAPTER 4

Penelope gazed beneath her lashes at the dashing London rake seated on one of her worn kitchen stools. As before, she very much saw what all the fuss was about.

The lushly chiseled mouth, the perfectly symmetrical features, the golden stature of tall enough to stand out but not so tall as to make kissing ungainly. With a form like his, anything would look sinful.

Then there was his proposition. Any price she might wish, if she would just sign away all control of the one invention that had ever gained her any recognition whatsoever.

Why had he made the offer? Did he think her driven more by wealth than science? Or perhaps he had been jesting, and had not expected her to consider his proposal for even this long.

She turned to gaze at him directly, giving up any pretense that both he and his proposition were not under intense scrutiny.

No doubt the man was as arrogant as his offer. But there

was something more. Something he wasn't telling her. A puzzle.

Although she had known him for less than five minutes, his impassioned criticism of her perfume as an unfair advantage to those who had not earned the privilege had rung true.

Given that perspective, she doubted he had any intention of continuing production of her perfume, were he to gain control of the process. She tilted her head. He had very carefully refrained from false promises. Perhaps due to honor. Or perhaps an old habit from his profession as a rake.

"Is 'rake' a profession?" she asked curiously.

"Are you even thinking about my offer?" he exploded in frustration.

No was on the tip of her tongue, so swift and so sour she could taste it. But she swallowed the urge rather than indulge it. She, too, could be careful with her words. Just because she intended to send him to the devil didn't mean she ought to be hasty in doing so.

"Your objection to *Duke*," she said instead, "is that men who would not otherwise attract certain women are now afforded the same opportunities as accomplished rakes like yourself."

"You see the problem." He gave her an encouraging smile.

She nodded. "I have always seen the problem. I created *Duke* specifically to upset the order you're trying to protect. To give *all* gentlemen the same chance. The shy ones, the bookish ones, the portly ones, the ugly ones, the awkward ones, or anyone else Society deems less worthy. Far from being unjust, *Duke* may be the closest to 'fair' that such gentlemen ever experience."

In fact, it was the reason she began *Duchess*. Women needed every advantage they could get. Particularly overlooked women who deserved to be seen. People like Gloria, who believed in love but lacked dancing partners.

If the right combination of scents afforded an opportunity a woman would not otherwise have had to connect with the perfect gentleman, didn't Penelope owe it to all women to do everything in her power to give them that chance?

"Balderdash," Saint Nick said flatly. "The whole point of earning something is to *earn* it. Not circumvent it with snake oil perfume or made-up science."

Her mouth fell open. "You don't believe in science?"

"How can anyone take it seriously?" he asked. "For centuries, alchemists have claimed they could turn lead into gold, purify the soul with mercury, cure consumption with an elixir. None of it has worked. These fools bumbling about as faux rakes are full of nothing more than false pretenses, just like the bottle those dreams were sold in."

The alarm went off, sending a rapid clockwork belt of three hundred nails pounding against a series of interlinked brass sheets connected to the closed door of her laboratory.

Penelope was glad for the distraction. She slid from her stool as if the unholy din wasn't vibrating through her bones, lifted the switch to stop the alarm, and strode to her oven.

Saint Nick might have meant his words to shock her. Or perhaps he thought *he* was the logical one, and she the poor befuddled female incapable of viewing the larger picture. Either way, she did not want him to see the excitement brimming in her blood. He had made a far more convincing argument than he even suspected.

Just not for the case he had in mind.

She slipped her wool-lined leather mitts over her hands and opened the oven door. Out of habit, she placed the tray of biscuits atop a cotton square designed for that purpose, and closed the oven door. But her mind was back in her laboratory.

Duchess had to be perfect. That was the only choice. It couldn't be as good as *Duke*. It had to surpass it.

But first, she had to prove the science. To show incontrovertible evidence that this new chemical combination worked exactly as advertised. All night, she had despaired of finding an unambiguous method of determining the latest compound's potency.

That was, until a non-believer walked through her door.

"Have a biscuit," she ordered.

He lifted his hand eagerly but then narrowed his eyes in suspicion. "I thought you said I had to leave when the alarm sounded."

"I only promised to listen to you until then." She tossed her leather mitts atop the counter and began to tidy the kitchen. "Are you peckish or not?"

The allure of fresh biscuits seemed to win out over his much-deserved suspicion. "May I have a plate?"

"Find one."

While her uninvited guest was thus occupied, Penelope slipped across the hallway into her laboratory to dab a drop of the working version of *Duchess* behind her ears and on her wrists.

Saint Nick was the perfect test subject. He didn't believe in perfume or science, but rather his own mind. Indeed, the deck was stacked delightfully against her.

He knew she was a perfumer. Believed she was the sort of alchemist who thought the right science could turn anything into something else. He would not trust her or her motives for a single second.

She was likewise a perfect control subject. Not only a spinster, not only a virgin, but one who had never been so much as flirted with before. If *Duchess* worked on Penelope, if it could win even the smallest token of affection from a rake who was already set against her, it would be an unarguable success.

'Twas the perfect experiment.

In order to prove her theory, Saint Nick needed to become overset with enough emotion to try to kiss her. Not that she would allow such a liberty.

For the kiss to be valid, it would need to be attempted for no reason other than him being unable to hold his passions at bay.

A peck of the cheek would not count. A brush of the lips against the back of her hand in greeting would not count. A manipulative wooing in an attempt to talk her into selling *Duke* would not count.

Only the sort of kiss that came from within would qualify. An unplanned kiss. The sort one fought against and only gave into when no choice remained but to indulge an overwhelming desire.

Not that Penelope had ever experienced any such event. She'd remained so far up on the shelf for so long that even wallflowers pitied her. She was old. Finished. She smirked. If the thought of kissing her were to cross any man's mind, it would be a miracle at thirty-four years.

Penelope didn't believe in miracles. She believed in science. Chemistry. Opportunity. It was time to start. She took a deep breath.

Well-meaning friends were always trying to get her to look different in order to be attractive, to *be* different in order to deserve love. Sweeter, flirtier, prettier. Become something men desired.

For this experiment to work, she was going to have to do the opposite. She narrowed her eyes. *Duchess* needed to let a woman bewitch a man without even trying.

First step: limit external influences.

There was no looking-glass in her laboratory, so she would have to do this part by feel. She tugged her already careless chignon a little more lopsided and tightened her battered smock about her neck. Next time, she would take care to make herself appear even more unappealing than usual. For now, she had to hurry. Saint Nick was bound to wonder where she was off to.

When she dashed back into the kitchen, she pulled up short. He was systematically demolishing biscuit after biscuit, consuming each with such care and sensual delight she quite doubted he had noticed her absence at all.

Her lips quirked at the sight. Although she hadn't baked the biscuits with Saint Nick in mind, she rather wished she had. Who knew watching a man consume something she created would be so satisfying?

"How are the biscuits?" she asked.

He jumped guiltily as if he'd forgotten Penelope altogether. She was not surprised. She hadn't been wearing *Duchess*. Now that she was, he would not forget her a second time.

"Does your offer still stand?" she asked.

He snuck the last crumb before setting his plate aside. "You'll sell me the rights to *Duke*?"

Under no circumstances. But Duchess needed time to work. Penelope was still refining the final characteristics. She didn't expect men to swoon at first sniff. Repeated exposure was the key. This could take days. She had to ensure he spent a measurable amount of time in scent range.

She leaned against the door jamb. "I promise to think it over. Come back tomorrow."

He abandoned the remaining biscuits with obvious remorse and reluctantly turned toward the doorway.

She was still standing there.

He could have squeezed past her.

She could have moved aside to give way.

Instead, they found themselves toe-to-toe, door jambs at their backs, with only a whisper of space between. Just enough room for *Duchess* to work.

"Thank you for the biscuits." He gave her a boyish smile.

She tried not to smile back. "Thank you for the flower."

"My pleasure." His eyes twinkled. "That is, until you left it lying on the ground like rubbish."

"It was rubbish," Penelope assured him. "Try harder next time."

His brow furrowed. "Try harder to what?"

"Whatever you're trying to do. Surprise me." There. *Duchess* should have reached his nostrils by now. Penelope moved out of arm's reach and motioned toward the door. "I'm sure the rose is still out there. There's time to give it to someone who would appreciate it."

"No," he said quietly, his blue eyes intense on hers. "You're right. The rose was meaningless. I'll do better."

But he made no move to exit.

Penelope's heart beat alarmingly fast. Something was happening. She tried to think rationally. A racing pulse was a good thing. Every beat of her heart was sending tiny pulses of *Duchess* from her pulse points to his nostrils. The scent was subtle. He would not know what was so intoxicating about her. It would just work.

She hoped.

Unfortunately, his scent was having an equally disruptive effect on her senses. This feeling of vertigo was not due to *Duke* or any other *eau de toilette*. She doubted he used one. He didn't have to. His scent was deeper than that, more real, more complex. A trace of his soap, the scent of his skin, an essence of arrogance and romance and danger. She swallowed hard.

Of course Saint Nick would not require cologne water. He was quite capable of being intoxicating all on his own.

At last, he dipped an extravagant bow followed by a cheeky grin. "Until tomorrow, Miss Mitchell."

"Until tomorrow," she murmured, unable to curtsy back.

He didn't so much as glance at the fallen rose as he strode back into the snow-covered streets and disappeared from view.

Penelope stood at the crack in her curtains for much longer. Her uneven breath steamed the window-glass until the wind stole away every last scarlet petal.

CHAPTER 5

Nicholas prowled through Marlowe Castle's public dining area in search of his brother. Not Miss Mitchell, he reminded himself for the third time. His brother.

The castle perched on the zenith of the mountain served as more than an iconic landmark for the village of Christmas. It was the largest employer for the townsfolk, and *the* fashionable place to see and be seen.

Even before the town's late founder had bequeathed the castle to the villagers in a philanthropic trust, its grand dining hall had been available to all residents, free of charge.

Most took every meal in the castle in order to fraternize with their fellow neighbors. Meeting over a dinner table after a day's work or before an evening out was a fundamental component of local tradition. The residents thought of themselves not as a town, but as a family.

Nicholas's brother was exactly the sort of gentleman who would find romance in such quaint notions. Nicholas had little doubt that Chris was already imagining himself starting a family in a cozy, snow-frosted cottage with a crackling fireplace and a panoramic vista of evergreen-studded hills.

Nicholas was only staying until his planned fortnight was over. He'd set aside limited time for a holiday. Half was now gone. His fingers itched to get back to work. The last thing he should be doing was stalking through some castle dining hall in search of Penelope Mitchell.

Er, in search of his brother. Nicholas was *definitely* searching for Christopher. The rascal had to be here somewhere.

There he was!

Nicholas made his way to his brother's table and sat down beside him.

Chris stared at him as if he'd sprouted antlers and a bright red nose.

"What is it?" Nicholas growled in irritation.

His brother smirked. "If only I could say I've never seen so many women sigh in unison as you walk by. I just witnessed a room full of ladies flutter every possible fluttery thing. Eyelashes, fans, handkerchiefs, fichus... A peacock would be impressed with their ingenuity—and your stoicism," he added, impressed. "It truly looked as if you didn't notice any of it happening."

Nicholas cleared his throat. He *hadn't* noticed any of it happening. He'd been looking right through all the other castle guests in search of the only one that mattered.

His brother, of course. He had one hundred percent been looking for his brother.

"Perhaps I'm not interested," he said.

Chris nearly spit ale out his nose. "When are you ever uninterested in women? The very night we arrived here, you—"

Nicholas waved this away. "Ancient history."

"It was last week," Chris pointed out. "It's not like one becomes a different person overnight."

He had made no such transformation, Nicholas promised himself.

The only reason he had been plagued by troubled dreams last night was because his visit with Miss Mitchell had been unsettling. She had gotten under his skin.

Not that he was interested in her. His strict code of conduct did not allow emotional indulgences.

That she was the first woman he'd ever purposefully planned to see two days in a row did not signify. They weren't in the midst of an *affaire de cœur*. There was nothing between them at all, save for a potential business arrangement.

One with which Nicholas intended to shut down this *Duke* nonsense once and for all.

"What were you thinking about just now?" Chris asked curiously. "You had the strangest expression. As if you were trying to solve a puzzle but could not."

"No one. Nothing." Nicholas leaned back. "Have you found a bride yet?"

"I'll make my inquiries when they regain consciousness from swooning. Witnessing so much rakish presence in one room must be exhausting."

Nicholas frowned. His brother's mouth might have curved in jest, but there was no humor in his eyes.

"I'm sorry," Nicholas said contritely. "I didn't mean to distract the ladies."

"You never mean to. It's what you do." Chris shrugged. "It's fine. I'm used to it."

Nicholas glanced about the wide chamber.

Dozens of startled gazes immediately swung away, followed by a rustle of whispers.

"Five quid says they're working up the nerve to talk with me." Chris took a sip of his ale. "In order to beg an introduction to you."

A rock formed in Nicholas's stomach. "The sort of woman who would be interested in me is not the right bride for you."

"Even the sort that wasn't previously the sort, turns *into* the sort after she sees you," Chris said and finished his ale.

Nicholas slid the empty mug away from his brother. "How many of these have you had?"

"One," Chris answered. "I'm not sotted. I'm bored of living in your shadow. I am ready to take a wife. But you are the worst person to have along when a man is out bride-hunting. I give up."

"You can't give up," Nicholas said in horror. "You've always wanted to get married."

Chris toyed with his empty glass. "It's not as easy for me as it is for you. I can't walk up to a stranger and start talking."

Balderdash. Nicholas tried to understand. "Because you need a formal introduction first?"

"Because I don't know what to say."

"That's a lie. You've made more friends in the week we've been here than I've made in the past year."

"I'm not looking for friends," Chris muttered. "I knew you wouldn't understand. How has your morning gone? Have you been forced to commission a new bedpost to mark your conquests on?"

Nicholas tilted his head uncertainly at his brother. "You never seemed critical of my choices before."

"I've been critical of your choices since I could talk." Chris arched a brow. "I'm always telling you to stop wasting your time with the wrong women so you can find the right one."

"You never seemed *resentful* of my choices before," Nicholas clarified.

Chris shrugged. "You never paused your conquests long enough to notice. I haven't figured out why you're still sitting with me right now instead of sweeping one of these fine maidens off for the best hour or two of her life."

Did he truly seem that cavalier? Nicholas swallowed a lump in his throat. The answer was clear.

Even at Oxford, the only times he and his brother saw each other were in social situations. Whenever Chris wasn't in class—or being dragged by Nicholas to some soirée or another—Chris was more likely to be found on a roof staring up through his telescope. Or staying up all night with the rest of the Junior Astronomers Club in hopes of glimpsing a shooting star or a new comet.

Or whatever aspiring astronomers did. Nicholas had no idea if comets and falling stars were the same thing.

He had his own interests. Interests he'd been too embarrassed to share with others. His brother knew, of course. Family was different. But even still, Nicholas had been happy to let everyone else believe he spent every possible moment dedicated to the fine art of wenching.

What had started as a convenient lie quickly took over his life.

Back at Eton, Nicholas had become the rake he'd pretended to be. And then he began to enjoy it. To revel in it. He liked the rules, the lines. "One night" was easy to understand. Fun. Predictable. Safe.

Becoming a rake had rescued him when he was adrift

without direction. It had given him someone to be. Rules to live by. One night was not enough time to get to know another person. Not enough time to *like* them. To be vulnerable. To have it all fall apart. Being a rake gave him control of his world.

He had never intended to ruin his brother's life in the process.

"Should I leave?" he asked quietly.

Chris shook his head. "You're paying for accommodations, too. Try the fish. I think you'll like the white sauce."

"I mean this village." Nicholas met his brother's eyes. "Should I leave?"

Chris let out a breath. "This is your holiday, too. Enjoy it."

"I'll be gone in a week," Nicholas promised. "Faster if I wrap up this business I'm trying to handle. In a few days, you'll be able to bride-hunt without my presence mucking up the works."

"You have actual business here?" His brother's eyes widened in shock. "Are you going to sell some of your—"

"No one knows about that," Nicholas said firmly. "Let's keep it that way."

"But you're good," Chris said. "One shouldn't keep one's talents a secret."

Nicholas's mouth curved dryly. "Some would say I don't."

"Not those talents." Chris rolled his eyes. "You should definitely keep those more secret. Give the rest of us a chance."

At that, Nicholas could not help but think of Miss Mitchell's words the previous afternoon. He straightened in alarm. "Please tell me you're not going to start bathing in *Duke* perfume."

"I said I agreed with you on the subject." Chris lifted a

shoulder. "If I cannot woo a woman with honest romance, I shan't take her as my wife."

Nicholas blinked. "What the devil is 'honest romance?'"

"Romance that means something." His brother's eyes took on a far-off sheen. "Not a dozen roses, but her favorite flower. Not poetry from the masters, but some truly awful rhyming couplets that come from one's heart. Not an afternoon promenade to march her before all of London, but a hundred quiet moments that mean everything. Moments only the two of you would understand."

It was Nicholas's turn to stare at his brother as though he had sprouted antlers.

Good God. *Nicholas* wouldn't be engaging in any such behavior. Not only was romance for people who intended to see the same person again and again, it was an exercise in futility.

When Mother and Father's love match had turned sour, he and his brother had watched the drama unfold before their eyes. The snide comments. Long silences. Father's mistresses. The night Mother never came back.

Chris had sworn to do better.

Nicholas had vowed never to love at all. By far, the safer choice.

"You don't look convinced," Chris said.

Nicholas was very convinced. They just held opposing beliefs.

"Love isn't for me," he said. Even if he were to find it, it wouldn't last. He didn't need the heartbreak. But he wished his brother well. "Keep looking. You'll find her eventually."

And he would. If anyone deserved to find the love of a lifetime, it was his brother. Chris would do it right. He'd be better than their father. He'd start a romance that never ended.

"I wish you would change your mind," Chris said softly. "You can't live life in single-night segments forever."

Nicholas gave him a crooked grin. "Why not? If I sum all the 'one nights' together, it adds up to the same thing."

Sort of.

"At least do something you like," Chris suggested. "There's that smithy on the edge of town. Didn't you say they would rent it?"

Nicholas's fingers itched again. The le Duc smithy wouldn't be the same as home, but maybe it would be close. "That's a good idea. I'll try."

Chris gave an exaggerated shudder. "How can you stand crouching in front of a fireplace for hours at a time?"

Nicholas shrugged. "I like chimneys."

"You're mad," Chris said. "Raking has to be more fun."

With a hint of a smile, Nicholas rose from the table and made his way out of the dining hall. A sliver of the afternoon was still free.

He had promised to meet Miss Mitchell again, but they hadn't formalized a certain hour. This errand would clear his head, give him time to think. Prepare him better than yesterday when she caught him so off-guard. He strode faster.

The smithy was a large wood-and-brick structure on the edge of the le Duc family property.

Nicholas knew little about the three siblings, save that they were French refugees fleeing Napoleon's regime, had become talented blacksmiths, and were willing to rent Nicholas the entire workshop for an hour at a time, no questions asked.

Perhaps they needed the money. Or perhaps they *didn't*

need the money, and preferred to spend the afternoon competing in one of their famed carriage races.

Nicholas was simply grateful for the borrowed space.

He stepped into the workshop and breathed in a warm, comforting mixture of iron, dust, and grease. His shoulders relaxed. The familiar scent alone was better than any massage.

Today he was not here to work, but to explore. Inspect the arrangement, test the equipment, gauge the privacy. He walked about the interior, taking his time.

He could only imagine the fun the caricaturists would have if it ever came out that Nicholas Pringle, avowed rake and man-about-town, spent every moment outside the London Season holed up in a private workshop not unlike this one, creating art from boiling glass and red-hot metal.

It would be the death of his reputation. Death of the life he had built for himself. Glassblowing and mold-casting were not the activities of a Casanova, but the pastime of a recluse just as happy with his hands covered in calluses as in dancing gloves.

By Jove, was this a wonderful workshop. Nicholas had missed smelling of bronze and fire. Hated being away from his forge, his kiln. He spent long minutes inspecting each shelf, and the treasures it contained. This was exactly what he needed.

No amount of riding in Hyde Park or boxing at Gentleman Jackson's or fencing with members of his club came close to the sensation of tumbling into bed at night after spending the entire day hard at work on his glass.

Nicholas did nothing with his creations, of course. Locked them in a wardrobe to gather dust. What else was he to do? He had no pretensions of becoming an *artiste*. That wasn't what the world wanted from him.

But it didn't mean he had to give it up completely. Not even here in Christmas. His pulse sang with joy as he inspected the workshop. It was perfect. Next time he would not rent it for an hour, but an afternoon. Or perhaps all night long. Once he started on a project, he was likely to forget all about time and—

Miss Mitchell! She was expecting him. He pulled out his pocket watch and grimaced. The hour had grown late so quickly. With a last glance toward the kiln, he forced himself to quit the smithy. He would come back soon. In the meantime, he didn't want to miss his opportunity to convince Miss Mitchell to sell *Duke*.

As he hurried back toward the street, a tiny stone caught his eye. Intrigued, he bent to pick it up. As big as a strawberry and as smooth as a grape, its oblong surface glittered in the late afternoon sun as if dusted with fool's gold. Nicholas grinned.

The color reminded him of Miss Mitchell's eyes. Complex. Full of mystery. More beautiful than they were given credit for. He rubbed the pad of his thumb across the pretty stone, then shoved it into his pocket, irritated with his flight of fancy.

Those were precisely the sort of foolish thoughts Father had castigated him for as a child. Rocks weren't *pretty*. A man's sons needn't always behave like gentlemen, but they ought to be *manly*, for God's sake. Did Nicholas want to be the laughingstock of Eton?

No, Nicholas had not wished to be the laughingstock of anywhere. Out of necessity, he'd learned to keep his inside separate from his outside. Make friends, seduce women, become the sort of man his father could be proud of. Publicly, at least.

Only his brother knew that Nicholas still dabbled with molten glass. But even Chris had not seen many of the painstaking creations. It was better that way. Easier. Nicholas couldn't disappoint people if they didn't know who he truly was.

He adjusted the rakish angle of his hat and strode up Miss Mitchell's front walk. As before, she was the one who answered his knock.

Today, she looked as though she had lost a battle with a fire-breathing dragon.

Her leather boots were badly scuffed. Her linen frock was worn at the elbows and missing half of its trim. Her thick gray smock was stained with every color imaginable, and featured three suspiciously large holes that appeared to have been singed with some sort of corrosive liquid. Her oversized gloves were burnt in odd places, as if she'd put out a runaway fire by smacking at it with her hands.

Her hair was mostly clumped together in some sort of knot that hung precariously to one side, a forgotten pencil poking haphazardly from tangled curls. One freckled cheekbone was streaked with the remnants of white powder, and a tiny spot of soot marred the tip of her nose. He grinned.

She looked positively magnificent.

Like a Greek painting come to life. A capricious goddess who cared not one whit what mere mortals thought of her. She didn't hide. Wasn't ashamed to be herself at all. The concept was as baffling as it was intoxicating.

"You smell like biscuits," he blurted.

"They're cold." She narrowed her eyes at him reprovingly. "You're late."

He pulled up short. "Did we agree upon a time?"

She craned her neck to peer behind him. "No flowers today?"

"You don't like flowers," he reminded her.

"Everyone likes flowers," she said with a laugh.

He shook his head. "You didn't like the one *I* brought."

"You didn't mean it. I believe you promised you'd do better." She leaned against the doorframe and crossed her arms. "Did you?"

Nicholas shifted his weight. He *had* said that, and then promptly forgot. Blast. Nothing he'd ever said had mattered the second day before. "Er…"

"As I thought." She moved out of the way. "Come on in, Mr. Disappointment."

"Wait. I brought you this." The stone was in his hand before he could stop himself.

She stared at it without changing expression. "It's a rock."

He nodded. "Yes."

Her forehead creased. "You brought me a rock instead of flowers."

"Yes," he said again, wishing very much that he had not. "I'll get rid of it."

He began to curl his fingers about the stone in order to toss it over his shoulder in embarrassment.

She clasped her gloved hands about his fist before he could do so. "Don't. I like it."

He didn't move.

She didn't lift her hands from his.

His heart gave a strange lurch.

"You like rocks better than flowers?" he asked uncertainly.

"I like *this* rock." She pried it from his hand and dropped it into the bib pocket of her smock. "You meant it. Well done."

She motioned toward the drawing room fireplace. "Your biscuits are on the mantel."

"Er... Thank you." He stepped inside and took off his hat. "Have you had enough time to consider my proposal?"

Too late.

She was gone.

Perhaps he had interrupted her in the midst of some experiment. No doubt she had disappeared to her dressing room in order to put herself to rights.

'Twas of no import. He had a moment to spare. After all, there were biscuits. He hurried over to the mantel where a stack of half a dozen rose from a single saucer.

"Don't mind if I do," he murmured, and lifted the first biscuit to his mouth. Mmm. Raisin and oat. He let his eyes close in happiness.

"Do they meet your approval?"

He spun around, neck growing hot. "That was fast. I expected you to—"

Change seemed an inopportune word if he still hoped to sweet-talk her out of *Duke*'s custody. It seemed Miss Mitchell had not gone to freshen up. She had gone to fetch more biscuits.

Nicholas much preferred this turn of events.

"These have cranberries," she said. "You may only have one. I'm working on a new recipe for the reception hall."

He lifted it from the tray with reverence. Some opined that the greatest magic of the local area was year-round Christmastide nestled high in a winter wonderland.

For Nicholas, the magic had begun when he and his brother walked into the castle's receiving area and were immediately greeted by an enormous buffet featuring spiced wine and tall platters of fresh biscuits.

With a crooked grin, he lifted his now-empty saucer. "These are delectable. I am happy to test as many recipes as you please."

She plucked the dish from his hand. "I'm done baking. I am far too busy to waste time on more than one new recipe a week."

A new recipe every week? Nicholas's breath caught. He was beginning to regret limiting his holiday to a single fortnight.

"Much too busy doing what?" he asked. With her, it could be anything.

"Experiments." She made a gesture toward the corridor. "In my laboratory."

At least he had guessed something right. He had begun to think he would never know what to expect with her.

Debutantes fit a certain pattern, courtesans another, the widows and fallen women who sought to spend their nights in the arms of a lover were yet another.

Miss Mitchell was different. If spinsters and bluestockings were supposed to be dull, she had broken that mold. She knew her own mind. She didn't need Nicholas or anyone. He doubted she even allowed Mother Nature to get in her way.

"Have you considered my proposal?" he asked anyway.

"Yes." She gave a brisk nod. "The answer is no."

"Any price," he reminded her with his most gallant smile. "Just name it."

She gave him a consoling look. "I don't need your money. I have my own."

"I could give you more." He no longer knew why he was so desperate for her to say yes. Was it to finally put paid to the ridiculous rakelings crawling out of the woodwork? Or was it so he would have an excuse to come back and see her? "What would it take for you to stop producing *Duke*?"

Her brow furrowed in thought as she considered the question carefully. "The apocalypse?"

A soft snort of laughter escaped before he could stifle it. He supposed he'd expected as much, but it had been worth the shot. "So definitely no?"

"Definitely no," she said firmly and motioned her free hand toward the door.

The startled laugh that escaped his throat this time held no humor at all.

He had never been dismissed from a woman's home before. The sensation was unnerving. He might not be a member of Parliament or a great inventor, but all the other ladies of his acquaintance had managed to put him to good use.

Nicholas frowned to realize that was not precisely what he wanted from Miss Mitchell. What on earth was happening? His throat tightened as he turned toward the door.

Perhaps her disinterest in making a good impression was what made Nicholas want to make a good impression on *her*. Or perhaps it was her surprising acceptance of a simple stone as a gift that made him wish he had more to offer.

What would it be like to have someone want to spend time with *him*, not just his body? To be able to be the person he truly was, not the person everyone expected to see?

A nightmare, he reminded himself firmly. He had built his walls for a reason. They kept him safe. Miss Mitchell was dangerous.

She followed him to the door and leaned one slim shoulder against the frame as he made his way out into the fading light. "If I ever catch you hanging about my doorstep again…"

He paused and glanced over his shoulder, eyebrows raised.

She grinned at him. "There may be biscuits."

The door shut tight before he could respond. Not that he was capable. He was smiling too widely to think of anything brilliant to say. To his surprise, the villagers had been right.

Coming here really did feel like Christmas.

CHAPTER 6

Penelope leaned against the wainscoting beside her friend Miss Virginia Underwood. From an unobtrusive corner, they watched guests wander in and out of the castle. Penelope was keeping tally-marks of which sorts of guests chose which biscuits.

Virginia was trying to impart an important lesson upon her. Or perhaps recounting a half-remembered dream. With Virginia, sometimes it was hard to tell.

"And although the noble turtledove can survive on its own," she was saying, "it is with both its mate and the rest of its flock that it thrives."

Penelope glanced at her sharply. "Are we talking about birds or about me? I have my flock. I don't need a mate."

Virginia sent her a sorrowful look. "You're keeping tally-marks of biscuit selection."

"That doesn't negate the point," Penelope muttered. "Observation is a key component of my methodology. The castle staff can report how many biscuits were consumed overall, but they won't know which people ate which ones, or how many, or under what circumstances no biscuits were chosen at all."

"Why do you need to know?" Virginia asked. "You provide the recipe and the kitchen bakes the biscuits. Whichever type is more popular, they will bake more of. Why must it be more complicated than that?"

"Aren't you curious?" Penelope asked. "If I told you men old enough to grow beards were less likely to choose lemon, and that blond children in pairs tended to choose cinnamon over nutmeg, wouldn't you want to know why?"

Virginia's eyes widened. "Is that true?"

"I don't know." Penelope lifted up her notebook. "I must observe and tally in order to find out."

Virginia harrumphed. "Is this your attempt to replace one obsession with another?"

"What?" Penelope stammered.

Virginia raised her brows. "Do you care a single fig about biscuit consumption, or are you hoping to spy a specific biscuit consumer?"

"What?" Penelope said again.

Virginia had an atrocious habit of being perceptive.

Penelope busied herself with her notebook.

"Spread your wings," Virginia suggested. "Show your true colors. The turtledove—"

"He is not some bird-mate," Penelope snapped. "He's a very bad idea."

"*Ohh*," Virginia said knowingly, as if this slip had given away everything. It probably had. "I understand. You're afraid he'll return to his own nest."

"I *know* he'll fly south. He's a migratory bird." Penelope

slammed down her pencil and glared at her friend. "See what you did? Now I'm talking like you."

Virginia crossed her arms. "What do the others say?"

"I have not asked anyone's opinion," Penelope enunciated clearly.

Virginia continued undaunted. "What do others say to women who do seek advice?"

"You've heard it all before. To attract a man, one must style one's hair like this, commission a gown like that, flutter one's eyes, swing one's hips, speak in a breathy little baby voice, but only when spoken to." Penelope snorted. "It's hogwash."

"Utter hogwash," Virginia agreed. "You made the right choice by looking as drab as possible."

Penelope blinked. "I look what?"

"After all," Virginia continued, "It is the male who must attract his mate. The robin's red breast, the peacock's plumage, the lion's mane. Beauty is *their* role. Your job is not to be desirable, but to be desired."

"Well, it's not working," Penelope muttered.

She'd spent all day in her laboratory with the door cracked open in order to be able to hear any fortuitous raps upon the knocker outside.

None had come.

Perhaps she hadn't worn quite enough *Duchess* yesterday afternoon. Perhaps Saint Nick was immune to her scent, faux or otherwise. Perhaps there were too many factors outside her control. Perhaps the experiment was over before it truly began.

"What's wrong?" Virginia asked, her brow furrowed in concern.

"I'm working on a new perfume," Penelope admitted. "It's not going well."

Virginia's eyes sparkled in understanding. "You don't want a mate. You'd like *to* mate."

"*Shh.*" Penelope darted her gaze about the entrance hall to ensure no one had overheard. "Fine. I wouldn't sob if he kissed me. But it's not going to happen. Worse, he wants me to stop what I'm doing."

Virginia nodded in commiseration. "He wants you to stop looking drab?"

"He wants me to stop using science." Penelope's teeth clenched. "He wants me to throw away my greatest success. He thinks it's a failure. A monster that should never have existed."

"He is probably smitten," Virginia said. "Men say the stupidest things when they're in love."

"He's not in love," Penelope burst out. "I doubt he believes in it any more than I do."

Virginia lifted her brows. "When has belief in love ever stopped it from happening?"

Penelope shook her head. "He lives for pleasure. I live for science. We're incompatible."

"Change your experiment," Virginia said. "Tally your observations of people in love until you prove to yourself it exists."

"I can't prove it's *forever*," Penelope said after a moment. "One can observe instances where love does not last, but not predict with any certainty when it will."

Virginia tilted her head. "Then what can you prove?"

"Desire," Penelope said simply. "All animals share an impulse to mate with one another. Yet they do not mate with all individuals of their kind. They choose. It is the selection process that interests me. If it can be influenced by chemistry, I will find a way to do so."

"Oh." Virginia cocked a brow. "You want to be the chosen biscuit. That's why you're tallying."

Penelope let out a frustrated sigh. "I do not want to be a..."

Did she? As soon as she'd heard the knock upon her door yesterday afternoon, she had dabbed on extra drops of *Duchess* for the experiment. Not for emotional reasons.

"I see." Virginia gave a smile of commiseration. "You don't want to just be part of the selection. You want to be the burnt biscuit that gets chosen first anyway."

Penelope glared at her friend.

Virginia had the strangest way of phrasing almost everything, but she was very rarely wrong.

Penelope *was* burnt. Drab. Left out cold. Crumbling at the edges. But she needed to be, for the perfume trial. Her clients would want to be chosen first. They would expect *Duchess* to help them achieve it. If such a feat could happen for Penelope, it could be recreated for anyone. Chemistry in a bottle.

Virginia lifted Penelope's wrist and sniffed. "Is that why you are drabber than usual?"

Penelope yanked her wrist out of Virginia's grasp. "Is 'drabber' a word?"

"There isn't a word for..." Virginia waved a hand in the direction of Penelope's carefully chosen attire. "*This.*"

"Yes, if you must know. To prove the effect is due to the perfume, I must be unattractive in every other way. I can wear the oldest, most comfortable clothes in my wardrobe—"

"This particular frock should be incinerated."

"—I can amuse myself spending an hour to make my hair as frizzy and lopsided as possible—"

"It doesn't look like you remembered it was on your head at all."

"—and I needn't bother attempting to be graceful or

coquettish or sultry. It's quite freeing. Why are you being so negative about it?"

"You're assuming the only way to attract a man is something you do with your body." Virginia cocked her head. "What if he likes your brain?"

"No man has ever liked a woman's brain. They're not even convinced we possess them," Penelope said dryly.

Virginia appeared to think this over. "He said *Duke* doesn't work?"

"He said it does work," Penelope clarified. "That's what he hates about it."

"Then he knows you have a brain." Virginia leaned back against the wainscoting and closed her eyes. "You should get a pet."

Penelope gazed up at the heavens for strength. "What would be the point of a pet?"

Virginia sighed happily. "Something to love."

"I told you," Penelope said. "I don't believe in love."

"Something to love *you*." Virginia opened her eyes and clapped her hands with excitement. "I have an extra bird."

"I do not want a bird," Penelope said quickly. "Do not give me a bird."

Virginia narrowed her eyes. "Are you afraid the bird won't like you?"

"I don't care if birds like me."

"Are you afraid the bird won't *choose* you?" Virginia insisted.

"I do not want any bird to choose me."

"Everyone cares when they're not chosen."

"I don't," Penelope said firmly. "If interest in another person is driven by chemistry rather than personal connection, the lack of it in one's life cannot reflect negatively on oneself."

"Ohh." Virginia nodded sagely. "You don't want to prove there's a lack in yourself."

"Are you trying to make me feel worse or better?" Penelope burst out. "You're doing a terrible job. If I tallied every single time you—"

"Put your plumage away," Virginia hissed. "Here comes your peacock."

Penelope jerked her spine up straight before she remembered she was trying to be slumpy and frumpy on purpose.

Too late. Saint Nick had seen her.

He and his brother were heading directly their way.

"Miss Mitchell." He sketched an elegant bow. "Allow me to present my brother, Mr. Christopher Pringle."

His brother bowed. "Do call me Christopher. Two Mr. Pringles are too many."

Saint Nick's smile widened. "I, of course, am Nicholas. Who is this lovely lady at your side?"

Penelope swallowed. Was she supposed to curtsy? She definitely wasn't going to curtsy. She was being dowdy and unattractive. "Virginia, meet… Nick and Christopher. Gentlemen, this is Miss Virginia Underwood."

Virginia clasped her hands to her chest. "I am glad the winds blew you this way."

Christopher frowned, then laughed in appreciation. "You mean to the refreshment table? All winds blow Nicholas toward biscuits. But when he saw you and Miss Mitchell, we had to ensure you ladies were enjoying your evening."

Virginia elbowed Penelope in the ribs. "Happy? He chose the burnt biscuit."

Penelope nudged her boot and hissed back, "Not now, Virginia."

Saint Nick smiled. "Chris informs me that only a fool would miss seeing the stars tonight, because there's a…" He pretended to think, and then shrugged. "I can never recall words longer than two syllables. My brother swears the sky will be lovely. Care to step outside with us and put his theory to the test?"

"Penelope loves theories," Virginia said. "Right now, she's working on—"

"By all means," Penelope said quickly. "I adore nature and multi-syllable words. Your brother sounds fascinating."

"You're right." Christopher grinned at Nicholas. "She *is* a spitfire."

"He talked about the biscuit," Virginia whispered in excitement.

"Stop it," Penelope whispered back.

"Satan," Nicholas corrected with a straight face. "If you wish to quote me correctly, I said she was Satan incarnate for having brought the latest plague upon England."

"Satan," Christopher mused. "No, it was a different synonym. 'Devilish tempting,' was it?"

"I will not help you find a wife if you keep meddling in my affairs," Nicholas scolded his brother. He turned to Penelope. "I did not call you tempting—"

"Or Satan," Christopher put in with a smile.

"—but I may have referred to your perfume as a plague on more than one occasion."

"On all possible occasions," Christopher added with a long-suffering grimace.

Virginia enveloped Penelope in a hug. "Your perfume is an

even bigger success than I dreamed. Congratulations on your first plague."

"Her… first plague?" Christopher prompted in concern.

"Aren't there some stars we're supposed to be seeing?" Penelope asked. "A bit difficult to do whilst still inside the castle."

"Quite right, quite right." Christopher proffered his elbow to Virginia. "If the mortal enemies will follow behind?"

Nicholas offered Penelope his arm and a grin. "My apologies. Chris loves stars the way wiser men love biscuits."

"Your brother is delightful," she replied as she took his arm. There. That would prove she wasn't giving any special attention to Nicholas.

"He is wearing a new waistcoat," he whispered. "Compliment him on it."

Penelope narrowed her eyes in his brother's direction. "It looks like the one you wore two days ago."

"New to him," Nicholas corrected. "Compliment him anyway."

She made a mental note to do so. "Is he really looking for a wife?"

"He really is." Nicholas groaned, as if the pursuit was on par with running off to become a sword-swallower in a circus.

A sudden thought soured her stomach. "You're not trying to matchmake me off to him, are you?"

Nicholas stopped so suddenly, Penelope nearly crashed into him. His eyes were unreadable. "No. I am definitely not trying to do that."

Because he couldn't stand the thought of her with his brother? Or because he didn't think her worthy of marriage? She was gently born, and had inherited a comfortable annuity.

Her life might not be as ostentatious as his usual crowd, but she was still respectable.

Penelope clenched her teeth. She shouldn't care. She didn't want to marry Christopher, Nicholas, or anyone. Their thoughts on her eligibility were completely irrelevant. All that mattered was the experiment.

Yet the uncertainty lingered.

When they stepped outside, the wind whipped away any other words she might say before she could have a chance to regret them. 'Twas better that way. The night was cold. The air was brisk, but not freezing. She stayed flush with Nicholas's warm side as she angled her head back to gaze up at the stars.

"Incredible," she breathed. Without a cloud in the sky, their view from the mountaintop was a perfect blanket of stars all around them. "Do you find it beautiful?"

Nicholas didn't say a word.

She tilted her head toward his and blinked to discover his hooded gaze on her, rather than the heavens. Her heart pounded.

They were standing too close. Their mouths were now inches apart. If he lowered his head or she rose on her toes, their lips could touch.

Her entire body tingled with proximity and awareness. She forgot about the stars, the castle, the cold. Her body had never felt warmer. Every molecule felt feverishly alive.

She needed to regain perspective posthaste.

Her rapid heartbeat was the cause of her elevated core temperature, she reminded herself. Her body's reaction to the signs of *Duchess*'s success. Not to Nicholas.

But it was no use. Of course it was him. Frozen, just like her. Not from cold, but from heat. The look in his eyes said he'd very much like to kiss her. That he was considering it even still. That he was as surprised as she was, but the shock had not extinguished the desire. She held her breath and waited.

Had his head lowered a tiny fraction? Were their mouths a little closer than they were before?

There was nothing Penelope wanted more than to rise up on her toes in order to give him easier access. To give him a sign. Give him—

"Do you see Cassiopeia?" Christopher called out from somewhere up ahead. "She is still a goddess of beauty."

The moment shattered. Penelope and Nicholas jerked their faces away from each other and up toward the sky as if nothing had happened.

Something had definitely happened.

Penelope's heart would not stop racing. It was her first almost-kiss. *Duchess* was working! Her breath caught. If his brother hadn't been a few yards ahead, if they hadn't been standing within sight of the castle, Nicholas might have lowered his mouth to hers and kissed her.

That was the next step, then. An almost-kiss wasn't the same as a kiss. She would adjust the formula and try again. If Nicholas kissed her—for no reason at all, other than wanting to kiss her—*Duchess* would be a success. She was almost there.

Her entire body thrilled at being so close to winning. Or maybe it thrilled at still being flush against the warm side of the handsome rake who had almost kissed her.

Her fingers still trembled where they curved about his arm. Her chest tightened. Devil take it, she was having a physical reaction! *Duchess* was designed to work on men, not women, which meant her body was responding this way because of… Nicholas.

Drat. She gritted her teeth. His biology must be a match for hers. Or perhaps his unique chemistry made him a universal attractor to women. She sighed. No wonder he was such a successful rake.

No matter. She could not allow emotion to get in the way of science. She would have to stay strong. Stoic. Tonight's marginal success would be an incremental tally in her notebook, and nothing more.

CHAPTER 7

Nicholas's fingers were still on the knocker when the door swung open.

Miss Mitchell smiled at him approvingly. "You're early."

He raised his brows. "Did we agree on a time?"

"I'll be in the kitchen." Her eyes twinkled at him before she disappeared from view.

He stepped inside the house and shut the door behind him. For the first time since arriving in Christmas, he had no need to stomp the snow from his feet before entering. Today was almost warm, and much of the snow had melted from the streets and walkways.

He hung his hat and coat on the rack near the door and crossed over to the mantel. No biscuits awaited, but from the rich, cinnamon-sugar smell of the cottage, they would be arriving at any moment.

Nicholas grinned. Miss Mitchell was right. He was early.

He reached into his pocket and pulled out a delicate glass disc in the shape of a flower petal. He had made it just that morning. He turned it over in his hand.

On its own, it didn't look like much. Certainly nothing like the flower he'd modeled it after. The smooth slip of glass could be a curl of anything. A scrap of nothing. Or a single glass petal. He placed it on the mantel where a saucer of biscuits had stood once before.

The glass disc was scarcely visible from a distance. A nearly invisible echo of the rose he'd brought and tossed aside because its intended recipient held no interest in meaningless gifts. Nicholas agreed. She deserved something genuine.

Glass was better than a rose. It didn't need water, wouldn't wilt, wasn't slowly dying after being cut off from its roots so that its beauty might be appreciated from the comfort of one's home.

This single petal would stay perfect forever. It would remain beautiful and whole long after Nicholas returned home and left Christmas behind.

He turned his back to the mantel and made his way into the kitchen.

The moment he took a seat on one of the wooden stools, Miss Mitchell pulled a tray of biscuits from the oven and placed it on a square towel atop the table.

"Let them set for twelve minutes," she said. "Then you can eat them."

"All of them?" He leaned toward them with interest.

Her lips twitched. "If you do, you'll be too full to try the new recipe."

"There's no such thing as 'too full' to eat biscuits," he protested.

"We'll see." She gave him a knowing look. "I'm making two dozen."

He placed his palm over his heart. "I solemnly pledge to do my very best to consume—"

"The other batch isn't for you," she said with a shake of her finger. "They're for your brother."

His mouth fell open. "*Christopher* gets the biscuits?"

"Christopher's potential love interests get the biscuits," she corrected. "He's to hand them out at will. It should work. The only thing miserable, corseted young ladies love more than biscuits is a man who lets her eat them."

He raised a brow. "Do you consider yourself a miserable, corseted young lady?"

"No on all four counts," she answered cheerfully. "I prefer biscuits to corsets, and I'm quite pleased to have made that decision. At four-and-thirty, I'm too old to be young. No need for pity. I consider myself a woman of science, not a spinster."

"You're four-and-thirty?" he repeated in surprise.

She curtsied. "Are you appalled?"

"I should hope not," he said. "Not when I'm six-and-thirty. We've got decades of 'young' ahead of us."

She leaned one hip against the table. "It's easier for men. You're not born with a 'wed-by' date. All your bits work indefinitely."

"Is 'bits' a scientific term?"

"It's the 'proper young lady' term. I am happy to use more precise vocabulary. Shouldn't we call things as they are properly named?"

"I'm not certain it is proper to refer to a man's—" he cleared his throat "—*bits,* regardless of terminology."

Her eyes shone with laughter. "Never say you are shocked and offended."

"Not in the least," he assured her. "I am always pleased when my bits are of interest. We can discuss their attributes in as much depth as you like."

"I'm fairly certain most of England has heard all they need

to know about your bits," she said wryly and held out her palm. "Flour, please."

He started and reflexively touched the empty pocket where he'd kept the glass petal. "I didn't bring—"

"Right behind you. Two cups, if you please."

He glanced over his shoulder and then back to her. "You want me to measure the baking flour?"

"I intend for you to measure all the ingredients." She affected an imperious stance. "'He who ate them, baked them.'"

He stared at her. "I am… fairly certain that's not a phrase."

"I just coined it." She wiggled her fingers toward the counter. "Are you done measuring?"

He leapt up from his stool and rushed to the bag of flour. "What do I measure with?"

"Bring it here. I'll show you."

For the next half hour, they worked side-by-side.

Nicholas had no doubt the mixing of the batter took twice as long with him helping, but he had never had more fun. The flour dusting both their clothes, the smudge of butter on her cheek, every brush of her fingers against his as she showed him how to mix the dough. He grinned to himself.

Baking biscuits was his new favorite pastime.

When the first tray was finally ready for the oven, he was surprised to realize that he'd forgotten all about the original dozen cooling on the table. Those twelve minutes had long since elapsed. His eyes widened. He'd been too busy enjoying his time with Miss Mitchell to bother eating shortbread biscuits. What on earth was happening?

Miss Mitchell perched on a stool and popped one of the biscuits into her mouth. "First time in the kitchen?"

"I've been in scads of kitchens," he protested.

"First time making something edible?"

"The biscuits are still in the oven," he reminded her. "We'll have to see."

"It's a good skill for you to develop," she said. "If you offer nice enough biscuits, perhaps people will still visit you after your good looks are gone."

He choked on his biscuit. "After my what?"

"It's nature," she said. "*Human* nature. Your features will never lose their appealing symmetry. But at some point, the rest of you will fail to meet the prevailing beauty standards. Perhaps you will be too fat or too skinny. Too bald or too hairy." She cocked her head. "Men do tend to sprout hairs from all sorts of interesting places as they get older."

"Is this another reference to my bits?" he asked. "I promise they haven't been sprouting anything."

Besides, there was no need to learn how to bake. His staff most certainly included a cook. If he wished to entertain at home, there would be no shortage of biscuits.

"You need a hobby," she continued. "Once the whole rake boom dries up, you'll need something to do."

He *had* something to do. A secret life, forging molten glass into works of art that would never fade or age. That side of him would have to stay private. The *ton* would never comprehend how menial tasks could bring so much joy. They would laugh him right out of London.

Miss Mitchell understood. She had a maid on staff fully capable of baking, but preferred to get her hands dirty herself. She thought he could be more than just a rake.

Then again, she was also an eccentric lady chemist living in a remote village in the northernmost corner of all of England. In such unusual circumstances, an independently wealthy spinster could be as peculiar as she pleased.

Nicholas did not share that freedom. His hobby would have to remain a secret. If anything, he did his best to ensure that life as he knew it would never change at all.

"Your vision of me in the future is some fat, balding, white-bearded old man who sits around eating biscuits?" he enquired politely.

She lifted her brows. "What's *your* vision of yourself in the future?"

He stared back at her without responding. Truth be told, he'd been concentrating too hard on each day as it passed to bother worrying about what the future held.

Her prediction terrified him. His looks were all he had. What would he be when they were gone? It would happen. Someday he would be too old or too tired or too roly-poly from excess biscuit consumption to carry on as he was now. He'd end up spending every day in his workshop. Alone.

Was loneliness his inevitable fate? Being a rake didn't fulfill any deep passion. It passed the days. Or more precisely, the nights. It gave him a part to play in the society he lived in. When that role was gone, perhaps his part in society would disappear with it. Perhaps he would cease to matter, too.

He forced the thought away and returned his focus to Miss Mitchell. "Where do you see yourself in the future?"

Her eyes lit up at once. "In my laboratory, inventing something new. On stage, accepting an award for breakthroughs in science. In London, finally presenting my work to the Natural Philosophers Society."

"You don't do that now?" he asked in surprise. "I could picture you lecturing them every day of the week."

Her smile turned brittle. "Membership is closed to lady chemists."

"Imbeciles," he said immediately. "Your left toe is more brilliant than any of those shortsighted fools."

"You haven't met my left toe," she reminded him, lips quirking.

He wiggled his brows. "Would you like to show it to me?"

"I'd be happy to kick you with it," she replied sweetly.

"I'd let you," he said with a grin. "I like a woman who knows what she wants."

"As long as the thing she wants is you?" she asked dryly.

"Or biscuits," he said, but his throat was now tight.

For the second time in the same conversation, her unveiled allusion to his rakish reputation caused a twinge of guilt. He knew she was teasing. If ever there was a woman who would find no fault in obeying the body's urges, that woman was Miss Penelope Mitchell. And yet Nicholas could not help but wish she was wrong about him. That he could do better. That he could *be* better.

It was unfamiliar ground. None of his previous interactions with women had involved much talking, much less quiet introspection and meaningful revelations. He'd had encounters, not relationships.

She was forcing him to change all that.

Somehow, they had become friends. Or something far more complicated.

When Chris had asked if Nicholas had ever had a day so perfect he'd wished all others were like it, the answer had been no.

Yet he'd returned to this cottage several days in a row, with the express purpose of repeating the previous day's delightful banter and delicious biscuits. His brother was wrong. With her, each day wasn't the same. It was better than the last. He hadn't expected to pour out cups of sugar and flour, squish it all together with eggs and butter, his forehead bumping hers between giggles as they bent over the same bowl of batter.

In that moment, he'd wanted nothing more than to kiss her. He could think of nothing else. Yet he also didn't want to ruin what they had. He wanted to be able to come back. He wanted whatever tomorrow might bring.

A horrific, mind-deadening racket filled the air. Miss Mitchell calmly rose to her feet. Nicholas narrowly avoided apoplexy. He would never get used to that alarm.

She switched off the noise and pulled the biscuits out of the oven.

"Let them cool," she warned him firmly. "Twelve minutes."

He widened his eyes innocently. "How ever could two young, stunningly attractive people with the perfect amount of hair, possibly pass twelve long minutes?"

"I've an idea." She walked out of the kitchen and crossed into an adjoining room. "Coming?"

Her idea was unlikely to be the same as his, but he was up for adventure.

He followed her into what was apparently her laboratory. It was filled with perfectly organized tools and flasks of every shape and size.

His spirits soared. He loved workshops. He wondered what she might think of his. This one was marvelous. He gazed about with pleasure. One section of the workbench held a project clearly in progress.

He edged closer with interest. "What's this?"

"*Duchess*," she answered. "I'm on iteration twenty-seven point five."

He blinked. "*Duchess?*"

"A perfume for women," she explained as she took a seat before a row of glass vials. "Men shouldn't have all the fun."

"You're making *Duke* for ladies," he repeated. Good God. It *was* the apocalypse.

She nodded. "*Duchess*. I've been working on the formula for months."

He swallowed his panic. "How does one work on a formula?"

"Field tests." She made an exaggerated pout and fluttered her eyelashes. "I tally how many gentlemen swoon at my feet."

An unreasonable surge of searing jealousy shot through him. No man could resist her. And now, with this…

He stared aghast at the slender vials. Perfume was perfume. It could not be targeted toward a single source. If the new concoction worked half as well as *Duke*, she would have to wield an umbrella about to shield herself from all the smitten swains.

The strange sensation in his stomach didn't go away. How many tally marks would that be? Nicholas might be heir presumptive to a dukedom he was unlikely to inherit, but he was far from the only gentleman in town.

The Duke of Azureford famously had a cottage right here in the village. Azureford! An actual handsome, single duke who did not require *eau de toilette* to attract young ladies. He was unequivocally the better catch.

"Are you going to sit?" she asked.

He sat.

There was no reason to be jealous, he told himself. Azureford had always been the better man. Almost everyone was. Nicholas wasn't the marrying type. He wasn't even going to stay in Christmas. His feelings were irrelevant. What Miss Mitchell did on her own time had absolutely nothing to do with him.

"I don't like it," he said.

"How do you know?" She lifted the stopper from a vial. "Would you like to smell it?"

He wanted to stop it. This was worse than *Duke*.

"Sell me exclusive production rights," he said quickly. "Name your price."

She lowered her nose to the vial. "Why do you think everything can be bought?"

Clearly it could not. He would have to find some other way to halt its production.

"If you're just going to glower at me over my shoulder, then you might as well go back into the kitchen." She stoppered the vial and placed it back with its siblings. "I knew having a guest in here would be a bad idea."

His heart skipped at her words. He stared at her speechlessly. She had brought the stool in for him. He was the first person she'd allowed in her private space. And he was about to lose that privilege due to a raging case of illogical jealousy.

"I'll stay," he said quickly. "I've finished glowering. Tell me what you do with these vials. Do you measure with them, like we did for the biscuits?"

"Not like the biscuits at all," she said with a chuckle. "The ones over here…"

So began a fascinating, if abbreviated, tour. There was far more in her laboratory than could be discovered in twelve short minutes. Nicholas doubted he could understand it all in twelve months or twelve years.

Miss Mitchell was nothing short of a genius. He loved listening to the passion in her voice as she described how the layer water between the nested containers of her *bain marie* allowed gentle heating at fixed temperatures, or the struggle to achieve the perfect drip rate and monitor appropriate volume levels without disrupting active experiments.

He drank it all in. He couldn't look away if he tried. Science made her so beautiful. Her eyes sparkled, her skin glowed, and her joyful smile could be felt all the way to his toes. He was forced to engage every shield in his arsenal.

She was exactly the wrong sort of woman. Not because of her interests or looks or mannerisms. But because he was going to miss her. His throat dried. He had never missed anyone before. Never known anyone for long enough. Every second spent with her would flay open his soul when it came time to leave.

And of course he would walk away. It was what he did. But more importantly, if she was wrong for him, he was very, very wrong for her. She knew it as well as he did.

All he had to offer was a body that she had helpfully pointed out would one day soon be going to shite, rendering him useless. What she had to offer was beauty and brains, science and sweetness, biscuits and friendship and laughter. She deserved more.

He wished he could impress her the way she impressed him. Their easy rapport was as terrifying as it was addictive. He enjoyed her company so much. Dreamt each night about coming back.

He thought again about the scrap of glass lying out on her mantel. It symbolized so much to him, although to any other observer it would look like nothing at all. Perhaps her maid would mistake it for rubbish and toss it directly in the bin. Perhaps she would do so herself.

After all, she didn't expect anything from him. To her, he was just some rake with nothing but wenching on his brain.

His stomach twisted. He could fix that, if he told her the truth. He could say *we both love creating things with our hands* or even *I have a workshop, too*. But what if she laughed? Or what if she believed him, but didn't care?

The only way to prove himself to her as something other than an aging gigolo would be to rip off the mask. He could not risk destroying the image he had so carefully crafted. It was all he had. Once it was gone, there would be nothing to fall back on.

A dull object crashed to the roof over their heads with a thud, followed by a strange, rhythmic scratching sound.

Her startled eyes met his. "Something's on my roof."

He nodded. "I hear it."

They listened for a moment in silence.

"What is it?" she whispered.

"No idea," he admitted. But perhaps this was a better way to show his usefulness. "Do you have a ladder?"

CHAPTER 8

Penelope stood in the center of her drawing room with one ear turned attentively toward the ceiling. Once the ladder was secured against the roof, Nicholas had ordered her back inside, so she would not catch cold. Nonsense, of course.

She could have argued that today was unseasonably warm. Or that the night they'd gazed up at the stars had been a half degree above freezing. But he wanted to handle the situation, and to be honest, it was lovely to have someone taking care of her.

Lovely in a terrifying sort of way.

She had never experienced anything like it. Never met anyone like him. Together, they formed a compound she was not quite able to identify.

To keep her mind off irrational matters like emotion, she glanced about the drawing room to see what might require tidying up.

Nothing, she realized with a sigh. Tidying up was what she did when she was trying to avoid uncomfortable thoughts in her mind, which was why her cottage stayed immaculately tidy.

A glint of sunlight from the front window refracted on a shiny surface atop the mantel. She hesitated. There should be no shiny surfaces atop her mantel. She moved closer to investigate.

It was a shard of glass. No, not a shard. A petal. It had been left there for her. Her stomach gave a little flip as she lifted it in her palm. This wasn't just any petal. It was a rose petal. One that would not be swept away by the wind or wilt and crumble into nothing.

She closed her fingers about the smooth, delicate glass and held it to her chest. Where on earth had Nicholas purchased such a perfect gift?

A frantic knock sounded upon her door. Penelope shoved the petal back upon the mantel and rushed to answer.

"You have a burglar," Virginia said, panting. "Someone is up on your roof."

Penelope dragged her inside and shut the door. "It's not a burglar. Saint Nick is up on the housetop."

Above them, footsteps paused, then began anew.

"You have a rake on your roof?" Virginia chuckled. "Isn't that a risky object to keep about?

Penelope was unamused. "What's wrong with being a rake?"

"What's good about it?" Virginia countered.

"It's honest," Penelope said without hesitation. "No promises or emotional manipulation. Men like Nicholas take extra care to ensure all parties not only know what they're getting, but get what they want. Come to think of it, he executes the role of rake rather scientifically."

Virginia's eyes widened. "You approve of the man you're interested in being a rake?"

"I'm not interested in him," Penelope protested. "I'm interested in science. Everything we do is an experiment."

"I thought a visit from Saint Nick was only supposed to be one night," Virginia said with a grin.

Penelope scowled at her. "He comes during the day."

"I imagined as much." Virginia tilted her head. "Have you fallen in love with him yet?"

"There is no love," Penelope said in exasperation. "So, no, I haven't fallen in it."

"Are you sure you don't believe in love?" Virginia asked. "Or is the problem that you believe other people aren't capable of loving you?"

"I..." Penelope glanced away. "Don't be ridiculous."

Blast Virginia and her razor-sharp questions. Penelope crossed her arms over her smock and wished she had something to tidy.

It had nothing to do with romance. Biologically speaking, of course, any member of any species would wish to be attractive to its own kind. If not to be loved, then to be chosen. Perhaps to come together in a reproductive ritual. Perhaps to form a more lasting mate bond. Those weren't emotions. It was nature.

A clatter sounded on the roof, followed by an extended silence.

Penelope and Virginia exchanged concerned glances.

Just when she couldn't stand the uncertainty any longer, the front door burst open and Nicholas strode inside bearing a wide grin and a small poof of fluffy brown feathers in his hands.

"You got a pet!" Virginia exclaimed in delight.

"It's not a pet." Penelope stepped closer to inspect the tiny chick shivering in Nicholas's hands. "This little thing made all that noise?"

He nodded. "I think it crashed into the chimney."

"You should name him Rudolph," Virginia suggested.

"No," Penelope said quickly.

"Randolph," Virginia tried again.

"No," Penelope repeated.

"I know," Virginia said slowly. "Name him 'Reindeer.'"

Penelope turned around. "It's a bird."

Virginia put her hands on her hips. "Have some whimsy."

"I could use some whiskey," Nicholas said. "Why are we naming the bird?"

"We're not." Penelope took another look at the trembling chick. "What's wrong with it?"

"Its wing is hurt," he said softly. "I'm afraid of making it worse."

Penelope glanced over her shoulder at Virginia. "Can you help it?"

Virginia's eyes narrowed as if sensing a trap.

"Please," Penelope coaxed. "I'll let you name it."

Virginia rushed forward to take the chick from Nicholas. "Dasher will be fine before you know it."

"Dasher?" Nicholas echoed.

"She dashed into your chimney," Virginia explained. "She's a chaffinch. You can tell by the white bars on her wings."

"Then she's in good hands," Nicholas said solemnly.

"The best," Virginia agreed. "I will get her situated at once."

She disappeared as quickly as she had come.

Laughing, Penelope turned to Nicholas.

He was standing right before her. Close enough to touch. Her heart lurched. She wanted to kiss him for a job well done.

Throw her arms about his neck, and lay her ear to his chest to calm her racing pulse with the beat of his heart.

She did no such thing. It would spoil the experiment. *Duchess* was a test to see if Nicholas would throw himself at her, not the other way around.

"What were you doing while I was on the roof?" His eyes widened. "Wait. You're a natural philosopher. Were you transmuting lead into silver?"

"I'm a chemist, not an alchemist." Her lips quirked. "Besides, you were only gone for eighteen minutes."

He widened his eyes. "How long does transmutation take?"

"Three hours and forty-seven minutes," she told him with a twitch of her lips. "If you're a madman who believes in such things."

"Like James Price?" Nicholas cast his gaze skyward. "I was still in leading strings when he published that ludicrous claim about inventing a powder that turned mercury into gold, but even back then I knew he was a charlatan."

Penelope frowned. Nicholas read essays on alchemy?

"Price has his shortcomings," she admitted. "As does his acolyte, Josias Humphries."

"Humphries doesn't have shortcomings. He's a blithering idiot," Nicholas said with a groan. "Do you know what happens to iron at 2,800 degrees? It melts."

"I did know that," Penelope said. "Why do you know that?"

The wry humor vanished from his eyes. "I... Doesn't everyone know that?"

"Most people don't know the temperature at which water boils, and it's a task they perform every day." She narrowed her eyes. "Do you melt iron every day?"

"I prefer to make tea out of water," he assured her. "Otherwise the leaves get all stuck. Have you ever tried to stir sugar into a glass of molten iron?"

"I don't imbibe more than the daily recommended dosage," she said with a straight face. "Now, confess. Why do you know about iron?"

"If you owned a carriage, you too could spend more time in a blacksmith's shop than actually driving. I'm thinking about getting a sleigh."

"I should've known," she said with a laugh. "Rakes have one interest, and it isn't science."

A shadow crossed his eyes. "I did pay attention to lectures. Does it surprise you?"

Did it? She supposed it should not. If she could be a woman and a spinster and a chemist, there was no reason he had to limit himself to being a single-minded rake.

"Did you get good marks?" she asked.

"The worst," he answered cheerfully. "Just to appease my father. He believed a man's interest should lie in women, not scholarly pursuits."

She arched a brow. "Were there many women at Eton?"

"Regrettably, it remains a school for boys." His blue gaze was intense. "You would have done very well there, I imagine. Been 'top prefect' in no time. The utterly obnoxious sort, with exemplary marks and perfect recall of every lecture."

She shook her head. "I like to think I would've been the one accidentally blowing up the chemistry laboratory."

He burst out laughing. "You'd like that? Is blowing up laboratories a particular dream of yours?"

"An occupational hazard," she corrected with a smile. "You've seen the metal door. Thick sheets of metal also span the interior of the walls all around the laboratory in case of fire. Even if it blows, the rest of the house should stay standing."

His brow furrowed. "But what about you? Is your smock some sort of anti-chemical, anti-fire material?"

"Oh, I would be incinerated with the rest of my equipment," she replied. "I'd be famous in no time."

"Please don't get famous," he said fervently. "I prefer seeing your molecules clumped together in their current form."

Her cheeks warmed. "Even my freckles?"

"Especially your freckles." His voice had grown hoarse.

Her stomach flipped.

"You do?" she whispered as he slowly lowered his head toward hers.

"I like these freckles." His lower lip brushed featherlight against her left cheekbone.

She shivered, her heart pounding.

"And I like these freckles…" His mouth brushed against the opposite cheek. "And…"

She held her breath, terrified she would vaporize from anticipation alone before she received her first kiss. "And what?"

"And I'm very interested in your mouth," he murmured huskily.

At last, his lips brushed hers.

Her pulse soared. Her breath caught. Her entire body surged with awareness.

She was going to swoon.

Heaven help her, she was going to embarrassingly and unscientifically melt into a puddle of quivering Penelope molecules right at his feet. He was finally kissing her. His mouth was warm and sweet and perfect. She was frozen solid in shock.

Wait, no she wasn't. Her legs trembled quite alarmingly. And her arms—dear God, when had she wrapped them about his neck? How was she supposed to mentally tally every interaction when she could no longer think about anything but this kiss?

His arms wrapped warm and tight about her. His lips were gentle against hers. Even if she swooned, he would keep her safe. But she did not dare swoon. She did not want to miss a single moment of his lips kissing hers.

The heady sensation of her heart pressed against his did not calm her pulse, but sent it racing even faster.

She had to regain her senses. This was just biology, she reminded herself urgently. The way her breasts grew sensitive and her nipples hardened, the desperate sensation of want deep in her core. It wasn't personal. This was how their species survived.

Kissing was a reflexive part of the human mating ritual, like the dance of the ostrich or the displays of the puffer-fish. It was nature, nothing more.

And yet, when his tongue touched hers, she was swept into another world. Their connection was not biology, but electricity. A lightning strike, again and again, anywhere their mouths or skin touched. It was the most dangerous storm she could have imagined. A hurricane of unprecedented feelings, overwhelming and unpredictable. A rush like nothing she had ever imagined. Something new that could only be achieved with him. Together.

"What am I doing?" he gasped, and reared back in obvious horror. "Miss Mitchell, please accept my deepest apologies. I—"

"Penelope," she whispered.

He ran a hand through his hair. "Penelope, I'm so sorry. This was… I have to go."

Before she could answer—if indeed she was capable of forming coherent thoughts—he swept his hat back onto his head and rushed out the door.

Penelope sagged against the closest wall and tried to catch her breath. Or her thoughts. At this point, regaining any sort of equilibrium would be a miracle. This afternoon had been a revelation.

He liked her freckles. He liked her mouth. He liked kissing her.

She closed her eyes and groaned. Devil take it, she liked him. It wasn't just an experiment. It had turned into something more. For her, anyway. For him… She brought her fingertips to her lips as if she could keep his kiss pressed there forever.

Foolish girl. She'd gotten what she wanted, hadn't she? The trial was over. *Duchess* worked. They were done.

No. She dropped her hand from her mouth and pressed her fists to the wall. It was a good start. *Duchess* might be working, but more evidence was needed.

Anyone could steal a kiss. No one purchased expensive perfumes for that. They wanted something more. They wanted everything. She could do no less.

The sexual act was an unequivocal criterion. A biological imperative. It was chemistry. Something she understood. Something *Duchess* ought to be able to help facilitate, if she was ever going to bring it to market. She could not give up field research now.

All in the name of science, she reminded herself firmly. Her sudden interest in participating in a mating ritual first-hand wasn't about her wants and desires. She wasn't falling for Nicholas. She was simply performing thorough research. As a student of nature.

She lifted her wrist to her nose. The scent was light, but still there. Not that there had been any doubt. He had *kissed* her. She could still taste him on her lips.

Penelope gazed bleakly in the direction of her laboratory, unable to smile at her success. The better her perfume worked, the less she wished it would.

She wanted Nicholas's kisses to be real.

CHAPTER 9

"Thank you for meeting me," Nicholas said as he strode into the castle library.

"The wind does not meet the river, but flow together until they part," Miss Virginia Underwood replied thoughtfully.

Nicholas blinked. "Am I the wind or the river?"

"Dasher is no longer in my possession," she announced. "He is being cared for in the aviary, along with Dancer."

He tried to follow along. "Who is Dancer?"

"The partridge." She clasped her hands in joy. "The aviary population has doubled in size."

"The aviary's inventory has soared all the way up to two birds?" he asked. "That's… Congratulations."

She gave him a beatific smile. "How can I help you?"

Nicholas was beyond help, really. He could not stop thinking about the kiss he'd shared with Penelope. It was only a kiss. How did he end up like this?

All of his previous liaisons had been with women with whom the scheduled activities were a foregone conclusion. There wasn't much else. Certainly no romantic kissing. And definitely no long conversations, or baking teams, or funny moments only the two of them understood.

He had no idea what to think about Penelope. Or what to think to do about any of it. So he had resolved to take his mind off her the only way he knew how. Return to his workshop.

What he needed was a new obsession. He'd rented the smithy for the rest of the week, and intended to lose himself in crafting a new mold. The more complicated, the better.

Although he doubted anything could be more complicated than the strange new emotions warring in his chest.

"They tell me you are an animal expert," he said.

Miss Underwood pursed her lips. "We all have passions."

"Do you know about turtles?" he asked quickly.

He didn't want to think about his passions. Turtles were a far safer topic. Their lives were simple, their shells complex. It would take intense concentration to design a mold with full accuracy. It was exactly the project he needed.

Miss Underwood's eyes grew wary. "Can anyone know turtles?"

"I don't mean their personalities." He pulled a small sketchbook from his pocket and opened to the most recent drawings. "I tried to capture as much detail as I could, but I'm relying mostly on memory. Is this turtle similar to the specimens local to Christmas?"

"Nothing is similar to that drawing." Miss Underwood wrinkled her nose. "It's an abomination."

"It is not an abomination." Nicholas straightened the sketchbook. "It's a turtle."

"Not any turtle known to man," she countered. "You've combined the retractable head of the Cryptodira with the larger carapace of the Pleurodira. And you've drawn the shell with fourteen scutes, which is either one or two scutes too many, depending on—"

His heart sang in relief as she listed her complaints. Turtles were complicated. He would have no time at all to think about Penelope. Researching the different shell contours and toe webbings would keep his mind more than occupied.

"What you meant to draw," Miss Underwood informed him, "are turtledoves."

"I absolutely meant to draw a turtle," he assured her.

"Because they come out of their shells?" she asked. "Noble and honorable creatures. But you meant to capture a turtle-dove. They mate for life."

"I'm not interested in mates," Nicholas said hastily. "Just a single, solitary turtle. One."

"Turtledoves," Miss Underwood repeated. "*Turr, turr.*"

He stared at her. "What?"

"*Turr, turr,*" she trilled, accompanying the coo with a gentle flap of her arms. "You may recognize the sound as the call of a turtledove seeking its mate."

"I'm not trying to learn its language," Nicholas said. "I'm trying to draw it."

"You should stop thinking of women like biscuits," she scolded him.

"What?" he choked out.

She crossed her arms. "You can't just eat one and then immediately go on to the next one."

"That is exactly how people eat biscuits," he said. "It is the only way. What does it have to do with anything?"

"Wait here." Miss Underwood made an about-face and disappeared amongst the stacks of books.

Before Nicholas could decide whether or not he was meant to follow, she reappeared with a slim volume in her hand. "Sketches from the Royal Ornithology Society. Turtledoves, pages eighty-eight to ninety-three."

He accepted the book. There was no other option. "Do I need to sign my name somewhere, or…?"

"Is your sketch for Penelope?" she asked.

"It is not for Penelope," he said quickly. "I doubt she's an aficionado of the genre. There are no *objets d'art* in her cottage."

Miss Underwood eyed him knowingly. "So when you enter her home, you know you are looking for something. You thought it was art. It is not."

"What is it I am searching for, O Wise One?" he said in exasperation.

She flapped her arms. "*Turr, turr.*"

"You're wrong," he said firmly. "You have no idea what I'm doing. This project is for me. I'm not looking for anything else."

"But is Penelope?" Miss Underwood asked archly, then turned and walked out of the library.

Nicholas glared after her in consternation.

The only thing Penelope sought was a chemical combination for her new perfume. She was far too busy for anything else. Her life was full of interests and hobbies and activities. The baking and laboratory experiments alone gave her little time to be sitting around thinking about life, or turtledoves, or Nicholas. She wasn't the least bit clingy. A trait he respected in a woman.

Penelope had never once paid him an unexpected call, or begged him not to leave when his visits came to a close, or—

Good God. Nicholas snapped up straight in horror. *He* was the clingy one.

He hurried from the library. He had to get to the smithy,

quick. Prove to himself he had plenty of better things to do than sit around reminiscing about a steamy kiss he'd shared with a lady chemist. He paused with his hand on the banister.

What if Penelope *would* consider mating for life? She might not believe in love, but she believed in nature. As a woman of science, she might very well select a biologically ideal candidate amongst the local gentlemen and wed him out of a sense of duty to the continued propagation of humankind.

Worse, she might find someone she *liked*. Someone truly perfect for her.

Nicholas's stomach turned. He didn't want her to fall for someone else. Nor could he see how such an eventuality could be prevented. Better gentlemen routinely offered things Nicholas had never considered. They were willing to promise an entire life, when Nicholas had only ever been willing to give a single night.

He forced his feet to continue their descent down the spiral stairs. It didn't matter. He was only here for a few more days. No need to complicate matters further.

Once he was gone, Penelope would forget him. And he… He would go back to the way things were. The way they'd always been.

Rather than lift his spirits, the realization made his chest feel empty.

He slid his hand into his pocket to ensure the sketchbook was still there, nestled against the slim volume of ornithology.

Feathers were a thousand times more intricate than turtle shells. He'd design a partridge. It would take hours of concentration to blow glass delicately enough to do it any justice. He might not leave the smithy for the rest of the week.

When he reached the foot of the stair, he strode toward the castle exit.

He didn't make it.

Penelope was standing near the refreshment buffet.

His feet were already turned in her direction.

Her eyes brightened when she saw him. She gestured to the young lady at her side. "Nicholas, this is my friend Miss Godwin. Gloria, this is Mr. Nicholas Pringle."

Gloria, who believed in love.

The first conversation he'd had with Penelope came rushing back. *Duchess* was for women like this one. Penelope was a good friend.

He made an elegant leg. "The pleasure is mine."

Miss Godwin neither simpered nor curtsied. She glanced between him and Penelope, widened her eyes, and took an unsettled step back. "Lovely to meet you. I have to go. The waxing gibbous moon is… waxing."

She all but ran off, as if the cosmos required her immediate attention.

"I don't think your friend approves of me," he said dryly.

Penelope's expression grew wicked. "She may have mentioned that she finds your brother superior."

Nicholas brightened. "Did she?"

"Don't be offended," Penelope assured him. "Attraction is the result of a complex mixture of factors, including olfactory scents and receptors."

"I wasn't offended," Nicholas answered. "I am thrilled to hear Christopher's olfactory whatsits are superior to mine."

"Or it could be Gloria's receptors," Penelope said slowly. "I'd have to test to be sure. Did you become a rake due to environmental influences or your innate chemistry?"

"What?" he stammered. "Is that something you can test for?"

"I don't know." She tilted her head to scrutinize him. "It would be a fascinating study. How would you describe the formative impact of the male figures in your life during your childhood?"

"Look at the time," Nicholas said quickly. "I turn into a pumpkin every day at..."

Penelope glanced at the clock in the receiving hall. "Half four in the afternoon?"

"Precisely at half four," he agreed. "It's a common condition. Details are well-known. No need to do any studies."

"Drat," she said with a little sigh. "I do love studies."

That was part of what made her so dangerous.

He didn't want to expose his childhood or his emotions. If he were a turtle, he would have no intention of giving up his thick shell. He didn't even like to talk about last week, much less his past. Life was simpler that way.

But a woman like Penelope would never take *Sorry, I'm a turtle* as an excuse. An experimental chemist like her would want to investigate all his hidden facets. Poke him, prod him, until every secret he had ever held was hers to judge, and react as she would.

Nicholas could not think of a worse end to a relationship.

"Did I catch you entering the castle or leaving?" he asked to change the subject.

"Leaving." She held up a small notebook. "I was just making some quick tallies of this afternoon's biscuit distribution."

Nicholas had no idea what that meant, but he did like biscuits.

And Penelope.

A frisson slid over his skin as he realized just how much he really liked her. It gave her power over him. It made him vulnerable. He did not want to consider how he would feel to discover the feeling was not reciprocated. That he was nothing more than a test subject to be studied.

He swallowed the agonizing thought, and proffered his elbow. "May I see you home?"

"Thank you, kind sir." Penelope curled her fingers about his arm with a smile.

A sudden flap of wind fluttered his coattails as someone ran past, right behind them.

"*Turr, turr,*" came the gurgling coo.

Penelope startled. "What was that?"

"Nothing." He all but dragged her toward the door before she could glance behind him.

"Was that Virginia?" she asked.

"I think it was a bird." He changed his mind. "Or a madwoman."

"They should put her in charge of the aviary," Penelope said. "Perhaps she would meet a nice gentleman who shared her interests."

"I don't think a two-bird aviary requires more than one person in charge," he said dryly.

"I meant a gentleman customer." Her eyes widened. "Are there two birds now?"

"Miss Underwood donated Dasher." He led her around a small puddle. "Are there many clients, male or otherwise, who visit a one-bird aviary?"

"If there are," she admitted with a smile, "I am certain they would have plenty in common with Virginia."

Nicholas tried to imagine Miss Underwood presiding over a two-bird aviary, giving her unique style of lecture to a gentleman who had traveled there for expressly that purpose. He could not decide if a comedy or a tragedy would ensue.

"She is such a kind soul," Penelope said softly. "She'd be the perfect candidate for *Duchess*."

"All men don't throw themselves at Miss Underwood's feet?" he teased.

Penelope frowned. "They should."

Nicholas tried to imagine a world in which England's most eligible bachelors were drawn to a remote village to swoon before Miss Underwood.

"God help us all," he muttered.

Penelope glanced up at the clouds. "I wonder if she'll ever marry."

He shrugged. "Does she want to?"

"Aren't all women supposed to want to?" she countered.

He paused. "Do *you* want to?"

"I've never wanted to." She glared at the horizon. "I don't see the point. Passion is chemistry. No other species complicates a perfectly natural act with dowries and courtships and boring sermons no one is listening to because their stomachs are growling."

"Is that all marriage is?" For some reason, the thought disappointed him. "Unnecessary pomp and circumstance tacked on to a purely biological coupling?"

He regretted the question as soon as it was out of his mouth. Why was he arguing against her? He wasn't trying to talk her into marriage. It would be beyond hypocritical to claim finding a bride as some sort of goal he had been working toward at any point in his life.

So why did it feel as though a knife twisted in his chest every time Penelope mentioned she had no need for love or passion or marriage? He should be glad. He'd be leaving soon.

What she did or didn't do with her life after he was gone was none of his business.

But it *felt* like his business. It was all he could think about. Her lack of interest in a romance with him. The possibility of her changing her mind with someone else. Someone better. Someone… marriageable.

He tightened his jaw and forced himself to rein in his fears. They didn't matter. He had to stay emotionless. These moments with Penelope were nothing more than an unusually prolonged encounter. He should treat it as no different than any other meaningless rendezvous.

Perhaps they would come together in… Natural human nocturnal behavior. Perhaps they wouldn't. Either way, it would soon be over. If she wished for physical intimacy, he would be delighted to oblige but he knew better than to involve his heart.

"What is it like to have a brother?" she asked.

He glanced over at her. "You have no siblings?"

"Does it show?" Her expression turned curious. "Is Christopher also a rake?"

"Christopher is not a rake." He forced himself to ask. "Does it bother you that I was one?"

Am. Surely he'd meant *am*.

"Not at all," she said in surprise. "One cannot fight one's nature. You're you. You should stay you."

His gut twisted. She had meant no insult, yet her easy acceptance felt more like a rebuke than a compliment.

Was being a rake truly his destiny? It might have become second nature over time, but that had been due to habit. If it was important for a man to be true to his essence, did he even know who that was?

Or was this another of her tests?

"You don't think there's anything wrong with being a rake?" he asked suspiciously.

She narrowed her eyes. "Do you think there's something wrong with being a spinster?"

"Do you think being a rake is like being a spinster?" he stammered.

She shrugged. "Both are happily unwed."

He arched his brows. "Are you certain all spinsters are happy to be unwed?"

"Are you certain all rakes prefer a life of solitude?" she countered.

He'd *thought* he was certain. Now he wasn't sure about anything.

"If I were to… not be a rake," he said carefully. "Would you like that better?"

"I would like you the same," she answered immediately. "I'd be interested in studying the variables that prompted such a change in behavior. But I would still find it in my heart to bake you biscuits."

She twinkled up at him.

He could not help but return her grin.

Penelope was unlike anyone he'd ever known. She didn't want him to fit any predetermined role. Not rake, not lover, not husband. She wanted to know him, not change him. *He* was the one who had begun to question his choices.

A crack of thunder sounded overhead.

They both lifted their heads to the sky in time for the first droplets of sleet to splash into their faces.

"It's coming," he said. He braced his muscles. "On your mark."

She gripped his arm tight. "Run!"

They tore off down the street, panting and laughing as the sky opened up and drenched them in cold rain.

By the time they arrived at Penelope's doorstep, they were both completely drenched, and their cheeks hurt from laughing.

"Coming inside?" she asked.

He shook his head. "I have an appointment across town."

"I'd tempt you with biscuits, but I've been so busy that I forgot to send my maid to market." She pushed a hunk of wet hair from her eyes. "I suppose I should get out of these damp clothes."

Nicholas imagined himself unrolling her stockings one by one, hanging them up by the mantel with care, then slowly unbuttoning her—

"Good plan," he said hoarsely.

Now that the overhang of her roof protected them from the rain, perhaps it was time to open his other coat pocket. The one without ornithology.

He shook the rain from his hand and pulled out a small, brown-paper package.

Her eyes widened. "What is—"

"It's nothing," he said quickly. "Open it later. When you're not busy."

"I will be stuck in my laboratory the next few days," she said with a sigh. "I've so much work to do."

He nodded. "I won't bother you."

"You can if you want," she said softly, then slipped inside her cottage and shut the door.

Nicholas raked a shaking hand through his soggy hair. Apparently, he'd lost his hat at some point and hadn't even noticed. All his attention had been on Penelope. He reached out to touch the knocker, then shoved his hands back into his pockets.

His whole life, he had limited far more than his interactions in an attempt to avoid becoming attached. He'd limited his hopes, his emotions, his happiness. Now look at him.

Clutching his coat, he turned from her door and stepped back out into the rain. His chest pounded. It was too late to stay safe.

He was in very, very deep trouble.

CHAPTER 10

Penelope carefully allowed a single drop of liquid to fall from one flask to another.

Duchess was nearly perfect. All she was adding now were flourishes. Floral notes above and beyond the underlying chemistry to mask science with sweetness. She inhaled the final aroma and smiled.

Ladies would try a perfume because it smelled nice. They would become repeat clients because it worked.

Since she'd begun testing *Duchess* herself, Penelope had noticed a distinct shift in her interactions with gentlemen in her community. Eye contact, where before there was none. Greetings that lasted longer than *how do you do*. Attention from a certain charming scoundrel she couldn't keep from her mind.

Everything about him was seductive.

She slid a glance to the package Nicholas had given her the day before. It sat unopened next to her *bain marie* and notebook. A brown paper temptation, when she ought to be working. Her fingers twitched. She wasn't a silly, rake-obsessed chit like the ladies he was used to.

Of course she could wait to complete a respectable day's work before opening a simple gift. Besides, it wasn't as if she were expecting romance.

Penelope turned back to her flask and adjusted the flame. Maintaining the proper volume was so troublesome. She could measure a given amount of liquid into a tube, but wouldn't know with certainty how much had evaporated unless she stopped the experiment to measure, at which point—

An unbidden memory heated her cheeks. In a fit of extreme non-coquettishness, she had complained to Nicholas about that very subject just the other day. She set down her tools and buried her face in her hands. Was it any wonder the man had other things to do?

A choked laugh escaped her throat. Nicholas had no doubt stopped listening the moment he realized "flask" had nothing to do with whiskey. Literally any other woman in Christmas would show him a more interesting time. Penelope's idea of excitement was Dalton's argument for atomic theory based on measurable mass.

Well, that was the test, wasn't it? Not if she could catch a man using artifice and feminine wiles, but if she could maintain a rake's attention whilst being utterly herself.

With a little help from *Duchess*.

She stared in frustration at the orange flame flickering beneath the vial before her. A strange unrest filled her. Using science to incite a man's passions was all well and good. Indeed, before *Duchess*, she'd never incited more than a yawn.

But she had begun to want more than passion. More than

biology. Her chest tightened. She wanted Nicholas to understand her. And like what he saw.

"Imbecile," she muttered under her breath. "Perfumes aren't magic."

She had to stay logical. Rational. Calm. Patient. Soon the trial would be over. He would return home; she would return to her laboratory. Who cared if—

Penelope snatched the package off the counter and sliced the cotton string binding it together.

She tried to calm her heart. The only reason Nicholas believed himself even cursorily attracted was due to an aromatic blend of chemical compounds. Not her personality. Any gifts he brought were therefore meaningless.

Her fingers trembled. What did she expect to find inside? Chocolates? An embarrassing flush heated her ears. Was that not what she wanted from him? To be wooed like any other woman, even if it wasn't real? Muscles tense, she unfolded the paper and pushed it aside.

Flasks.

Her breath caught.

He'd bought her *flasks*.

Her heart beat out of control. She lifted one of the delicate glass cylinders to inspect it.

It was the same as the model she normally purchased, save for a few key modifications. The lip was not completely round, but contained an external dip on one side, allowing the wielder to control the pour of liquid with greater precision.

The base was the same roundness, the body the same thickness, but tiny indicators on the glass would allow her to gauge the volume of liquid inside and whether its value had changed. The design was perfect.

She clutched all four flasks to her chest. He did see her. He did know her. He understood her. She couldn't stop smiling. This gift wasn't the traditional fare any gentleman purchased for any woman, but something meant specifically for *her*.

So where on earth was he? Since delivering the gift, he had disappeared. Her smile dipped at the edges.

He was not promised to her. A rake, by definition, did not promise himself to anyone. The gift might mean nothing.

Perhaps his natural wanderlust had led him to other women. Those who could be won with a single red rose. She swallowed a sour taste. The moment he exited *Duchess*'s scent range, she would no longer be foremost in his thoughts.

No matter. Science was the only thought she intended to keep in mind. Chemistry was the sole commitment she had time for. Anything else was an unnecessary complication.

She stared down at the flasks in her hands. Her shoulders curved. She would thank him for his thoughtful gift. He was a nice person. A temporary tourist who would soon return where he belonged. She placed the flasks back onto the table. There was no room in the equation for emotion.

She shouldn't make more of it than what it was.

A knock sounded from outside.

She blew out the candle and went to answer.

Before she could finish opening the door, Nicholas barreled in hefting a large wicker basket.

Her heart filled with joy. "What are you doing?"

He grinned at her. "I come bearing gifts."

"Frankincense, gold, and myrrh?" The corners of her mouth twitched.

"Close." He strode past her into the kitchen and dropped the basket on her table with a thud. "Flour, sugar, and butter."

"How *much* flour, sugar, and butter?" she asked suspiciously. "That basket looks like it weighs two stone."

"I panicked." His eyes were impish. "Running out of biscuits is like running out of..."

"Oxygen?" she guessed.

He shook his head. "Hot chocolate."

"Humans can live very long lives with no consumption of chocolate," she informed him gently.

"But without chocolate, are we truly living?" He shot a stern glance over his shoulder before continuing to unload the basket. "I think that's everything. I added each ingredient to my list when we made the last batch."

"You did? I didn't see you write anything down."

"Mental list," he clarified. "I'm almost as good at list-keeping as I am at biscuit-eating."

He was right. Everything she needed was there.

"You purchased all of this because I chanced to mention I hadn't had time to go to market?"

He nodded. "Confession: after long and careful consideration, I concluded that your lack of biscuit ingredients was at least partially my fault."

"Very self-aware," she murmured. "But that was yesterday. What if I've been to market in the meantime?"

"Then we'll have even more biscuits." His eyes brightened. "Did you?"

"No." She stifled a giggle at his crestfallen expression.

"You are a cruel, cruel woman," he chastised her. "I shall write your name on the 'wicked' list for teasing me."

"It's not teasing," she protested. "I'm a natural philosopher. Science deals with hypotheticals."

"And I will deal with *you* later." He gathered her measuring cups and a mixing bowl, then pointed toward the stools. "Sit. Allow me to demonstrate the only chemistry lesson I ever paid attention to."

Penelope selected the closest stool and rested her elbows on the counter behind her in order to watch as he worked. Her insides felt warm and her normally tight muscles were unusually relaxed.

This was what it felt like to have someone take care of her, she realized. No—not to take care of her. To care *about* her. A delicious shiver skated across her skin. She hadn't just crossed his mind. He had acted on his feelings. She couldn't stop smiling.

She did her best to focus on the recipe. "Make sure the eggs—"

"No interruptions, Natural Philosopher," he scolded her. "Your kitchen is not my first workshop. Science is about observation, is it not? Your job is to observe silently."

She tried to keep a straight face. "What if, in the name of science, I happen to observe that you look especially fine today?"

He gestured with his fingers. "More detail, please."

She affected a dry, scientific tone. "One might observe that the tailoring of today's coat emphasizes the strength of your muscles. That the gold in your waistcoat brings an extra sparkle to your eyes. Or how the smudge of flour on your left eyebrow makes an unusual sartorial touch."

"You may comment upon your uncontrollable attraction to me at will," he assured her. "Do continue. What were you saying about how the sight of me sets your loins a-quiver?"

She burst out laughing. "I didn't—"

"How gravely you wound me, madam." He sent her a faux petulant glare. "Just as I was debating sharing these biscuits with you."

She clutched her hands to her chest in shock. "Who is this

imposter in my kitchen? The real Saint Nick would never voluntarily share biscuits."

"I was tricking you," he agreed. "The biscuits are for me. Your gift is the empty basket."

"It's a lovely basket," she said solemnly. "It smells of wicker and unrealized potential."

"There might be a single portion of fine chocolate inside," he said. "Also only for me."

She grinned and hopped off the stool to investigate. There was indeed fine chocolate inside. More than enough for two. He'd thought of everything.

Her heart gave a little flip as she surveyed the kitchen. As much as she loved the pretty stone, the glass petal, the incredible flasks... His other presents had been static objects meant to be enjoyed by her alone. Today's gift was an experience meant to be shared together.

She could not think of anything more romantic. But it was all thanks to *Duchess*.

After a quick taste of the batter, he slid the first tray of biscuits into the oven and grimaced. "As much as it pains me to say this... Can you set that abominable alarm?"

"As you wish." She started the kitchen chronometer and then positioned herself directly before him. "I've only one question. How ever will we pass twelve long minutes?"

He moved closer, sending her a sultry glance from beneath his lashes. "Mmm. I doubt your suggestion at all resembles my—"

She twined her arms about his neck and pressed her lips to his before he could continue.

He immediately enveloped her in his warm embrace and returned her kiss with passion. She felt her heart melting. He tasted of sugar and nutmeg and long, cozy nights. Each kiss was a promise of something more, something better. He did not want to change her into someone she was not. He wanted to bring her pleasure, exactly as she was. And she absolutely intended to let him. Starting with—

The experiment, she reminded herself with a start. This was a trial for *Duchess,* not a fantasy for Penelope. She'd almost ruined it by kissing him, instead of waiting for him to kiss her.

It was too late to stop now. But to keep the results pure, she could not allow herself to be the aggressor, even in something as simple as a kiss. If their physical interactions were to progress further, he would need to instigate each step from his own free will.

Please let there be additional physical interactions, she begged the fragrant drops of perfume on her pulse points. His every kiss incited a whirlpool of emotion, a surge of desire so intense it took her breath away. And when his tongue touched hers…

Every molecule of her body wanted this man more than she'd dreamed possible. It was as if she was hydrogen and he was carbon and together their irresistible chemical bond had joined to form ethylene, a substance so flammable that any spark could cause it to combust.

At this rate, her entire kitchen was going to ignite.

Each delicious, drugging kiss caused an instant reaction of subsequent sparks from her mouth to her core. Her pulse raced for him. Her body begged for him. Her—

He lifted her waist and swung her onto the edge of the table. Her heart pounded in excitement. The sudden arrival of her derrière knocked one of the eggs off the other side of the table and to the floor.

Penelope did not care a button about broken eggs or

melting butter or the puff of flour that her skirts had sent flying. From this angle, her hips were now at the same height as Nicholas's, aligning their sexual organs perfectly.

She couldn't wait to find out what he intended to do about it.

Without breaking their kiss, he slid his hands over the curve of her hips, up the dip in her waist, coming to rest so close to her bodice that the edge of his fingers brushed against the curve of her breasts.

Her nipples immediately responded. The pad of his thumb stroked the side of her breast. She held her breath. Her skin tightened in anticipation, yearning for a touch that did not come.

He lifted his lips a fraction from hers. "May I—"

"Yes," she gasped. "Immediately."

His mouth once again claimed hers.

Slowly, inexorably, his hand at last cupped her breast. Her entire body came alive at the touch. His fingers teased her nipple lightly, devastatingly, flooding the pleasure regions in her brain with a strong urge to rip her clothes from her body in order to give him greater access. To give him anything he wanted.

She couldn't say so aloud. All she could do was respond to his kiss.

He hiked the hems of her skirts up just high enough to allow his hips to nestle between her thighs. Her breath caught. Even though several layers of clothing still separated them, there was no mistaking the hardness pressing against her core.

Experimentally, she rubbed against him.

He gasped into her mouth and grabbed her hips tight. "Good God, woman."

"I liked it," she whispered against his lips. She should not have done that. "Should I stop?"

"I like it, too." His voice was scratchy and tortured. "Do it again."

As his kisses once again robbed her of thought, she gave up on tally-marks for the experiment. This was so much better. His talented hands caressed her breasts, her trembling legs were locked tight about his hips, and the throbbing of—

A deafening clamor rent the air as the mechanical alarm sent hundreds of nails pounding against sheets of metal.

He leaped back and glanced wildly about the kitchen in desperate search for the switch. "Where do I…? How can we…?"

She slid from the table and raced to the switch, sliding perilously on a patch of runny egg in the process. Her hand slapped at the control until the racket finally stopped.

Unfortunately, so had their intimate moment.

"I should've set it for twelve hours," she muttered.

His eyes twinkled. "I don't know what you've heard… but the middle eight hours would probably be me sleeping."

She leaned forward with interest. "And the other four hours?"

"Spent exactly how you think," he responded at once, unrepentant wickedness glinting in his eyes. "Toss me a towel?"

She handed him her wool-lined baking mitts, still reeling from their kiss… and the idea of experiencing far more for hours.

He pulled the tray out of the oven and set it on the cooling cloth in the middle of the table.

"Should I start the chocolate?" she asked. Her voice was

surprisingly steady, but her trembling legs threatened to melt into a puddle at his feet at any moment.

"The chocolate is for you." He stepped close and lifted her hand as if to kiss it, then turned it over to press a soft kiss to her wrist instead. "You smell delicious."

"It's the biscuits," she blurted. But she deserved the awkward reminder.

It wasn't the biscuits. It was *Duchess*, rudely reminding her that Nicholas was simply responding to biological urges she'd chemically engineered for precisely this purpose. Her stomach twisted.

She wished she was worse at chemistry. That his extremely pleasing reaction was to *her*, not to a complex blend of compounds and extractions. That she had never started this trial at all.

He straightened his jacket and gave her a crooked smile. "Thank you for a lovely afternoon."

"You aren't staying for biscuits?" Her heart gave a lurch of disappointment.

He paused. "Is that what you want?"

"Are we… still talking about biscuits?" she stammered.

"We should figure that out," he said, his gaze intense. "And possibly allot ourselves more than twelve minutes."

"But you're a rake," she babbled. For a man famed for his conquests, Nicholas was proceeding remarkably slow. Curse her inability to instigate properly! "What is there to figure out? This is what you do."

"Wrong," he said, his voice rough. "You are not 'what I do.' This is something else entirely. Something I'm not certain either of us is ready for."

She hesitated. "Because I'm a virgin and you're not?"

"Perhaps there's more than one way to be a virgin," he said

at last. His brow furrowed as he ran a hand through his hair. “I’m always ready for a tumble. I’ve never had it mean something before.”

Her heart stopped. “What does it mean?”

His intense gaze focused on hers. “That continuing down this path would be dangerous.”

And with that, he was gone.

CHAPTER 11

Nicholas warmed the tip of his blowpipe in the fire. The simple, calming act should have made him relax. Made him feel at peace with the world and himself.

It did not.

He clenched his jaw. Although this rented space did not fully replicate his workshop back home, the smithy was not the cause of Nicholas's unrest. A certain tempting chemist was. She had haunted his thoughts since the moment he walked out of her home.

Perhaps he *should* have stayed for biscuits. He shoved the tip of his blowpipe into molten glass. No. He should not stay for biscuits. There were no biscuits. There was only hot, sweaty lovemaking, which was especially odd phrasing, given he had never made love to anyone before. His liaisons had just been meaningless tumbles.

Not that he was in *love*. He wasn't that foolish. This was a mere infatuation. His first. No wonder it was so confusing.

Every moment with Penelope was like being with… what? A friend? A lover? Something in-between?

That was the problem. He had friends and he'd had lovers, but he'd never had an "in-between" before. It marked a perilous crossroads. Friends were forever. Lovers were temporary. If Penelope crossed from one side to the other…

He whirled the molten glass onto the end of his blowpipe. Being afraid of losing Penelope was ridiculous. Walking away had always been the plan. He was on holiday, not some bride-hunting expedition like his brother.

Not that Penelope was the sort to seek empty promises or try to change him. Was that what stung? That there was no ambiguity?

She had clearly been open to full physical intimacy. The reason was clearly because he was a rake, therefore loving and leaving was "what he did." And he clearly should have taken her up on the offer because great Zeus, he could not concentrate on blowing glass into a mold.

What had he been hoping for? That *she* would fall in love with *him*? He snorted. That would also be a first.

He slumped forward and rubbed his temples with one hand. She expected things from him. All the wrong things.

Or perhaps logical things, and he was the one who had changed. He didn't want his old life anymore. He wanted something better.

He wanted *her*.

Nicholas broke the blowpipe from the clay. There he went again. He had planned to craft a turtle. Or a pheasant. Anything would do, as long as it had nothing to do with Penelope.

Of course, that was not what happened. Even as he'd fashioned this mold, he'd known its glass figurine wasn't for him, but for her.

It would get locked in his cupboard with all the others just the same.

He shoved the clay mold aside and began to pace the workshop. He despised not knowing what to do. Penelope wanted a liaison with a rake. Nicholas happened to be a rake. An obvious solution presented itself.

Except he didn't *want* to be a rake. Had unconsciously stopped the same day he met her. Now that they'd spent so much time together, he had thought she'd seen something more in him than a caricature.

He had been wrong.

Wanting a true connection, dreaming of "love" like an utter lunatic, those things weren't for him. He'd learned long ago not to reach for what he wasn't meant to have.

He had to go back to what he knew. Penelope wanted one night with a rake? He would give it to her. It would have to be enough for both of them.

~

After cleaning up the workshop and himself, Nicholas made his way straight to Penelope.

"One night?" he demanded.

His heart pounded. For the first time, he had arrived empty-handed. Today he had nothing to give but himself.

She peered up at him. "What?"

"One night?" he repeated, his voice cracking. "That's what you want?"

A frown marred her brow. "Isn't it what *you* want?"

"Yes or no." He jerked a hand through his hair in nervousness. "We can be intimate, or we can leave things as they are. I need to know before I come inside."

She bit her lip. "You'll come inside either way?"

There was his answer. He gave a crooked smile. "I'm satisfied with a simple plate of biscuits."

"I'm not." Her cheeks flushed pink, but she didn't look away. "I want it all."

Even better. He swung her into the house, kicked the door shut behind them, and covered her mouth with his.

Her lips were warm, and familiar, and welcoming. Returning to her arms was like coming home. A cozy fire, protected from all the snow. He could not help but deepen the kiss.

She smelled heavenly, and she tasted like… cinnamon sugar? His pulse jumped. He fervently hoped the kitchen alarm wasn't about to sound.

He lifted his mouth from hers. "Are you baking?"

"I was." Her lips curved as she gestured behind him. "I set your biscuits out by the chimney. Do you want to start with a snack?"

"I do not." Yet he made no attempt to drag her to the closest horizontal surface. He needed to make certain they both understood what they were agreeing to. "I'm here on holiday."

She nodded. "I know."

"A fortnight," he clarified. He wished he could stay longer, but he had given his word to his brother. Chris deserved the chance to bride-hunt without Nicholas's presence getting in his way. He let out his breath. "My holiday will be over in two days."

She nodded again. "And then you return home."

"Yes." He gazed into her eyes, willing her to understand. "At present, I have no plans to come back to Christmas."

She tilted her head in confusion. "I know all that. What does it have to do with tonight?"

"I…" His mouth dried.

Blast it, his logical chemist understood perfectly. *He* was the dreamer.

"It has nothing to do with tonight," he admitted. He lifted her chin with his knuckle and brushed his lips over hers. "Tonight is about us."

"You smell different." She nuzzled closer, as though to breathe in his aroma. "I like it."

He couldn't help but laugh. "It's not a perfume. I smell like…"

His laughter cut off with a start. Had he really been about to say, "a blacksmith?" Was he *mad?*

He was heir presumptive to a dukedom. Society's most celebrated scoundrel. The only thing a man like him was expected to do with his hands was to—

"You smell like what?" she prompted, her wide brown eyes gazing up at him.

His heart stuttered. He'd come here to make love to her, not to lie to her. If puncturing the bubble of his "dashing rake" persona made him no longer of interest because it spoiled the fantasy…

At least she would know who he truly was.

"The smithy." He cleared his throat. "I smell like a smithy. I've been renting it to use as a workshop."

She seemed to think this over. "Your hobby is… blacksmithing?"

"Art," he said hesitantly. "I know it's foolish mummery, but—"

"The petal," she breathed. "You made the petal?"

The back of his neck heated. He hadn't expected her to guess what it was, much less that he'd made it by hand. He gave a short nod.

"It's not mummery, you daft man." She put her hands to his chest and pushed him aside. "It's beautiful. Even prettier than the rock you gave me. You're very talented."

He watched, immobile, as she crossed to the mantel. First, to inspect the stone that had reminded him of her eyes, and then the glass petal.

"This rose petal is perfection. Delicate and strong." She turned it over in her hand. "I can't believe the papers don't give as much ink to your art as they do to your bedsport."

Nicholas was glad of it. He had gone to great lengths to keep the secret.

She glanced up when he didn't answer. Her eyes widened in shock. "They don't know?"

"Nobody knows." He rubbed the back of his neck. "Except Chris. And now you."

"Nobody knows?" she repeated in disbelief. "Why doesn't anybody know?"

Because Father's lack of patience for unmanly behaviors had resulted in some of the worst moments of Nicholas's childhood. The harsh punishments for each infraction had caused art to intertwine with self-recrimination until he could no longer separate the two.

"Just a lad trying to make his father proud," he muttered.

Her brow furrowed. "With art?"

"Without it." Nicholas cleared his throat. He hated discussing private embarrassments. "Father felt it wasn't manly."

Penelope stared at him as if he'd lost his mind. "But art *isn't* manly."

His stomach hollowed in shame and guilt. "I know. That's... literally what Father always said."

"Was he a man of science?" she demanded. "Because I am a student of the genre, and I find his conclusions lacking."

Nicholas blinked. "What?"

"Art isn't manly or womanly or anything else. It's *humanly*." She frowned in thought. "I haven't done enough research to determine if other animals display a similar trait."

"What?" he repeated blankly.

"Facts. I can name hundreds of 'manly' artists," she continued. "Titian married his housekeeper after she gave him two sons. When Rembrandt's wife took ill, he took her nurse as his lover. If by 'manly' you mean 'shameless roués.' I shall refrain from listing the countless men who painted erotic nudes of their paramours to keep them warm on lonely nights, or I won't cease talking all evening."

"You know about art?" he stammered.

"The artifacts on display at the Egyptian Hall in London made me curious about the chemical progression of paint composition over the centuries, which led me to—" She snapped her teeth closed and took his hands firmly in hers. "Nicholas. I regret to inform you that your sire was a blithering idiot."

He stared back at her speechlessly. What if she was right? His heart pounded. What if she was wrong, and unmasking his true passions earned him nothing but scorn and humiliation?

She bit her lip. "I'm sorry. Too direct?"

"Your mind may be scientific," he said at last. "But other people—"

"The opinions of strangers are irrelevant. Live for yourself." She squeezed his hands. "*Be* yourself. All they'll have is gossip. You'll have *art*."

Vertigo assailed him. Tonight he would have something

even more precious than art. He would have Penelope.

He pulled her into his arms and kissed her from somewhere deep in his soul. A secret place he'd been hiding his entire life. She'd seen through his defenses, torn away his shell, and *liked* what she found.

With her, he was not some empty Lothario, but an artist. Which meant tonight, he could come to her not as a rake, but as a man.

As himself.

He slid his fingers into her hair as he kissed her. *She* was the work of art. He savored the softness of her skin, the sweetness of her scent, and the heat of her mouth. Yet her kisses were more than just Eden for his senses.

Touching her was no mindless diversion, but a startling bond that grabbed his heart and refused to let go.

The thought of an emotional connection terrified him. His pulse would not stop racing. Wild thoughts slashed through him like lightning strikes. Kissing her was a perfect storm of pleasure and vulnerability and desire.

But with her, he didn't want some forgettable encounter. He wanted to cherish this night for the rest of his life. No matter how much it scared him.

"One night?" he murmured between kisses. "You're certain?"

She grinned up at him. "This very night, if you're so inclined."

"I'm actually here for two more days." He kissed each corner of her smile. "I can make room in my schedule for a second visit."

She twined her arms about his neck. "Let's start with tonight."

A lead weight punched into his gut.

Not a yes.

His first time asking to prolong a liaison. The first woman with whom he could not begin to guess how many nights together could ever be enough. And she did not feel the same. *Yet,* he reminded himself.

The evening was not over. He would make it perfect.

He swung her up into his arms and kissed her with everything he'd been holding back.

"Bed?" he gasped, when he came up for air.

"Too far." She gestured behind them, panting. "Chaise longue. Much closer."

He would have preferred a bedchamber. More romantic, more special, more… *official.* But the evening wasn't about him. It was about Penelope. Anything she wanted, he would give her.

In less than a heartbeat, they were reclined on the chaise and back in each other's arms. His pulse galloped in urgency. Perhaps it was their proximity to the fire that simmered his blood and fogged his brain.

Or perhaps it was the knowledge that this might be their last night. Their *only* night, if he didn't do this right. He cradled her face and kissed her.

"Touch me," she whispered. "Like you did before."

With pleasure.

That was, until a belated thought struck him.

"The alarm isn't set, is it?" he asked suspiciously. He loved the taste of spiced sugar but did not look forward to falling off the chaise in a blind panic. "How much time do we have?"

Her gorgeous brown eyes twinkled up at him. "Is sunrise long enough?"

He gave her a lopsided smile. He rather suspected a thousand sunrises wouldn't be enough.

CHAPTER 12

Penelope's heart raced in anticipation of Nicholas's touch. Although she now knew how intimate her breast would feel in his hand, the decadent sensation still took her breath away when at last he gave her the delicious torture she sought.

His kisses were just as magical. Heady and disorienting, full of wicked promise and incredible sweetness. She wanted it all.

When he broke their kiss, she raised her head to complain —until he tugged down her bodice and placed his mouth to her breast. With a gasp, her head fell back against the cushion to revel in the sensation.

Had she thought his fingers were delicious torture? This was a hundred times worse and a thousand times better. It defied science. It was pure feeling, pure desire. Her body didn't just yearn for the sex act. She yearned for *him*.

Nicholas was the active ingredient in this combustible formula. His kisses made her lightheaded because *he* was the one doing the kissing. His touch made her desperate for more because it was him that she wanted.

He saw her as more than some bluestocking spinster. More than a science-obsessed lady chemist. He saw her as a passionate, sensual woman who was all those things and so much more. Worthy of his desire, and her own. She threaded her fingers into his hair.

He, too, was far more complex than appeared at first glance.

Although she did not know art as well as chemistry, she understood wanting to make new things with one's hands. She happened to do so in a laboratory, and he with a kiln. They were more alike than one might think. It frightened her.

Any woman with a pulse would beg for a chance to share physical pleasure with a man like Nicholas. The realization that they might form a compatible compound made her glad he was going away. She could not stand to have him close, and still not *have* him.

But for a few hours, he was hers.

Her back arched with pleasure at his touch. She could not wait to copulate with him. He was all she could think about.

Today, she wore extra droplets of *Duchess* on each pulse point. Everything else could come off. She'd happily burn her clothes in the fire to bring her body in closer contact with Nicholas. He was magnificent. The sensations his mouth teased from her nipples made her want—

Cool air kissed her bare thighs as his warm hand slid to cup her core. Her mind fogged. When had he lifted her skirts? Were they even still clothed? She didn't know and didn't care. He'd begun to dip a fingertip inside. Rhythmically. Deliciously.

He returned his mouth to hers as he continued to work his magic.

Her lungs forgot how to breathe as the inexorable coil of want began to expand and build within her. She recognized the warning signs. Her fingers were not nearly as talented as his but had often brought release she could not find elsewhere.

He was bringing her close to the edge, but she didn't want his fingers. She wanted him. All of him. This was a moment that was meant to be shared.

She tugged his shirt from his waistband, fumbled for the buttons of his fall.

He lifted his lips a breath above hers. "What are you doing?"

"Trying to free your sex organ," she panted. His fingers had not ceased their ministrations and it was becoming increasingly difficult to form coherent words. "I want it inside of me."

He paused. "What did you just say?"

"I want your sex organ inside me right now," she repeated, then hesitated. "Is the suggestion unclear?"

"Very clear," he assured her, and claimed her mouth in a long kiss. "And a splendid idea. My sex organ thinks your idea is the best suggestion it's ever heard. I was just thinking that before we get to that step, I might pleasure you in a few other ways first. Specifically, I could—"

"You could stop talking." She grabbed the sides of his face and pulled his mouth back down to hers. "You might also—"

"Take your suggestion." He lifted his hips and unbuttoned his fall without delay.

She knew the precise moment because the heat and weight

of his shaft now pressed just inside her thigh. Her pulse skipped. They were closer, but not close enough.

She'd waited her entire life for this. She now realized she'd been waiting for *him*. It was time. She could not bear a moment more. Not when every molecule of her body yearned for him. Her hands ran over his hard muscles. She longed to combust together. Didn't he?

Her heart pounded uncertainly. "Aren't you—"

"I'm getting there." He took a ragged breath. "Penelope, I've never... There might be pain." His words were husky, his gaze agonized. "I'm so sorry. The last thing I want to do is hurt you."

She shook her head. "You won't. I'm ready."

Very ready. His fingers had already brought her close to her peak. There might be some pain upon entry, but not much. After all, there was no barrier for him to breach. She'd taken care of that years ago with an accidental discovery.

Since long before the ancient Greeks, women had been using artificial phalluses to pleasure themselves. Evidence could be found in paintings and antiquities collections all over the world.

After investigating the evolution of methods and varieties, what woman of science could resist the professional obligation to perform empirical personal research?

As enjoyable as artificial phalluses turned out to be, the experience would be nothing like this one. Penetration substitutes were sturdy, but lifeless. Meant to be used in solitary circumstances.

Or were they? A scandalous experiment flashed through her mind. What if she were to wield her false phallus, whilst Nicholas—

All thoughts of future erotic experiments vanished as he

nestled his very real phallus at her entrance. She wrapped her legs about his hips and gasped at the sensation. It was not pain at all, but a thick delicious fullness. A connection unlike any other.

This was perfect. *He* was perfect. Hot and hard, sensual and strong, carnal and caring… She cupped his face and kissed him with a fervor she could not control. Their chemistry was magical.

That their union should occur on the chaise before the fire was even more perfect. She'd chosen the drawing room on purpose. Here, where they always exchanged their gifts. The pretty stone upon the mantel, the glass petal, the plates of fresh biscuits… and now each other.

Her spine arched with pleasure. The wet friction of each stroke, the sweet heat of each kiss—nothing could stop the chemical reaction building between them. At any moment, the explosion would happen.

She gripped her legs tighter about him, matching him stroke for stroke. "Nicholas, I think I'm going to…"

"Don't hold back," he murmured between kisses. "I'll join you."

She couldn't hold back if she tried. The knowledge that they were about to reach their peak together pushed her over the edge. Release flooded her. She cried out as dizzying waves of pleasure took her higher than she had ever been. All because of him.

She thought she detected complementary throbbing begin in his phallus, but after one final pump he jerked free from her embrace, bucked his hips beneath a handkerchief, and collapsed back on top of her.

Progeny. He'd had the presence of mind to prevent potential progeny. She swallowed hard.

Thank heavens one of them had behaved rationally.

A woman of science would never admit being swept away by illogical emotions. Next thing you knew, she'd claim to believe in miracles and true love. Nonsense. She brushed a damp curl from Nicholas's forehead and tried to calm her pulse.

"One night to slake our lust," he mumbled. "Do you feel well and truly slaked?"

The corners of her mouth twitched. "If I say no, will you do it again?"

"We'll do it even better," he promised sleepily. "You skipped a lot of good bits."

Her heart thumped. "I might like that. After you wake up."

"I might stay just like this forever," he murmured, and nestled close. "I love the way you smell."

At his words, cold sliced through her heart. He hadn't made a connection with *her*. His instincts had responded to a chemical compound. She stopped stroking his hair and tried to blink the hot stinging from her eyes instead. He was here in response to her *scent*. Exactly as she manufactured it.

She hated *Duchess* a little more every day.

Her throat tightened. She'd wanted this moment to be true. But it wasn't. None of this was real. This was an illusion of intimacy engineered in her laboratory, with no regard for his feelings on the matter or her own. She deserved exactly what she got.

Even if that meant nothing at all.

CHAPTER 13

Penelope wrapped her scarf tighter about her neck. She was standing in the makeshift observatory at the rear of Gloria's cottage, but the open window was not the source of her cold. Penelope's emptiness came from within.

Gloria glanced up from her telescope, her gaze concerned. "Are you ready to talk?"

"No."

There was nothing to discuss. That was why Penelope had ushered Nicholas out the door as soon he had re-buttoned his fall, washed off every trace of perfume, and buried herself alone in her bed with only her thoughts and the darkness of the night to accompany her.

Gloria gave her a sympathetic look. "Then why are you at my house before dawn?"

"I knew you'd be awake," Penelope answered immediately. "You stay up all night to watch the stars."

"I know why I'm awake." Gloria narrowed her eyes. "Why are *you* awake?"

Because no matter how far Penelope hid beneath her

blankets, sleep had refused to come. She had gravely miscalculated the aftereffects of *Duchess* achieving a successful trial.

She did not feel as though she'd won. She feared she had lost much more than her virginity. She had lost her focus. Her rationality. She needed to get it back.

Gloria turned back to her telescope. "I stopped by the castle for supper last night."

"Hm," Penelope responded distantly. "Anyone there?"

"Only every female in Christmas," Gloria said with a laugh. "The dining hall has been overflowing with women for two weeks. Every lady in there is hoping to catch sight of—or spend the night with—Saint Nick."

Penelope's stomach filled with nausea. She longed to ask if Nicholas had been present to bask in the adoration, but she dreaded the answer. Either way, if he had not returned to the castle after leaving her cottage, that meant he had gone somewhere else. Possibly to someone else. And if so, she didn't want to know.

"Trust me," Gloria said with a roll of her eyes. "If *Duchess* was ready for sale, you could make a fortune in the next half hour."

The knife in Penelope's stomach gave another twist. *Duchess* was ready. Penelope was not. She certainly did not want other women using it on Nicholas.

The thought of him engaged in intimate activities with someone else… White-hot jealousy roiled her stomach. Based on observable history and empirical patterns, a rake engaging in consensual copulation with everyone he pleased was not a hypothetical situation but a foregone certainty.

Gloria angled her head. "What's wrong? You used to find such antics amusing."

Had she? Penelope wrapped her arms about her aching chest. Apparently, she used to be an idiot.

"You can't possibly be jealous," Gloria scoffed. "The moment you met him, you could not think of a worse sort of man. After you argued over *Duke,* I was certain that would be the end of it. Did you see him again after that time at the refreshment buffet?"

Penelope focused her gaze at the wall as though she no longer spoke English.

"You *did* see him again," Gloria breathed. "Good heavens, this isn't envy. This is possessiveness."

"I do not possess him." Penelope's voice cracked.

"No one could," Gloria agreed. "Luckily, it's not as if you two…"

Penelope pretended to be deaf.

"Did you?" Gloria demanded, hands on her hips.

Penelope wished she were invisible.

"You *did*." Gloria's eyes widened in disbelief. "When? How?"

Penelope sighed. "First…"

"Don't tell me," Gloria interrupted quickly. "I understand the mechanics. I just don't understand how they happened between the two of you. I thought you disliked him."

"I thought so, too." Penelope hugged herself tighter. "For a day or two. And then I…"

"And then you what?" Gloria arched a brow. "You thought the best way to settle your differences was to get naked and let biology take over?"

"Turns out," Penelope said, "that's a terrible way to settle anything."

"Good to know." Gloria stepped closer, her tone soft. "Then why did you do it?"

"I didn't mean to, at first. It was supposed to be a simple test. I wanted to prove that passion and emotion were illogical human behaviors, and that chemistry was not only more dependable, but more powerful."

"And now?" Gloria prompted when Penelope didn't continue.

She sighed. "Emotion is definitely illogical, and passion is as powerful as chemistry."

Gloria crossed her arms. "Did you truly believe women of science were exempt from emotion?"

"It's illogical," Penelope repeated. "I thought women of science were logical."

"You can be a chemist and aware of your emotions."

Penelope shook her head. "No one wants an emotional chemist."

"You mean, Saint Nick doesn't?" Gloria asked softly.

"He's not attracted to *me*," Penelope said. "I manipulated his brain into a false attraction to a chemical compound on my wrists."

"Dynasties have been built on less," Gloria assured her. "But what is your excuse? If he is a mindless gnat drawn to your honey-like wrists, what made you attracted to him?"

"Gnats aren't drawn to honey," Penelope mumbled. "Most feed on plants, although there are some carnivorous varieties that—"

"Penelope." Gloria sent her a warning look.

She let out a long, slow breath.

"He's kind," she said at last. "He's charming and handsome, yes, but so much more than that. He's… complex."

Gloria blinked. "Saint Nick, London's favorite rake, is complex?"

Penelope nodded. "I'm beginning to suspect everyone is. Until I met him, I thought I was simple, too."

Nicholas was more than just skillful in the bedchamber. He was funny, he was sweet, he was thoughtful. He was also a talented artisan.

Especially given the damage his father had caused, she respected Nicholas's commitment to art. Aware his peers would judge him or change their opinions about him if the truth were to come out, Nicholas hid that facet of himself, but he did not stop. He held nothing from his passions.

"No wonder everyone swoons over him," Gloria said.

"I wish I could swoon," Penelope said. "Lying unconscious would be preferable to my current state. All this emotion is overwhelming. I have no control over it. It's something that can only be experienced, not quantified. It's terrifying. I don't know what to do."

"Because he's a rake?" Gloria asked.

"Because he makes me feel like there's more to life," Penelope admitted.

Gloria cocked her head. "Like what?"

"Like… believing in love."

"Believing?" Gloria lay a hand on Penelope's arm. "You *are* in love."

Penelope's stomach bottomed. Bloody hell. This was not the result she'd been looking for.

"That's your hypothesis," she stammered.

Gloria was undeterred. "Are you afraid he doesn't feel the same about you?"

"I know he doesn't."

That was the part that hurt. Her perfume had worked. It made a man as amazing as him believe he was interested in her.

Unbeknownst to him, it wasn't true. It was just science. Carefully constructed aromas designed to fool his brain. Chemistry. Alchemy. Manipulation.

And Penelope was the one who had fallen for it.

"Why don't you tell him how you feel?" Gloria asked softly.

Penelope scoffed. "What would that do?"

Gloria pursed her lips. "You don't believe in reformed rakes?"

"No," Penelope answered bluntly. "Even if I did, I wouldn't want to change him. That's not what love is."

Gloria arched her brows. "Now you're an expert on love?"

Penelope was pretty sure she no longer considered herself an expert in anything. But if she found it objectionable for others to demand Nicholas give up his art, she could not ask him to forsake any other passions. Even the ones that made her want to cry.

"Do *you* believe in reformed rakes?" she countered.

"He's *ton*," Gloria admitted. "Isn't keeping mistresses acceptable Society behavior, as long as it's discreet? I am certain he wouldn't flaunt his other lovers in front of you—"

"He wouldn't have to. The caricaturists and the society papers flaunt all his indiscretions for him. I don't want the image in my head at all." Penelope rubbed her temples. "He's leaving tomorrow. That is the best thing for both of us."

Gloria crossed her arms. "What about love?"

"He's not in love," Penelope said in exasperation. "Once he is out of scent range, the effects of the perfume will wear off and he'll forget me completely. Life will return to normal."

"*His* life," maybe," Gloria said doubtfully. "What about yours?"

Penelope touched her fingertips to Gloria's telescope

stand. "You have the stars. I have science to keep me busy. I'll be in my laboratory."

With the door shut tight to ensure she be unable to hear anyone knock. If she saw Nicholas again, she would have to confess the truth about the trial. She could not continue living a lie.

Gloria hesitated. "You plan to lock yourself in your laboratory until he's gone?"

"No," Penelope said. "That would be an ineffectual half measure."

She planned to cocoon herself in her laboratory for the rest of her life.

CHAPTER 14

Nicholas shoved his blowpipe into the fire and glared at the dancing orange flames. Normally, nothing was as calming as blowing glass or crafting an intricate mold. This morning, he was far from calm. He had bolloxed things with Penelope.

He had wanted their first lovemaking to be perfect. Slow, gentle, romantic. Instead it had been fast and carnal. They hadn't paused to kick their shoes off, much less get undressed. And as soon as it was over, they were done. Goodbye.

For a rake, that specific sequence of events was often considered an ideal encounter. It was not what Nicholas had wanted to give Penelope at all. He wasn't certain how he felt to discover that it was all she had wanted from him.

Oh, very well, he knew exactly how he felt.

Miserable.

He gathered molten glass onto the tip of his blowpipe and sighed.

Penelope was marvelous. Smart and sensual, funny and logical. A scientist and a surprise. Any man would be lucky to have her. Nicholas preferred that the man in question... be him. But he couldn't blame her for turning him away.

What had he offered her? Not one night, but two? How generous of him. Imbecile. She should have made him exit through the chimney.

He locked the molten glass inside the clay mold and began to blow. It was all his lungs were good for. What could he have said to Penelope? The more he opened up, the more he risked being found not good enough.

As a rake, he was more than serviceable. He was splendid. London knew what to expect, and Saint Nick delivered.

As Nicholas the bachelor glassblower, however, he became an oddity. A hobby that would raise no eyebrows for a man outside the *beau monde* would make Nicholas a laughingstock.

He would not offer Penelope a laughingstock. Nor had he any intention of forcing her to mix with his fast London crowd. Not that it mattered. He had already been dismissed.

He snapped his blowpipe from the clay mold. Was he cleaving to the persona of Saint Nick for Penelope's sake, or for his own safety? Just because something was easy didn't mean it was right. Or good.

Devil take it, he didn't want two nights with this woman. He wanted *all* the nights. Now unto infinity.

He dropped his head into his hands and groaned. He was in love, damn it all. And he only had two days left in Christmas. Time was disappearing fast.

He was going to have to tell her.

His legs shook as he jumped from the stool. Declaring himself to a woman was possibly the most terrifying undertaking he had ever attempted in his life, but Penelope was worth it. His heart thumped. They were a good match. She had to feel it, too.

He retrieved two molds from a hidden shelf. This was his gift. He had made them for her, and this was the perfect moment to deliver them. He cracked open the molds and carefully withdrew two glass figurines.

Turtledoves. One-of-a-kind, just like Penelope. Delicate to the eye. Stronger than they looked. The perfect gift to bring when informing a woman that one had fallen in love with her.

He hoped.

His muscles twitched. He'd never been in such a position. No one had ever loved him, chosen him, wanted him to stay. He knew not to expect too much.

But Penelope was worth the risk. What they were building was real. Not some temporary distraction, but a relationship based on mutual respect, honesty, and the sheer joy of each other's company. Only a fool would walk away without trying to make it last.

He set the birds down just long enough to put the smithy to rights, then started for the road.

To label himself nervous would be a gross understatement. Penelope was clever. If she returned his affection, he would be vindicated. If she didn't… Then he supposed he really was the shallow, otherwise useless rake he had always pretended to be.

He tilted the top of his head into the wind and strode faster. The one thing that scared him more than rejection was missing the opportunity to try.

She was stepping onto her front stoop just as he turned up her walk.

His insides warmed, and an involuntary smile curved his lips. The sight of her always made him happy. He could not fathom where she might have been at this hour of the morning.

He caught up with her as she was about to shut the door.

She did not move aside. Or invite him in. Or smile.

"You said one night," she stammered. "It's daytime."

Not the most auspicious start. He pressed on anyway.

"Here," he said. "I made these for you."

Her hands seemed to accept his offering reflexively, rather than out of any particular desire to receive a gift. She did not even glance down to see what it was. "Nicholas—"

"They're turtledoves," he blurted out. So much for his grand romantic gesture. It could not possibly go worse, and he was powerless to solve it. Or stop his mouth from babbling. "Glass figurines. They stand alone, and they can interlock. Turtledoves mate for life."

Splendid. Now he sounded like Virginia.

To his horror, Penelope's beautiful brown eyes took on a wet sheen. Not in a *this-is-so-romantic-I-could-just-cry* sort of way, but in a *this-is-so-horrible-I-could-just-die* sort of way. "Nicholas—"

"I love you," he announced, using his last scraps of courage. "That's what I came to say. Even if you don't feel the same, I thought you should know."

"It's not love," she said, her eyes tortured. "It wasn't supposed to be like this."

He tried his best to hide the tornado of disappointment within. There was his answer.

He was not what she wanted.

"Very well," he said despite the swaying in his head. "There's no need to ask why. I can well imagine."

"I don't think you can. You don't know the whole truth." She took a deep breath. "It was me. Rather, it was *Duchess*. I believed I had perfected a formula that could manipulate male emotion—"

"You what?" he stammered.

"—but I couldn't be certain until I proved it. I needed a test subject in order to run the trials—"

"A what?" he repeated, taking a jerking step backwards.

"—and I gave the trial a strict time limit in which to accomplish predetermined tasks." Her voice cracked as she met his eyes. "The experiment worked beyond my wildest dreams."

"It *worked?"* he repeated, banging a trembling fist to his chest in anger. "You toyed with my heart to prove a theory?"

"That wasn't the intended goal." Her voice cracked. "I only meant to—"

"I was listening," he said, not bothering to hide his bitterness. "Your intent was to manipulate my emotions in order to trick me into playing the lovesick swain for your own amusement."

"Not amusement," she said quickly. "Science—"

He scoffed. "You are very amused by science. Don't shift the blame." His hands shook. "I believed you of all people would treat others with unfailing honesty, and you purposefully misled me."

"I…" She closed her eyes. "Yes. I did."

"It was a game to you." His heart lurched in humiliation. "See how long it took me to exhibit whatever behaviors you've been marking behind my back with your little tally marks."

She winced.

"I'm surprised you didn't enter your wager in the betting book at White's," he said, each word scratchy and raw. "Then everyone could laugh at the silly laboratory specimen who believed he had finally unlocked his cage."

She shook her head, cheeks pale. "I never thought of you as a specimen."

"Didn't you?" His voice was empty. "Wasn't that how you chose me to be an unwitting part of your little experiment? You saw me as a *thing* instead of a person."

He had been such a fool. He'd believed he had found love, but he hadn't even found a real connection. He was just a research subject. An animal, like any other. Useful for a brief moment, then dumped back in the wild.

It had been a farce all along.

He should have known better. Of course she didn't love him back. Back when she'd selected him for a laboratory experiment, the one true thing she had told him was that she didn't believe in love. His useless heart banged against his ribs.

It didn't matter how real the past fortnight felt to him. To her... it wasn't. This was nothing more than the successful conclusion of a routine perfume trial. His chest tightened. She could skip back to her laboratory and concoct another potion, but he was done being part of her tests.

"I don't love you, then," he said hollowly. "As it happens, I don't even know you."

He spun around on stiff legs and strode as fast as he could from her door.

CHAPTER 15

Penelope hurried off her front stoop after Nicholas, but he was already heading back out in the street. Her chest ached at the damage she'd caused. He had deserved to know the truth, but she hadn't meant to hurt him.

"Wait," she called out. "Nicholas, please stop! Where are you going?"

"To fetch my belongings," he said without turning around. "I'm done here."

He did not slow down.

She forced herself not to chase him. She had no right to. Although she knew her own feelings were real, his interest had been caused by chemical compounds designed to manipulate him.

His affection was a mirage, no matter how much Penelope might wish otherwise. He had deserved to know the truth. She just hadn't expected it to hurt this much.

In one single moment, Penelope had destroyed everything. The haunted look in his eyes when she'd told him it was all a farce...

Her heart had broken along with his. She swore under her breath. *Duchess* had caused nothing but damage.

No. Penelope had achieved it herself.

She loved Nicholas, yet she had used him and hurt him. She deserved to lose him.

Penelope trudged back out into the street, not to chase him to the castle, but to allow him free will. She turned her leaden feet in the opposite direction.

Gloria's maid answered her door and allowed Penelope back inside without question. Less than an hour had passed. It felt as though she had spent it in a hell of her own making.

Penelope plodded into the observatory on heavy limbs and stood out of the way of the telescope. She hadn't come to talk. She just didn't want to be alone right now. Her home was too full of memory of Nicholas. Back when he thought he loved her.

Gloria was cleaning her telescope with a cotton rag. "I thought you were going to stay in your laboratory for the rest of your life."

"My life is over," Penelope said wearily. "Thanks to me."

Gloria turned from the telescope and squinted in Penelope's direction. "What are you carrying?"

"Turtledoves." Penelope clutched them to her chest. "They stand alone but fit together."

Gloria's eyes widened. "May I see?"

Penelope forced herself to relinquish the precious figurines.

"These are incredible." Gloria's eyes lit with wonder. "What an ingenious way to interlock the two. Where did you buy them? I want a pair, too."

Of course she would. The only thing Gloria loved more than the stars were mechanical puzzles. When the heavens were too cloudy for sky gazing, she spent long hours with her grand orrery, a mechanical device rotating a model of all eight planets. Gloria claimed she used it to unlock the mysteries in the sky.

Unfortunately, Penelope could offer no puzzle to solve. Everything was devastatingly, humiliatingly clear.

"The doves were a gift from Nicholas." Right before she'd informed him he was an unwilling participant in a chemistry experiment. She was surprised he hadn't taken them back and smashed them.

Gloria set down her cleaning rag. "If you still refuse to believe in love because 'it's not visible to the naked eye,' I'd say these doves are indisputably tangible evidence."

"I made a mistake." Penelope's shoulders slumped. "*Duchess* inflated my confidence, and I used misplaced pride to cause nothing but harm."

"'Misplaced' is right." Gloria put a hand on her hip. "Your perfume didn't help your confidence at all. Your only faith was in chemical compounds, when you should have had it in yourself."

"I am now incredibly confident in my ability to destroy the best thing that ever happened to me," Penelope assured her. "I interrupted a declaration of love to tell him it wasn't real. Now he's gone."

"Do you remember why you two argued when you first met?" Gloria asked after a moment. "What did you tell me?"

"That Saint Nick was on a mission to stop *Duke*," Penelope said with a bitter smile. She'd been so sanctimonious. "That the gallant rake feared confused, hapless women would find themselves leg-shackled to all the wrong men."

Gloria crossed her arms. "And what did you say to that argument?"

Penelope sighed. "I told him women aren't hapless. *Duke* starts the conversation. Women decide where it goes."

"Listen close," Gloria said. "Men aren't hapless either. He chose you. Not your scent. The whole package."

Hope pricked Penelope's heart. Might it be true? Could *Duchess* have worked as designed, yet not have manipulated the final outcome?

"You have to trust," Gloria said softly. "Have faith that what you feel is right. All sorts of non-verifiable things exist. If a rake can choose love, surely a lady chemist is capable of the same."

"I want to believe more than anything," Penelope whispered. "But it would truly be a miracle. The chemical compounds used in *Duchess*—"

"Are you wearing it?" Gloria asked, coming closer.

Penelope took a step backward. "What?"

"Are you wearing it right now?" Gloria sniffed behind Penelope's ears. "You don't smell like anything but Penelope."

Penelope pushed her away. "I washed it off as soon as I realized it had been a mistake. The trial is over. I'll never wear perfume again."

"When did you get rid of it?" Gloria insisted. "Did you pause to have a quick wash-up between accepting his gift and breaking his heart?"

"Of course not," Penelope said, exasperated. "If you must have every detail, I scrubbed it off last night before curling into a ball and failing to sleep."

Gloria grinned. "Then you weren't wearing it."

"What?" Penelope stammered.

"You weren't contaminated with your evil perfume." Gloria lifted her chin in triumph. "When he declared himself to you, *Duchess* was out of smell range. You were talking to the real Nicholas."

Penelope sniffed both wrists, then stared at Gloria.

"*Duchess* started the conversation," Gloria reminded her. "You had the power to finish it."

The power to ruin it, rather.

"It happened too fast. This was my first kiss, my first sexual encounter, my first—"

"Your first time glancing up from your notes," Gloria put in dryly. "You never came out of your laboratory. Not completely. Eligible gentlemen could leer at you all day long and you wouldn't notice. Until *Duchess* gave you a reason to start."

That… sounded uncomfortably accurate.

Penelope had done everything in her power to block herself off from the outside world. She hadn't realized just how well she had succeeded.

"He said he doesn't love me." Penelope's chest tightened with shame. "That he didn't know me at all. He's already gone."

Her heart cracked. She'd managed to realize both her worst fears at once.

Love was real.

And she'd lost it.

CHAPTER 16

Nicholas attempted to enter his guest chamber without being spotted. In his current mood, he had no wish to converse with anyone, much less pretend to feel carefree and flirtatious.

Unfortunately, the door to his brother's chamber across the corridor was ajar, and Nicholas's arrival did not go unnoticed.

Before Nicholas even had a chance to ring for a footman to load his trunks into his carriage, Chris was standing in the doorway.

"Have you been to the roof of the castle?" he asked. "I have to fix my telescope. The view is astonishing."

"I'm leaving," Nicholas said. There was no sense keeping it from his brother. Nicholas's accelerated departure worked out in Chris's favor.

His brother frowned. "You have until tomorrow. Why would you leave early? This village is positively brimming with comely young ladies."

"I don't care about them," Nicholas muttered.

His brother stepped into the room and lowered his voice. "Is it the lady chemist?"

Nicholas did not respond.

His brother's mouth fell open. "Never say you've developed an infatuation!"

"It doesn't matter what I feel." Nicholas shrugged. "She was never interested in a lasting relationship. I was a convenient subject upon which to test the efficacy of her new perfume."

Chris raised his brows. "How exactly did the lady test you?"

Nicholas glared back at him stonily.

"Let me see if I understand." Chris came closer, stroking his chin as if deep in thought. "The individual in question slept with a willing partner, on precisely one occasion, with no inclination or promise, spoken or otherwise, to continue interaction after the deed was done?"

Nicholas crossed his arms.

"You got raked and don't like it." Chris's eyes lit with mirth. "She 'Saint Penelope'ed you."

Sometimes, Nicholas wanted nothing more than to throttle his brother.

"You cannot possibly be angry with her over it," Chris said in disbelief. "Do unto others, and all that. Weren't you always worried that someday a woman would agree to one night and not really mean it? Penelope meant it. Huzzah."

"It's worse than that. One night was what I wanted, too." Nicholas sighed. "Until I didn't."

Chris stared at him for a long moment, all humor gone. "You fell in *love?*"

Nicholas shrugged. "She didn't. So, it doesn't matter."

Chris stepped forward, his initial humor now replaced by wonder. "Good God. I never thought you'd fall before me."

"I never thought I'd fall at all." Nicholas scowled. "The landing is hell."

Chris reached out. "Nick, I'm sorry. Do you want me to—"

"No." Nicholas clenched his jaw tight and turned away before his brother could touch him.

He didn't want Chris's pity. He wanted to be as far away as possible.

It wasn't the village of Christmas he was running from, but stacks of warm biscuits placed by the fire. Afternoons side-by-side on stools in her laboratory or in the kitchen. Laughing at private jokes. Their hands touching as they kneaded a bowl of dough. Heated kisses that tasted of spice and sugar. The scent of her skin. The softness of her hair.

The finality in her tone when she admitted his time with her had been a test trial that had now concluded. She didn't need him anymore.

"Where will you go?" his brother asked, his voice concerned. "Home?"

"My workshop," Nicholas answered.

"What about London?" his brother insisted. "Parties. Dancing. Other women."

Nicholas shook his head. "You warned me one day I would become too old to be a rake, and now that day is here."

"I said that two weeks ago," Chris pointed out. "You've barely aged a fortnight. I understand that rejection hurts. You don't have to be a rake, but you're too young to become a hermit."

Nicholas lifted his head with interest. "What is the minimum age? I hear the Weld family constructed a lovely hermitage on their country pile."

"You shall not take a post as a garden hermit," Chris said

firmly. "You do realize the position requires you not just to live alone, but to avoid all contact with others."

"Exactly." Nicholas nodded. "The answer to a prayer."

All that awaited him in London was some new series of meaningless affairs. It was no longer what he wanted. He wasn't certain it had ever been something he desired.

He now suspected he'd been searching all this time for someone who would want more, someone he'd be unable to live without.

Playing the part of rake helped save his pride. He could convince himself that the emptiness in his life wasn't because he was unworthy of love, but because he had not yet met the right woman.

Well, now they'd met. And he was still unworthy of love.

Chest tight, Nicholas stalked to his dressing room and yanked the bell pull. "As soon as my trunks are packed, I'm gone. There's no reason to stay."

"Isn't there?"

Of course Chris would think that. He still believed in *happy ever after*.

"No," Nicholas said flatly. "It's over. If Penelope doesn't even want a two-night liaison, she's not going to marry me."

His brother raised his brows. "Did you ask her to marry you?"

"What would that have done?" Nicholas asked wearily.

Chris lifted a shoulder. "Why don't you find out?"

Nicholas scoffed. "No woman wants to marry a rake."

"You just said you weren't a rake anymore," Chris pointed out. "Marry her."

"I was a test subject in an experiment." Nicholas enunciated each word.

"You said that was over, too."

Nicholas clenched his fists, throat stinging. "I am…"

"All out of excuses?" his brother suggested.

"Hurt," Nicholas admitted in a low voice. "I tried to be honest and forthcoming in all my interactions. She let me believe we were creating something that didn't exist. I'm better off alone."

CHAPTER 17

Penelope was still slumped against the frigid wall in her best friend's private observatory. She stared across the telescope at Gloria.

"What are you looking for?" she asked at last.

"Answers." Gloria lifted her gaze from the eyepiece. "What are you looking for?"

Penelope cast her gaze down at the interlocking glass figurines cradled in her arms. "Impossible things."

If she hadn't created *Duke,* Nicholas would never have approached her. If she hadn't decided to experiment with *Duchess,* none of the past two weeks would have happened. She had lost him for the same reason that she had found him.

"You don't believe in impossible things." Gloria returned her gaze to the lens before her. "Which means whatever you're thinking about must still be possible."

"It's not," Penelope said. She had been dishonest. He wouldn't forgive that.

Gloria shot her a knowing look. "How do you know if you don't experiment?"

Penelope lowered her head in thought. If what had attracted Nicholas's attention was also what had caused her to lose it, could the same work in reverse? The original experiment had been about what Penelope wanted. What did Nicholas want?

Observation, she reminded herself. What were the observable facts? He never spent more than one night with a single woman. He had spent a night with Penelope. Ergo, he wanted her body. He had come back again. Ergo, one night wasn't all he wanted.

More facts. He designed superior measuring flasks for her. Ergo, he supported her interest in chemistry. He hand-delivered biscuit ingredients in order to bake for her. Ergo, he wanted to take care of her. To spend time together. He designed her the sort of bird that mates for life. And he said…

"He loves me?" she asked in a small voice.

Gloria's gaze softened. "Did he use those words?"

Penelope nodded.

"Then he does." Gloria's eyes shone with satisfaction. "What are you going to do about it?"

Penelope's stomach turned. "He also said he didn't love me anymore."

"And one of those statements was true," Gloria agreed. "Which one do you believe?"

A fortnight ago, Penelope did not believe in love. Today, there was nothing she wanted more.

She just needed to convince Nicholas.

Up until now, he had always come to Penelope. It was past time for her to go to him. Or at least try her damnedest.

It might be too late.

She rushed from Gloria's house without another word. She had taken too long already. The castle was enormous, but the staff was swift. They could have trunks packed and carriages ready in the wink of an eye.

Penelope raced up the snow-packed road toward the castle. If she did not catch him in time, she would lose more than her chance at a second trial. She didn't even have an address to send him a letter. If she couldn't find him, there wouldn't be another opportunity.

She dashed in through the castle's front doors and made her way past the reception buffet to the head housekeeper.

"Mrs. Blair," she gasped, her lungs burning from racing up the steep hill.

The housekeeper smiled. "How can I help you, Miss Mitchell?"

Penelope took a deep breath. "Which guest chamber belongs to Nicholas Pringle?"

The housekeeper folded her arms across her ample bosom and gave Penelope a disapproving stare. "Just like I tell all the other ladies. The day after the party, milord gave me explicit instructions not to share that information with anyone."

Penelope's heart skipped. "He did?"

That was the same day Nicholas had first come to visit Penelope.

The housekeeper harrumphed. "And I won't be making an exception for you. Marlowe Castle respects our guests' privacy."

A perfectly reasonable stance, and impossible to argue with. What next?

Penelope spun from the housekeeper in frustration and darted a panicked glance about the reception chamber.

Nicholas was nowhere to be seen, of course. He didn't want biscuits and spiced wine. He wanted to be far away from a woman he believed didn't love him.

"What are those?" came a dreamy voice from over Penelope's shoulder.

She jumped and jerked around, clutching the glass figurines to her chest for safety. "Virginia! I didn't see you. These are birds."

"Turtledoves," Virginia corrected, a self-satisfied smile spreading across her face. "Of course they are."

Penelope waved Virginia's cryptic comment away impatiently. Time was running out. "You live here. Do you know which guest chamber belongs to Nicholas?"

"Sixth floor," Virginia answered without hesitation. "South wing, left side, fourth door. Did you know that the nuptial flight of the European turtledove is often—"

"Thank you," Penelope called over her shoulder as she fled the reception area and dashed up the spiral stairs.

She could swear she heard Virginia trilling *turr, turr* after her as she ran.

Penelope flew up the stairs. Even though it might already be too late, even though love was scary and unknowable, even though she might have already broken things past all repair, she had to try. Nothing else mattered. She skidded off the landing and into the corridor.

The door to his guest chamber was open. Shadows moved inside. Nicholas might still be here!

She burst inside, out of breath and half wild. *"I love you!"*

Christopher Pringle stared back at her, eyes wide. His startled gaze dropped to the figurines. "Did Nick make those?"

"Er, not you." Penelope hugged the turtledoves closer to her chest. "I meant—"

Nicholas stepped out from his dressing room, his eyes dark and unreadable. "*Out.*"

"Does he mean you or me?" Penelope whispered to his brother.

"Definitely me," Christopher said cheerfully. He slipped past her into the corridor, shutting the door as he left.

"I love you," she said again, her heart racing.

"People 'of science' perform experiments on animals," Nicholas said. "You don't fall in love with them."

"I'm not proud that I set out to manipulate you," Penelope admitted. "It was wrong of me. To be honest, I didn't believe it possible."

"Congratulations," he said icily. "Now you know."

Penelope bit her lip. "You don't understand. The experiment was whether I could attract a man as myself. We might have begun on false pretenses, but every moment we shared was you being you and me being me. Nothing could be more real."

He arched a brow. "Nothing?"

"You met the true me. You know the true me. You made love to the true me." She took a half step forward. "I'm so sorry I hurt you in the process. I was foolish. I don't deserve your forgiveness."

He let out a slow breath. "Penelope—"

"I won't sell it," she said quickly. "*Duchess* is dead. I'll stop *Duke*, too. I never expected a perfume to become my greatest achievement, and when I saw what it could do, my only thought was to give women the same advantages. I never meant to bring heartache."

"Perfumes can't break hearts," he reminded her. "Women who manipulate men into falling in love with them, despite having no interest in keeping them, break hearts."

"There's nothing I want *more* than to keep—" Penelope's voice caught. "You still love me?"

He cocked his head. "You want to keep me?"

"Of course I want to keep you," she choked out. "The experiment was to attract your attention, nothing more. I changed it to flirtation, in order to have another day with you. And then I changed it to a kiss, in order to have another. And then I changed it to—"

"Last night... wasn't part of the experiment?"

"The trial was successful on the first day," she admitted. "I couldn't give up the experiment because it meant giving up you. I thought the only reason you kept coming by was because the chemical scent engineered for my pulse points had bewitched you."

"Many things about you bewitched me." His lips quirked. "The chemicals behind your ears, however..."

"It's science," she babbled. "I could never have attracted you on my own. You can't deny it. *Duchess* was the one—"

"My turn," he said, and took a step forward. "You're right. I knocked on your door because I wanted to halt *Duke*, not seduce its creator. But that changed."

She nodded. "The 'one night' rule. I know."

"You don't know because I didn't tell you." His gaze was intense. "I realized I didn't want a night with you. I wanted all the nights. All the days. All the sunsets, and twilights, and sunrises..."

She bit her lip uncertainly, her throat scratchy. "You did?"

"No." He took another step forward. "I do. I always will."

"Me too," she whispered and threw herself into his arms. "I want you every single second. You are the reason I know love is real."

"You love me?" he whispered into her hair.

"With everything I have." She hiccupped into his cravat. "I love you more than alchemy and chemistry and biscuits—"

"Bad news," he told her. "I never said I loved you more than biscuits."

She slapped his chest and gazed up at him with hope in her heart. "I love you, Nicholas Pringle."

"I love you, Penelope Mitchell." His eyes twinkled. "Even more than biscuits. Will you be my wife?"

"*Yes.*" She pressed her mouth to his and kissed him.

The door swung open. "Your trunks are in the carriage, milord. What shall I tell the driver?"

Penelope's eyes met Nicholas's. "My house?"

"Your cottage contains a shockingly insufficient quantity of workshops," Nicholas said with a straight face.

The footman cleared his throat. "You're staying, milord?"

"I'm definitely staying." Nicholas tossed the footman a sovereign for his troubles and returned his mouth to Penelope's. "Banns take three weeks. Think we can build something more appropriate in that amount of time?"

CHAPTER 18

"Are you ready?" Nicholas gazed down at his beautiful bride.

Penelope grinned back up at him. "For anything."

She lifted her fingers to his elbow.

He swung her up into his arms instead. "Allow me to carry you across the threshold and into our new life."

Penelope's eyes twinkled up at him. "Does it count as new if we're going to be doing the same things as before?"

"Newer and better," he assured her. "Now we'll be doing the same old things together."

He turned toward the open door. Although the reading of the banns only required three weeks to complete, construction had taken months.

Their splendid fireproof home boasted what Nicholas considered to be not one, but three workshops. A chemical laboratory for Penelope. A glassblowing and mold-making workshop for Nicholas. And a well-stocked kitchen for endless supplies of biscuits.

Not to mention an oversized chaise longue reclining beside their new chimney, just waiting to be christened.

Heart full, Nicholas stepped over the threshold with his wife in his arms. He swung her in a circle, then paused when he noticed the empty mantel. "Blast. I should have brought you a gift."

"You are my gift." She tilted her head towards the cozy chaise. "But if you really want to give me something…"

Their bodies entwined atop the plush surface in no time.

"Welcome home," he murmured between kisses.

Her eyes held a naughty glint. "I can't wait to spend the rest of my nights with Saint Nick."

"And your days," he said firmly. "Allow me to demonstrate what I have in mind."

They wouldn't leave their cottage for a week.

EPILOGUE

For the second time in Penelope's life, the castle ballroom brimmed with merry villagers. All her neighbors once again gathered under one roof to celebrate a perfume of her creation.

But this time, she hadn't done it alone. Nicholas was by her side, and had worked with her to make *Duchess* a runaway success.

"Can you believe this is happening?" she whispered.

He squeezed her hand. "You did this."

"*We* did this," she corrected him with a smile. "I cannot tell if demand is due to my perfume or the gorgeous bottles it's sold in."

Nicholas had changed his turtledove design from figurines to decorative perfume bottles. The intricate, delicate construction of the interlocking glass birds had more than doubled the price.

Cost didn't seem to matter. Clients who previously would have selected one or the other, now purchased *Duke* and *Duchess* together in order to own the collection.

"Speech, speech!" cried the crowd.

"What do you plan to say?" Nicholas asked.

"I'll start with the chemical composition of civet excretions," Penelope said with a straight face. "What are you going to tell them?"

"Turtledoves mate for life," he said, eyes twinkling. "Even glass ones."

She nodded sagely. *"Turr, turr."*

"Speech!" the crowd shouted.

"I love you," Nicholas murmured into her ear.

"I love you, too," she whispered back and looped her arm through his.

They exchanged a mischievous grin and climbed upon the dais to make their speech together.

AUTHOR'S NOTE

I've had so much fun writing the twelve romances in this series. One of the best parts has been in the in-joke of deciding who—or what—the next "duke" will be.

You can grab a free bonus novella here:
https://BookHip.com/HKLJDP

Thank you so much for visiting Cressmouth! I hope you enjoy reading these stories as much as I've enjoyed writing them. Happy holidays!

xoxo,
Erica

THANK YOU FOR READING

Love talking books with fellow readers?

Join the ***Historical Romance Book Club*** for prizes, books, and live chats with your favorite romance authors:
Facebook.com/groups/HistRomBookClub

And check out the official website for sneak peeks and more:
www.EricaRidley.com/books

WISH UPON A DUKE

12 DUKES OF CHRISTMAS #3

A star-crossed lovers, opposites attract, feel good romance from a *New York Times* bestselling author:

Rumor has it, charming adventurer Christopher Pringle is finally ready to settle down. He's searching for a free-spirited bride to join him on his travels. But when the matchmaker he hires turns out to be the woman he had a public spat with the day before, nothing goes as planned!

Miss Gloria Godwin loves exploring the world... from the safety of a book. She detests her dashing client's attempts to force her from her comfort zone. It should be easy to marry off the handsome heir to a dukedom. But the more she tries to match him to other women, the harder it gets to say goodbye.

SNEAK PEEK

WISH UPON A DUKE

Gloria's heart pounded with pleasure.

Christopher was bending a rule, just for her. He wasn't merely allowing her to be herself, no matter how silly that might be, but actively joining his imagination with hers.

She'd like to join a few more bits together.

He was temptation incarnate. Everything about him with something she shouldn't have or couldn't have, but wanted very much. She sank her fingers into his hair as she kissed him.

His lips were firm and generous, his tongue hot and demanding. She would relinquish anything he wanted if he would give her everything she needed. Her body yearned for him, from her banging heart to the rush of desire racing through her blood. She might lose him on the morrow, but she would not allow tonight to pass them by.

"Tell me about your travels," she murmured between kisses. "Do all cultures require cravats?"

He murmured *No* without separating his mouth from hers.

She slid her fingers from his hair down to his neckcloth. In moments, she untied the knot. With a flourish, she tossed the soft square of white silk aside.

"Tourists," she murmured. "Always with the neckcloths. Tell me about this very interesting coat of black superfine." She ran her hands over his hard muscles. "Do men in all places hide their gorgeous arms in such things?"

"They do not," he said between kisses. "Horrid custom."

She wriggled her skirts up so that she could better straddle his thighs, then pulled him upright in order to divest him of his coat. When she'd dreamed of what it might be like to undress him, she hadn't realized her fingers would fumble with each button because her hands trembled so. Or that removing each layer of clothing would feel like stripping away another shield from her heart.

When the well-tailored superfine and accompanying waistcoat joined the forgotten neckcloth outside the blanket, he moved to lay back down.

She stopped him.

"This linen shirt," she said as she ran a fingertip along his shoulder. "It offends my sensibilities."

"A thousand apologies, madam." He crossed his arms at his waistline and removed his shirt in a single fluid movement.

Her breath caught. Having him to command was headier than any brandy. Seeing his naked flesh with her eyes, feeling his strong thighs trapped beneath hers, made her feel more powerful than any star in the sky. He wasn't looking at his telescope. He was looking at her. Submitting to her every wish because his desire matched her own.

His hot gaze never wavered from hers. "How else may I be of service?"

THE DUKE HEIST

WILD WYNCHESTERS #1

A secret identities, forbidden love, opposites attract romance from a *New York Times* bestselling author: Why seduce a duke the normal way, when you can accidentally kidnap one in an elaborately planned heist?

Chloe Wynchester is completely forgettable -- a curse that gives her the ability to blend into any crowd. When the only father she's ever known makes a dying wish for his adopted family of orphans to recover a missing painting, she's the first one her siblings turn to for stealing it back. No one expects that in doing so, she'll also abduct a handsome duke.

Lawrence Gosling, the Duke of Faircliffe, is tortured by his father's mistakes. To repair his estate's ruined reputation, he must wed a highborn heiress. Yet when he finds himself in a carriage being driven hell-for-leather down the cobblestone streets of London by a beautiful woman who refuses to heed his commands, he fears his heart is hers. But how can he sacrifice his family's legacy to follow true love?

"Erica Ridley is a delight!"
—Julia Quinn

"Irresistible romance and a family of delightful scoundrels... I want to be a Wynchester!"
—Eloisa James

Register your preorder by February 2021 and receive a **FREE BOOK** as a bonus gift!
https://www.EricaRidley.com/preorder

SNEAK PEEK

THE DUKE HEIST

Miss Chloe Wynchester folded her hands in her lap and did her best not to glare a hole right through the handsome, haughty Duke of Faircliffe. His frigid blue gaze had looked right at her—and slid away just as quickly, having glimpsed nothing to attract his interest.

How many times had she and Faircliffe been in the same room? Eight? Ten? Every disdainful glance in her direction as indifferent as the last. She lifted her chin. Her father had taught her that to the right person, she would be visible and memorable. Faircliffe was clearly the wrong person.

Not that she *wanted* him to notice her, Chloe reminded herself. The continued success of "Jane Brown" hinged on her uncanny ability to be wholly unremarkable under any circumstances. She gripped the soft muslin of her skirt and took in all the other ladies in the parlor.

Mrs. York clapped her hands together. "And now… a celebratory tea!"

The duke's face displayed a comical look of alarm. "I don't think—"

"You must join us!" Mrs. York's hands flapped like frightened birds. "The girls were about to have oatcakes and cucumber sandwiches before you arrived."

"We were about to discuss epistolary structure in eighteenth-century French novels," Philippa murmured.

"I never meant to interrupt," Faircliffe said with haste. "I mustn't stay, and in fact—"

"Nonsense! Come, come, all of you." Mrs. York waved her arms about the room, driving her guests into the dining room like a shepherd herding sheep.

Chloe and Faircliffe were both caught in the flow.

Once they reached the door, however, Chloe stepped to one side. She could not take a seat at the table, or she would be stuck there for the next hour.

While everyone else was occupied, *this* was her chance to liberate the painting. But first, she needed an excuse to disappear. An adorable, furry reason.

She released Tiglet from the large wicker basket. The calico kitten darted between boots and beneath petticoats with a formidable *rawr.*

Mrs. York gave a dramatic shriek in response.

Tiglet scaled several curtains in search of an open window before darting out of the dining room and flying off down the corridor as though his tail were afire.

Chloe gasped, as if shocked that her homing kitten was attempting to dash home. "How embarrassing! I'll run and find the naughty little scamp at once. Go on ahead. Please don't wait for me."

With her basket hanging from her arm, she ducked into the parlor and closed the door behind her. She hurried to lift the painting from the wall and carried it behind a chinoiserie folding screen in the corner. Up came the frame's grips, off came the backing, out came Bean's painting. She rolled it carefully and tucked it into the basket before stretching the forgery she'd brought over the wooden frame.

She ran to open the parlor door before anyone noticed it had been shut and hurried past the dining room to the front door without taking her leave from the guests. Would anyone notice she failed to return? Doubtful. If anything, the ladies would assume Jane Brown had slunk off in mortification.

Still, there was no time to waste. Any caper's success depended upon a timely exit.

Keeping her head down, she headed down the front walk toward the first carriage in the queue. Only when she glimpsed the red curtains and a pair of leather gloves on the box did she lift her head toward the driver's perch.

It was empty.

Her lungs caught. Where was Graham?

Distant shouts reached her ears, and her tight muscles relaxed. Something unexpected must have occurred, and her siblings' distraction was underway.

This was her cue to flee.

Chloe pushed the basket inside, unhooked the carriage from its post, and leapt onto the coachman's seat. Female drivers weren't unheard of, but all the same, she was glad she never went outside without garbing herself in the plainest, dullest, dowdiest clothes in her wardrobe. No one who glanced her way would bother looking for long.

She set the horses on a swift path out of Mayfair.

Only when Grosvenor Square was no longer visible behind her did she allow herself a small smile of victory.

"Did we escape?" came a low, velvet voice from within the carriage.

Chloe's skin went cold. Who was *that?* Graham wouldn't

be hiding in the back of the carriage. A stranger was in the coach! She twisted about and wrenched the privacy curtain to one side.

A handsome visage with soft brown hair and sculpted cheekbones stared back at her, glacial blue eyes wide with surprise.

"*Faircliffe?*" she blurted in disbelief.

"Miss… er… *you*?" he spluttered when he found his voice. "What the devil are you doing driving my carriage?"

ABOUT THE AUTHOR

Erica Ridley is a *New York Times* and *USA Today* best-selling author of witty, feel-good historical romance novels, including the upcoming THE DUKE HEIST, featuring the Wild Wynchesters. Why seduce a duke the normal way, when you can accidentally kidnap one in an elaborately planned heist?

In the *12 Dukes of Christmas* series, enjoy witty, heart-warming Regency romps nestled in a picturesque snow-covered village. After all, nothing heats up a winter night quite like finding oneself in the arms of a duke!

Two popular series, the *Dukes of War* and *Rogues to Riches*, feature roguish peers and dashing war heroes who find love amongst the splendor and madness of Regency England.

When not reading or writing romances, Erica can be found riding camels in Africa, zip-lining through rainforests in Central America, or getting hopelessly lost in the middle of Budapest.

Let's be friends! Find Erica on:

www.EricaRidley.com

Made in the USA
Middletown, DE
12 May 2022

65712166R00205